FOR LAUREN

Your love of books always made me want to write my own. You were always happy to listen to my ideas, and ultimately, you were the first to read this story from front to back. You've been there with me since I wrote the first word, and now you're still with me when it's at its completion. I'm thankful to have you as my sister. This one's for you.

Homecoming
by Kate Hasbrouck

ISBN 9781940192215

Published by
◄ köehlerbooks ™

210 60th Street
Virginia Beach, VA 23451
212-574-7939
www.koehlerbooks.com

Publisher
John Köehler

Executive Editor
Joe Coccaro

Cover design by Dalitopia Media

HOMECOMING

KATE HASBROUCK

VIRGINIA BEACH
CAPE CHARLES

†

For he will command his angels

Concerning you

To guard you in all your ways.

On their hands

they will bear you up,

so that you will not dash your foot

against a stone.

†

Psalm 91: 11-12

1 KERANA

From the very edge of the branch I could see nearly everything in the forest. The sun had reached its peak and cast long shadows between the trees, wrapping the world in a cool blanket below me.

Today my life will change forever. I will go to Earth, and I will essentially become a Human.

It was time for me to be on my way.

The breeze was soft, but at these heights, the slightest wind sent the branches swaying.

I looked down through the tree and the forest floor seemed miles away. I took another step onto the branch, feeling it bow.

And I smiled, for what was a thirty-foot drop to an Eldurian?

I leapt from the end of the branch, fell through the air for a few seconds of blissful flight, and landed lightly onto a lower branch. I loved feeling the wind rush through my hair as I fell. I eyed the next branch below me, which was closer, but not by much, and quickly jumped down to it. I continued down the tree until at last I reached the forest floor.

"Kerana?" I smiled and turned to see the most beautiful woman in Eden approach me through the spotted pools of sunlight. Long brunette hair flowed over her shoulders like a waterfall, and blue eyes radiated a light that stars would envy. Her face was flawless and smooth. She had a smile that was contagious and beautiful, that conveyed a story of love and wisdom.

"Mother!" I replied. "How did you know where to find me?"

She said nothing at first, but opened her arms and I lingered a few moments more than usual in her embrace. She smelled like fresh pine and mint.

Then, "Kerana, really. Do you think I know you that little?"

I smiled. Of course she would know.

"It is getting late, dear. You need to get going. Your father is with the twins and insisted that I come to see you off." She ran her hands through my long hair affectionately. She hadn't done that since I was eight or nine. "He sends his love."

She paused, looked at me, and brushed her hands up and down my arms. "Your first day wearing the Eldurian robe—I can't believe it!"

I couldn't either; it still seemed surreal to me that I had just that morning changed from the uniform of the Elduns to the robe that meant I was no longer considered a child among my people, but an adult.

"Well, come on, we should get you going."

I fell into step beside her. My thoughts were tangled up in one another, and I couldn't quite straighten them out. I was sure that this was what every Eldurian felt before they left for Earth.

"How are you feeling?" Mother asked me as we walked together.

"I am feeling confident, just a bit curious about what to expect." I smiled at her. "I do not fear it," I added honestly. I wasn't afraid at all and really never experienced fear in Eden. But then again, I had never seen a Human before and we were taught in school that fear was a part of everyday life experiences on Earth. It was my first time away from home and I was to set out entirely by myself into a world that I was only familiar with through books and drawings.

She nodded her head. "I remember feeling the same way. But I trust that you will do well."

"I believe I will too."

"And of course," she added, "Adonai will be there with you. You won't have to remain in Earth's fear when He is at your side."

I smiled. "That is a very large part of why I am confident. I know I am supposed to go. I know that it is my time."

"I know it is too," she replied.

We walked side by side as almost equals now, I realized. It was strange to speak with her eye to eye, and to know that I would no longer rely on her help.

"You know, I still remember my first day on Earth," she murmured, pulling me out of my musings.

"The very first?"

"Kerana, I doubt that you will ever forget your first day in the world of the Humans. I walked out of the Portal and into a place that was nothing like Eden." She grew quiet, and looked down at her feet as we walked. "I remember I walked out of the Portal and immediately I wanted to go back. Everything felt wrong. The world smelled strange, it sounded strange. I began to think that Adonai was wrong, and that I wasn't ready to go into this world."

She smiled at me then. "But Adonai is never wrong, I reminded myself in that moment. And I knew that He was there because He reminded me in His ever so gentle way. So I picked up my bags and made my way to the busy streets to take a taxicab to the nearest airport, so that I could reach Maine."

Silence fell again as we continued to walk. I knew that we were coming close to where we would part ways. I wondered what was waiting for me only a short distance away, through the Portal.

Would the Humans smile the same way? Would they laugh like the Eldurians did? Would they love like the Eldurians did? It was hard to know the answers, knowing that the Humans were the Fallen, and the Eldurians were not. The darkness that lived in them did not live in us.

Against a tree along the edge of the path were two bags packed full of clothing, books, and other necessities. I laid them out before wandering back to the trees—before I had one last glimpse of Eden. I was fully aware that when I returned, my view of it will have changed. I wanted to retain an innocent, naïve memory of it, of the way I had always known it.

"Here," Mother said. She opened a bag and pulled out some clothing and handed the neatly folded stack to me. "I am glad that the clothes I passed on to you fit as well as they do. You should change quickly before you leave. I will take your robe and keep it safe."

I nodded at her, and quickly changed into the clothes she had given me. I handed Mother my newly acquired Eldurian robe somewhat regretfully. I was just getting used to wearing it.

Mother called the stiff pants I wore "jeans," and the shirt I wore was made from a soft cotton material and was a warm pink color.

"How do I look?" I asked, turning for her to see me from all angles.

Her face lit up, and her eyes shone. She considered my appearance, and after a moment said, "Here, come see for yourself."

She gestured behind the tree to a gentle stream that collected into a deep pool, the water calm. I strode to it and looked down at myself. It was strange to see these colored clothes; I was used to seeing my long blonde hair that hung to my elbows against the white of the Eldun clothes. I adjusted the shirt, pulling it down. The outfit was honestly a bit uncomfortable.

My mother smiled again at me as I straightened up. I grabbed a bag of books beside my feet that were required of me at the new place I was going to be educated at—a place called "University."

"You will do fine, dear," she reassured me.

I reached down to pick up the other bag, and then looked up

at her. There were tears in her eyes.

"Mother—"

She shook her head. "I'm fine, dear. But you should get going: it is getting late."

I looked at the watch on my wrist. It still felt strange to wear one, and I still had trouble understanding the meaning of the numbers. But she was right—I needed to get going.

"May the grace and peace of Adonai be with you always." She cupped her hand over my cheek and smiled at me.

I hugged her tightly, and she held on a moment or two longer than usual.

"Go," she said.

I threw the second bag over my shoulder, as was the custom of the Humans, though terribly uncomfortable on my back, and set off through the forest. I looked over my shoulder and saw Mother watching me. I waved at her. She continued to wave until I was out of sight.

I slowed my pace and filled my lungs with fresh air. I wasn't anxious to leave Eden. Not quite yet.

"Are you ready to go?" I heard in my ear, just slightly louder than a whisper. It was Adonai's voice.

"I think so," I replied, coming to a stop. I looked around and through the trees nearby, but I couldn't see Adonai anywhere. I heard a laugh that reminded me of a faint breeze.

"Do you remember what your job is?"

"To protect and guard the Humans," I said, almost methodically as if I were in class.

There was another small laugh. "You have always been so thoughtful of others, so compassionate. But remember, I have plans for you too, Kerana."

I continued to look through the trees around, but I could not see Him. He had chosen not to show Himself this time.

"You were created with a unique purpose. Don't forget that. Your time on Earth will help you to see exactly who you are, and what you are capable of."

I nodded, unsure of what else to say.

"You are ready, my dear one. Go in peace, and know that I am with you always."

I could feel myself growing more confident now as I approached the Portal. I had never approached the unknown before, but Adonai's peace was tangible now, when I needed it most.

The trees on either side of the end of the path formed a small arch above my head, almost like a doorframe, where woven branches created the passage onto Earth. There didn't seem to be anything on the other side of the arch. But I knew better. I walked right up to the threshold of the doorway, and took a deep breath. I had seen every book, talked to many Eldurians, and learned every necessary fact about these Humans.

I was ready.

I took a deep breath, and I crossed the threshold.

I stepped out into dim light, and it took a moment for my eyes to adjust. My stomach lurched uncomfortably as I looked around. I saw that I stood among many trees still, but these were not the trees from Eden. The sunlight that streamed through the tops of them wasn't as bright, or as warm. The branches that hung low on them showed leaves that had holes in them, or were torn. Some were browning and dry. The acrid, sour air caught at my throat and my mouth went dry. *Breathe.* I attempted a steady breath, but my lungs seized in my chest and I coughed and sputtered and gasped for air. Finally, I regained control of myself, though I trembled slightly from head to toe. A haze in the air made it hard to see very far.

Loud roaring sounds reeled through the Earth forest—probably from a mile or so away. Birds called to each other mournfully overhead. A shout, a blaring horn, and a rushing, angry, mechanical sound. My Eldurian hearing subsided slowly, and the loud, fierce sounds became dull roars at the back of my mind. I was grateful. But I couldn't move. I stood rooted to the spot, transfixed by all of the chaos around me, desperately willing myself to take it all in. And I hadn't taken two steps on Earth yet.

Was this really where the Humans *lived*?

I recalled the map in my pocket, and quickly drew it out. I scanned it and saw I needed to head north through the forest about half a mile, and right across the street would be the college. I neatly refolded the map, slipped it into the back pocket of my blue pants. It wasn't terribly long before I reached the edge of the forest. My acute hearing was either going to hinder me or help me in this realm. There was loud roaring from the vehicles on the road beside the forest. I recognized the speeding metal machines on the black pavement from the books back home. They were quite a bit more alarming in person. They flew by me at high speed as I stood on the side of the road.

Inside each of the cars sat a Human. The cars were moving too fast for me to get a very good look, but I could make out their faces for a second or two before they blew past me. Along the sidewalk, other Humans walked by, their heads bent down or a small rectangular box pressed tightly to their ears. Not a single one looked up at me.

How am I going to get across? I wondered. I could see the large red and gold sign across the street stating in large, bold letters the name of the school: *Cornerstone State*. At least I was at the right location.

Overhead, a streetlight glowed green. I remembered this was how Humans governed traffic. I continued to watch it as it turned yellow, and then red.

A group of Humans congregated at the corner of the sidewalk started to make their way across the street, and the rushing cars slowed, then stopped. I hurried to the spot where the Humans had crossed, and tentatively looked at the cars. They were still. I blinked and began to cross the street.

I was halfway across the street when the red light turned green again.

My stomach dropped as I heard the cars begin to move, and I looked over just as a car, its driver clearly not paying any attention to the road, raced right toward me. "Whoa!" I screamed. I jumped out of the way and onto the sidewalk. The green car hurtled past me and didn't even attempt to slow down. *Whoosh!* My head rattled with the force and the sound.

I dropped my bag on the sidewalk, clutched my chest, and bent over. My heart hammered against my ribs. I had never experienced this in Eden and I was certain I did not want to experience it a second time. I felt tears well up in my eyes.

This must be fear, I thought as I wiped the tears off my face, trying to control myself. *This must be what it feels like.*

2 ELI

I turned off the ignition and put my head back against the headrest. I really didn't want to do this anyway, so why rush it? It seemed so logical to everybody else. Go to college, get a degree, move on with life.

At least that is what good old Dad always taught me.

I'd already rehearsed all this with my Dad and, of course, he won—again. I closed my eyes and ran my fingers around the familiar steering wheel and tried to relax. It irritated me to think that after all this time Dad still treated me like a child—like a puppet. And I was a junior in college.

Ridiculous.

All of my things for the upcoming year were crammed into the passenger seat, the backseat, and trunk of my small Stratus—my mini fridge, suitcase, laptop, and pillows. I felt claustrophobic. I had left the one place I hated most for the place I hated second most. This year was sure to be a fun one. More lacrosse, more classes, more just existing.

I shut my eyes against the glaring California sun and sighed heavily. School just filled up time for me. Sure, I was good at it. I was especially good at lacrosse, just like I was in high school—no one could better me. But what was the point?

Lacrosse was only one small part of me. A very, *very* small part of me. To everyone else though, that's who I was. I saw how pig-headed some of the football players became in high school and vowed I'd never be one of them. With that vow, I sacrificed any social status that lacrosse would yield. But that was all right. I would rather be alone, anyway.

I turned on the car and ran the air conditioner for a moment and then pulled the lever beside my seat and let it fall back—as far as my desk lamp, trash can, and blankets behind it would allow. Something just wouldn't let go and it gnawed at the back of my brain. Was it the fight with my dad right before I walked out the door? The excruciatingly long drive from Colorado? Or was it just my poor expectations for this year? Maybe it was all of the above.

Maybe it was the heat, or maybe it was the exhaustion, but whatever happened in that second, I was struck with an idea. I looked under my seat and in the center console for something to write with, and something to write on. I settled for a pencil and a napkin from a fast food stop on the way here.

Frustrating madness, surrounded by blinding light,
No matter where I go, it's always as dark as night.

Yep, I smirked at myself in dark humor. That was about right. Ugh. I sounded like an angst-ridden teenager.

I figured there was a side of me that no one could see, a side that used to be there anyway. I didn't exactly remember who that person was, because I hid it long ago, or it was gone—I didn't really know. I had morphed into a mask I created when my dad pushed sports on me instead of letting me pursue music. A mask that I wore when the school only saw me as the star player of the team. A mask that I hid behind so no one could see who I really was, or what I cared about. No one really cared when I was younger, so why would anyone feel any differently now?

I let my eyes open and stare up at the blazing sun in the bright blue sky. It was harsh to me, all the sunshine. I would rather be somewhere surrounded by less sun, somewhere more peaceful. Less intensity everywhere. Less pressure.

There is a downside to a lacrosse scholarship.

I stared out into the campus grounds, and farther away where I couldn't see was the playing field where I played lacrosse every Saturday. It was what was expected of me. It is the whole reason I got to go to this school. That is why I wasn't currently at the school of my choosing. The stupid school picked me.

I wonder what my mom would have thought of me attending a state college in California. Her dream had been for me to attend the small-town college in Seattle where she grew up and to play the piano, just like her.

Since she passed away, my dad never let me near that dream ever again.

I ran my hand through my damp hair. *He barely lets me near her piano.* I had to get out of the car. The hot interior threatened to fry my brain; I needed fresh air before I actually went insane. I grabbed my keys and stepped out.

I don't think I'll ever get used to this heat.

I grabbed the small backpack that held my laptop from the passenger seat, and slung it over my shoulder. I wanted to keep the laptop out of the heat, but really didn't want to haul all of my stuff out to the dorm yet. So I locked my car and strode slowly into the grounds, my eyes glued to my feet.

Campus was pretty busy. I saw a few familiar faces from the lacrosse team wander down onto the grassy quad between the dormitory buildings, one of them carrying a football under his arm. Alex Luther, I thought. Across the parking lot, a few of the young girls that had to be freshmen said goodbyes with tears in their eyes, their arms wrapped tightly around their parents' necks.

A few people waved at me as they passed, but for the most part I walked in silence. The scene made me smile a little. Finally back at school, I realized I didn't quite feel the dread I felt when I left home.

I trudged up the steps.

"Eli!"

I turned and looked down the stairs. I couldn't help myself. I smiled. There at the bottom stood my loud, rambunctious, carrying-on teammate, roommate and something of a friend, Steven.

"Eli! Hey man, what's up?" Steven ran up the steps three at a time to catch up with me. He looked taller, somehow, and wore old sweats and a university tee. I hadn't seen him since May, but still. I thought being six feet two was tall enough. Guess his genes didn't think so. And his hair was shorter. Cut all that stupid long blonde hair off—that blonde hair that he just had to keep last season, even when coach told him to shave it off. He argued, "The ladies dig it, Coach." And Coach bought it. Of course.

"Steven," I responded, smile still intact. He grasped my hand like a gorilla and shook it roughly while he clapped me on the shoulder with his free hand.

"How was your summer?" he asked, all too enthusiastic. I didn't know if I wanted to punch him or hug him. Such was my relationship with the kid.

I shrugged. "The usual."

He cocked an eye brow at me. "That bad, huh?" Steven cut in before I could really answer anymore. He knew my relationship with my dad was shaky, at best.

"Not bad, just—long." I shrugged. "How was yours?" I tacked on to deter him from pestering about me too much more.

He brushed it off and shrugged too. "Not bad. I played lifeguard, slept, talked to the ladies." He considered his words for a second. "Yeah, that's pretty much it." He smiled at me.

I returned the smile. I pulled the doors open to the dormitory and lead the way inside. I was tired of standing in that sterile California sunshine already.

"Where's the rest of your stuff?" Steven wondered aloud when he eyed my only bag on my back. I shrugged.

"It's back in my car."

He eyed me suspiciously. "Across campus? Why?"

"I didn't feel like bringing it all at once, and didn't exactly have enough hands to take it all in one trip," I replied.

"Whatever, dude," he sighed. He rolled his eyes sarcastically. Again with the wanting-to-punch-him thing.

Steven joined me and we made our way to the RA seated behind the counter in the middle of the large lobby. People were scattered around on the overstuffed sofas and uncomfortable arm chairs acting like school was in session.

"So where's your stuff?"

A smug grin flashed across his face.

"Already in the room. I just checked my car to make sure I had it all."

I nodded in response, and stepped up to the counter before he did.

After we checked in, we hopped onto the next available elevator, honestly too lazy to take the stairs, and rode in a companionable silence. One thing I really appreciated about Steven was that he respected my tendency to be silent a lot. I couldn't put up with anyone else as my roommate—I'd go crazy or strangle them. Or both. So, somehow, we developed a sort of mutual friendship agreement. Or something close to it. Whatever it was, it was a small thing that I appreciated about this school. A small thing that helped me to come back this year.

"So how about these new dorms, eh?" Steven said. His words pulled me out of my mental wanderings. I didn't miss a beat, though.

"Nice, I guess. But I won't say much until we get to the actual room where we'll live for the next nine months." I saw Steven agree with me in my peripheral vision.

"They are better than what we had before." He let out a small chuckle. I knew what he was thinking—that anything could be better than the state they were in before.

He got to the door before me, unlocked it, and stepped aside to let me in. And sure enough, the rooms were nicer. Even somewhat bigger. I dropped my bag on the bed that was empty. Steven had already strewn his things all over the bed farthest from the door, beside the window. Both of the headboards of the beds were pressed up against the right wall, so the sunlight would wash over our pillows early in the morning. I didn't mind that Steven took the bed that would get hit first. At least I would get an extra twenty minutes of sleep before the sun hit my not-fond-of-early-morning-sun face. I sat on the end of bed that was now mine to test it out. Even the small mattresses seemed to be better.

"You want me to help you cart your stuff up here so you aren't out 'til midnight bringing it in?" he offered. I looked up at him. This kid got a gold star in my book today for that.

"Yeah, man. Thanks."

The sun started to set over the tops of the buildings and the trees as Steven and I made our way back through the winding paths of the campus. We caught up about our summers and compared thoughts on the coming semester.

"Even you would have liked this girl," said Steven. "She's kind of quiet, like you. Yet easy to talk to. I just—"

"Whoa." I stopped in my tracks. A girl stood on the path ahead of us. Her long blonde hair caught the lighted gold and the amber of the setting sun. She emitted this glow—but no, that wasn't possible.

Was it?

How incredibly beautiful!

"And so that's when I said, I said, 'You can't be serious!'" Steven said. He was still walking, ahead of me now. He looked back. "Hey!" Clearly I was supposed to laugh at a joke I missed, because his eyes were on me.

"What's up?" Steven asked as he looked around. At first, I couldn't register an answer.

"Uh, nothing. Sorry, it's nothing," I said, and shook my head.

Steven shrugged his shoulders and continued towards the parking lot.

I looked back at her. *Is she for real?* A long shudder raced down my spine. The weirdest thing was that I couldn't figure out *why.*

She was thin, I noticed, fit with nice curves. I looked at her long, slender legs as she walked up the path. But she didn't seem immediately remarkable. It wasn't as if I hadn't seen a well-built blonde before. I frowned, and my brain felt fuzzy. *What is it? Why can't I just look away?*

A picture flashed across my mind. I saw a dark theater with a familiar face seated at a piano that shone in the bright stage lights. I sat in the front row beside my father, and my five-year-old feet swung lazily, unable to touch the floor. Mother played on stage, and the rush of exhilaration I felt as I heard those first notes were oddly similar to how I felt when I saw this girl. But why?

Her eyes sparkled as she stared at the buildings in front of her, as blue as a July afternoon sky. Was it the sunset? Her face glimmered too, just like her hair. But that was the sunlight, it had to be. Had to.

I felt strange and exposed, like I had gawked at something sacred. I tried to force myself to look at my feet. I managed to fall back into step with Steven, who looked at me as if I were crazy, but my eyes continued to flick up towards her. She was just *so* beautiful. And on our sidewalk!

She was twenty steps from us, ten, five. I blinked, and my brain just sort of shut down on me. I let Steven walk ahead and without a word I stepped to the left and found myself directly in front of her.

3 KERANA

I made my way through the intertwining paths between the buildings at Cornerstone University. I snatched the map out of my pocket one more time. I took note of all the trees and natural elements that the Humans who built this establishment attempted to retain. It settled my nerves slightly to see the familiar.

Stop thinking about home, I scolded myself. I was disappointed in my inability to endure the Earth realm, but it was hard to ignore the small weight on my chest that made it hard to breathe. I knew that Earth was a troublesome place, but I didn't think it would have begun to affect me already. *Why, I've not even talked to a Human yet!*

But I was used to endless trees, open fields, and wide skies. These tall walls here on Earth blocked the natural elements. Humans seemed content to live in their own structures, a curious trait. I checked the position of the sun. It was early afternoon, and I could hear Humans starting to filter onto the grounds. I was genuinely surprised that I had been alone up until that point. *What am I supposed to do?*

I stood still and glanced around for some kind of clue. I could hear people in the building in front of me. Panic started to seep through my body. *Maybe I'm not ready to come into this realm yet. I feel so lost.*

Get a hold of yourself, Kerana! It was so odd to be out of control—to not know what to do next.

I closed my eyes and inhaled the scent of the nearby trees and the warm air. There was no sense in completely losing it. It was irrational, a moment of unwanted weakness. My heart beat slowed, and I relaxed. I heard the first Human approaching—on my right! I swallowed hard. I focused my gaze up on the building in front of me, analyzing every detail. I didn't know what else to look at. From the reaction of the Humans who ignored me on the street, I wasn't sure if I should look directly at the Human or look away. My stomach flipped. As soon as I felt safe, I glanced over.

It was a male; muscular and much larger than almost all Eldurians. He had dark hair that hung in his face slightly. His mouth was set in a frown, as if he was concentrating on something very hard. His head was down, so I knew he hadn't seen me yet. I studied the contours of his frame, and the structure of his strong face. He seemed rougher than anyone I had ever seen, but I was very intrigued. Then he looked up at me.

He stopped a few feet in front of me, which startled me. A wave of shock passed over his face. Perhaps awe. His midnight blue eyes, once shadowed and hazy, opened wide and bright. The bag hanging over his shoulder slipped slightly, but his attention was focused entirely on me. He looked at me as if I were something he had never seen.

I smiled at him slightly, the same smile my father would use on me when I was little to instantly cheer me up. Then I looked away. He didn't move an inch! I turned off the path and walked through the grassy area toward the dorms.

"Wait!" he called after me. It was the first Human to address me. His voice was deep and rough, not like the soft, clear sound of the men back home. I wanted to react the way a Human would. I turned around slowly to face him, and kept my expression pleasant and innocent. His face froze again, as if he were made of stone. He stared. I felt slightly uncomfortable.

"I—uh—" he started. He ran his fingers through his hair and broke eye contact with me.

Am I supposed to say something? Is this normal behavior for a Human? I waited politely for him to continue, for him to do *anything*. His face fell back into the frown, and his eyebrows furrowed together. I realized he was frustrated again, but for some reason, it was because of me.

Our eyes locked.

"Who—what's your name?" The eye contact felt so different with a Human than an Eldurian. I couldn't quite explain why it was different, but I could see the depth in his eyes, and there was something else there that I wasn't accustomed to.

It was a simple question, probably the most simple of all questions. Yet, I couldn't find my voice. My first encounter with a Human wasn't going as smoothly as I expected. I took a quick breath. "Kerana."

He stared. Blinked. Shook his head.

But no, I only said my name, so he still should have understood me.

"I'm Eli." His response was simple too, which confused me somewhat. I didn't know what to say from this point, so I hoped that he would continue to speak.

He simply shook his head again and smirked at nothing in particular—almost laughing to himself. He walked towards the other dormitories. I stood rooted on the spot and watched him walk away from me. *How very odd*, I thought. That wasn't quite the reaction I expected. *Is that normal?* Abashed and slightly set off now by the experience, I turned away from the boy named Eli and walked up the pathway to the steps of the dormitory that would be my new home.

The dormitories for the females were quite a bit nicer than the males; I had heard from some passing students. Apparently they had remodeled them. They all seemed nice, but I grimaced slightly. They weren't as nice as home. Here, there was no soaring tree above me to comfort me, no bright green leaves with the perfect Eden sun shining through them, no songs of the Eldurians in the air all around. Here, it was eerily quiet. The warmth was gone.

With some practice, I managed to unlock the door with the card. A rude buzzer alerted me to enter. I looked around my small room—two small beds, simple desks, and sturdy wooden dressers. The walls were an odd green color that turned my stomach. I think they were attempting to mimic the dew in the morning grass. It wasn't comforting at all. I dropped my small bags across the bed nearest the window. *I wonder if my roommate is coming soon.*

I opened the window beside my bed and let out some of the stale, suffocating air. Small birds chirped and sang. Human voices bounced off the buildings and around the campus. The gentle wind flowing through the room helped to settle my raw nerves.

I set my thoughts to the task of unpacking. I didn't have very much because I fully intended on going home often, every night if I was able. I figured my roommate wouldn't say much if I didn't come back to the dorm often, or was gone while she slept. She wouldn't be any the wiser most of the time.

I made a neat stack of clothes in the bottom drawer of the dresser. My eyes caught the very deep blue sweater that my mother had given me just the day before. I lifted it to my face and drank in the smell. *Home. It smells like home.* I loved the color; it reminded me of the night sky. But now when I saw it, my mind also drifted to the eyes of the strange male I had met named Eli. He had such dark, stormy eyes. It almost hurt me to look at him. There seemed to be a lot of hurt pent up inside. But he walked away from me, probably a signal that he wanted me to steer clear of him.

I frowned slightly and sat on my bed. I didn't exactly believe that I would be the most well-liked person when I arrived, but I certainly hadn't expected a cold shoulder. I thought he was pleasant, introducing himself the way he did. But then just walking away? Smirking and laughing no less? I thought it was downright rude, whether I was Human or not.

I stood to my feet again, brushed my long hair out of my face, and stiffened in frustration. There really was no reason for me to be so upset. Maybe that was just how certain Humans were, and I most likely wasn't going to get that reaction from everyone. At least that is what I told myself. With effort, I shut my mind off from Eli and his rudeness.

Just then, I stiffened again, but this time because of what I was now hearing outside my door. My hearing being so acute, I had started to tune everything out here already. Everything was so loud in the Human realm. I stood still, even though it was unnecessary. I could hear the girl's voices as if they were standing right beside me.

"Did you see the girl who walked in here?" one of the voices insisted incredulously. There was a hint of desperation in her voice. I wasn't sure I liked it.

"No I didn't, but Rachel said that she looked like she came straight from a runway."

That was odd. I considered these words for a moment, trying to mentally reexamine my prior lessons for that word "runway." My thoughts immediately jumped to a "run away," or someone that ran away from home or something. I had even heard of people running away from prison or when they were wanted for a criminal act. I shook my head, making no connection between what the Humans said and myself. Maybe I looked like a convict? I froze.

"Oh man, you will know her when you see her," the first voice added impulsively. There was that tone that I didn't like again.

"She was that bad?"

"She will break every girl's heart on campus."

They thought there was something wrong with me. That I

stood out. I wasn't fitting in, and I hadn't even been here a full day. I sunk down on my bed, weary and depressed, trying to remember every detail of the Human world I could, trying to find a way to right this. As far as I could remember, I was doing everything correctly. I was saying the right things, gesturing the right way. I thought I even dressed the correct way. But apparently, I was doing something wrong. Something devastatingly wrong. I had to correct it and fast. I was sure that any other Eldurian would have been prepared enough to fix the situation if they were standing out the way I was. The fact that it was my first day playing Human made it that much worse. These girls had just said something I know they didn't intend for me to hear. I wonder how often that happened in the Human world.

Adonai, what do I do now? Please, I need help.

A whisper of fresh air flew through the open window, ruffling my hair. I stared out into the sunshine, and immediately felt better. The wind swirled through the room, making things dance.

Peace be with you, my child, the wind breathed in my ear.

Thank you, my heart sighed in return.

I reevaluated my standpoint and wondered about how I could possibly be "more Human." I decided that the next day I was going to wear clothing that was as simple as possible, something that couldn't be confused with any other things that would make the Humans talk about me. Then I would note what the other females were wearing. Just as I was finalizing these plans in my head, the door to my dorm room opened. I jumped up, startled because I had been so lost in my own thoughts. In front of me stood another female, about a head shorter than me, with colorful, loud clothing. She wore a sunshine yellow shirt that hung off her shoulders with a large red necklace that was lying at her throat, with tight pants that were vibrant blue. She had a thick belt wrapped around her waist that had bottle caps all the way around it. A wide red ribbon tied her hair in place, and bright purple shoes donned her small feet.

Her clothing really caught my attention. She seemed very out of place compared to some of the other Humans I had seen up to this point. I listened out into the hallway. Not a murmur about her clothing or how she looked.

She can dress like this and not have a word said against her, and I get ridiculed for a simple shirt and jeans? I am not sure I will ever be able to understand this world.

Even still, I couldn't help but stare at this female. She threw her heavy luggage onto her bed without a thought and then sighed heavily as she stood up right.

She was very pretty, but naturally so. She didn't wear makeup, but her skin looked almost pearl-like, and her eyes were wide and an aqua blue. Her long hair was a rich amber color, but it didn't look as if she had tampered with it to create that color. I figured most Human females were envious of that color. I almost was.

But the thing that I liked most about her was her wide smile. It brightened her whole face as she grinned at me from across the room, and her vibrant eyes matched the happiness now etched onto her face. I couldn't help but smile back at her; she made it very easy to do so.

"Wow. I can see why everyone has been talking," she said, plopping down onto the end of her bed, her lucid eyes never leaving mine. I blinked at her, and frowned again, following her motives and sitting on the end of my small bed. I couldn't find the words to say, so I avoided eye contact. I heard her snicker.

"What?" I asked, returning my gaze to her. Her face was warm, and gentle. It loosened the knot in my stomach slightly.

"You mean you don't know?" She asked, her face changing. She looked like she was really trying to analyze me and what I was thinking. Her stare was powerful, and I found I couldn't look away. It made my skin itch, like she knew what I was thinking. Then she sat back, breaking eye contact and laughed out loud. This really threw me off.

"I assume you know what people think of you?"

"Not exactly."

Her eyes grew wide in disbelief, and she laughed again. "Have you looked in a mirror lately?"

I reached up, touching my face. I had looked into a mirror just the night before. I hadn't seen anything wrong.

"You are gorgeous. Absolutely stunning." she exclaimed, the grin she had greeted me with dancing back onto her pretty face.

I felt my eyes grow wide, shock coursing through me. I couldn't believe it. I had convinced myself that the Humans thought I was an oddity. Well, I suppose I still was. But at least there wasn't something wrong with me like I had originally thought. The next thought that passed through my head was embarrassment. I felt my face flush red. I guess I had a lot to learn, still.

I could feel my roommate staring at me. "You seriously had no idea? Wow. I think I am gonna like you!" I heard her hop up from her bed, and a moment later, she had sat down beside me on my bed.

"You see, I know a lot of girls who are pretty, too. But they would *kill* to look like you," I noticed her quick glance at my figure. "If I had to paint you a picture, I would compare two kinds of girls; one I would compare to goddesses and the others to their faithful worshippers. But here you are, well worthy of being slotted into my category of 'goddess,' and you have the attitude of a saint. Wow." She looked away from me, and stared ahead of her into space for a moment, thinking something over, I assumed. "Don't let this go to your head, though. I think I am gonna like you better if you aren't narcissistic." Then she winked at me, which made me laugh. "Seriously, you never noticed?"

I shrugged. "I didn't realize that was out of the ordinary, because where I'm from, everyone has similar features."

She brightened, turning her whole body to face me, crossing her legs on my bed. "Where are you from, exactly?" she inquired, attentive.

I froze for half a second. *What do I say?*

I knew it would be wrong to lie, but I also knew that telling her the full truth was out of the question. Adonai required me to be honest, but protect our ways from the mortals.

"I am from a small town a long ways away. You would never have heard of it, so I won't even try to explain it."

The girl studied me for a moment with those intense, aqua eyes, but let whatever questions I was sure were whirring through her mind pass.

"Where are you from?" I asked, hoping she wouldn't return the topic of conversation to me, in case she asked too many questions that I didn't know how to answer.

"I am actually from near Chicago. I live about half an hour from the city with my folks. Came to this school for their photography program. It's one of the best in the country, I guess. So far, I'm impressed with it. It can't be so bad if I like it," she said, winking at me again.

"I am being so impolite. Forgive me for that! I haven't even introduced myself, and I don't know your name!" she exclaimed, with sudden fervor.

"I am Kerana," I said.

"You can call me Ev. My full name is Evelyn, but it is too prim and proper for my liking. Ev is more artsy."

"It is an honor to make your acquaintance, Ev." I said, just like I had learned back home.

Ev grinned at me, laughing a little, her whole face lighting up again. Then she reached out, and embraced me.

"We live together, honey. I think we are more than acquaintances now."

I spent quite a bit of the afternoon with Ev, getting to know her. By the time we made our way to the dining hall, which was something I had been both anxious and excited about, I had learned that Ev was an enthusiastic bird watcher, had a Labrador retriever by the name of Spunky whom she missed terribly already, and she tended to sleep in so late that the sun was going down before she surfaced. She made me laugh, and she made me happy. I felt as if I had discovered another Eldurian. If I hadn't heard some of the pain in her voice as she spoke of her late grandfather that had passed away that summer, or the flippant way in which she talked about her life, I would have almost believed her to be from Eden.

The dining experience was sorely disappointing. No fresh foods. Everything smelled wrong, as if it had been tampered with. Ev didn't seem to mind, as she chattered away happily to me and piled food onto her plate. I decided on an apple and a glass of water.

Ev cocked an eyebrow at me. "That's really all you are eating?"

I shrugged my shoulders, and she smiled. "That's all right, honey. I understand the first day nerves. Everyone gets them. Well, I never did, but that's okay," she patted my shoulder affectionately. "I understand to the best of my ability."

I smiled in reply.

Late that night, after Ev was finally asleep, I sat on my bed, my knees curled up to my chest. I felt very tired, but not horribly so. I looked up at the moon that streamed in through our window, and crossed to the window sill. I leaned against it and closed my eyes.

Adonai, You have blessed me in so many ways today that I can't count them all. It has been far different than what I expected it to be.

My thoughts drifted to the first few moments of being on Earth. *Fear. That moment was terrible. I don't understand Your plan fully, but I pray You will reveal it to me.*

I waited.

There was no reply.

I bit my lip as I withdrew from the window. I knew that Adonai didn't always answer prayers immediately, and knew that He was listening.

I just hoped that You would answer me this time. I really need some answers, some peace.

I longed to step into the trees and to sit beside Adonai. How could Humans stand being away from the presence of Adonai? I felt as if I were impossibly far away from Him.

I crossed to my bed and slipped underneath the covers, the silence unsettling. As I closed my eyes, I felt a weight settle onto my chest; a weight that I had never felt before.

4 ELI

Stupid! Why did you stand there and just gawk at her?

I skipped the cafeteria food and worked on unpacking my stuff. I was so aggravated. *Why was I such an idiot in front of that girl?* Sure, I had seen girls before. Plenty of times. Everywhere. Some girls begged me to take them out, but I never found a lot of interest in dating. I was a loner, and that was who I wanted to be.

Right, because I *was* an idiot. Plain and simple.

I had to be the most ridiculous—I wanted to kick myself.

She is only another girl.

Yeah, but I'd never seen another girl quite like her. My thoughts drifted uncontrollably.

Wow. I had to shake this. I was just tired, that's all. Tired and stressed.

What an awesome way to start off the semester.

Thoughts of the girl I just saw crowded my frontal lobes. I skipped the sheets and blankets routine and threw my sleeping bag on the bed instead. It was time to crash. Exhausted, I drifted into the realm of sleep.

I woke up with a start. The red digits on the clock read 2:10AM. I ran my hands through my hair. From the street lights outside our window I could see the outline of Steven and heard his even breathing. Man, I must have been tired.

My dreams had been anything but pleasant. I was playing a beautiful black baby grand piano in the middle of a big lacrosse game, my whole team watching me and hurling colorful profanities.

I fell back on the bed again and put the other pillow over my head. I slipped back into the same dream again.

My dad was the coach, and all he did was yell at me on my piano in the middle of the field from the sidelines. It was against our rival school in southern California, and I wasn't playing my part, mentally or physically. The other team's score shot up constantly, so fast that the numbers started to blur together. I couldn't stop playing my piano. The ending buzzer started to sound across the field as a death march for my team...

I opened my eyes. My dorm room was filled with sunlight. I squinted. I slapped the snooze button on my alarm and stiffly sat up, stretching. 10:48.

I swore so loud that the people three floors below me probably heard. I hopped up, ran to my dresser, ripped out a pair of jeans and a clean shirt, and jumped into them. I ran down the hall to the bathroom, and quickly brushed my teeth. I slapped water on my bed head hairdo and tried to straighten it out. I ran back to my room, grabbed my schedule and my book bag, locked the door, and tore off down the hall at a sprint.

Just my luck to be late on the first day of classes. And to my first class no less.

Class had started roughly half an hour ago.

I had to make up some excuse for why I was late. I couldn't tell the truth.

"Uh yeah... um... I uh... slept in." That's gonna sound really good.

But what else could I use? Something that wasn't going to make my teacher second-guess me. But what?

I reached the lobby, and charged through the front doors, not even glancing at the RA behind the counter. My body started to complain with the exertion. It wasn't used to sprinting this much since last lacrosse season.

My car broke down.

No, that one is too common. If I lived somewhere where there was snow, it might be a better one to use.

There was a death in the family.

Too common again, and this one is pretty much used as a last resort. I wasn't quite that desperate. Maybe on the due date of a term paper.

I locked myself out of my dorm room this morning.

That one was better, but still not thought out very well. There were still loopholes. I couldn't have those, or at least really obvious ones.

I had a last minute schedule change.

Hmm. This one had potential. As I reached the building where my class was, I thought through exactly what I would say to the teacher as I walked in. I could see it all in my head, and it was an innocent enough excuse.

I had originally planned to take a philosophy class at this time, but since I needed this physics credit more than I needed philosophy, I decided last minute that I should still see if there was room. And lucky me, there were a few spots open.

I knew it was safe because physics classes were usually small. Being such a difficult science, it didn't have very many people actively pursuing it. And I also knew the professor, which is exactly why I knew he would grill me about why I was late.

I reached the stairs to the second floor, took them two at a time, and raced down the hall, passed classrooms on both sides as I flew by. I assumed people in the classrooms were startled by my thundering footsteps, staring at me out the door, but I didn't have a chance to take a good look around me. I saw my classroom at the end of the hall, so I slowed down, and tried to catch my breath. I didn't want to be seen racing into the room; it would blow my innocent cover story.

As I approached the open classroom, I realized that it was oddly quiet. I couldn't even hear the professor speaking. My eyes were drawn to a piece of bright green paper posted on the wall near the door:

Physics 303 with Prof. Steinbach has been canceled due to lack of enrollment.

I didn't know whether I wanted to laugh or cry. Still catching my breath, I leaned against the wall, my eyes still glued to the piece of paper. What a waste of my time. I could still be sleeping! I could have saved myself the effort if I had only known.

I wonder.

I reached into my pocket of my jeans, and checked my cell phone. I had two texts from Steve. One was asking me a pointless question about where iced tea came from, and the other was saying that he heard my physics class was canceled. I also realized I had a voicemail from a number here at the school. Listening to it, I realized it was my advisor, also telling me that many dropped the class this morning or found a different time to take it. I looked back at my schedule; I still had four hours before my next class. Fuming and frustrated, I stalked back the way I had come, heading back to bed to sleep off my building ferocity.

Later that afternoon I caught up with Steven at the cafeteria. After lunch we headed off to lacrosse practice.

The first practice back at school is always the hardest.

I stood with my hands on my knees, completely out of breath as Steven ran up beside me. He stumbled to a stop and gasped for breath.

"I," he began, a wheeze in his words. "Hate. Everything."

I smiled in spite of the fact that my lungs felt like they were on fire.

I watched as a teammate named Kyle Hanley fell to his knees and hurled all over the tartan track beneath him.

"Oh, come on," Steven moaned, disgusted.

"Ladies!" we heard. Coach Clarkson made his way down the bleachers to where the rest of the team gathered. "Welcome to my new training regime! It's nice to see you all again."

He wore his *Cornerstone State* hat, bearing the school's C in bright red and gold. I noticed his little red whistle that he loved to blow at us so much. I was glad to see it was hanging from his neck, not his mouth at the moment. Coach looked down at Hanley, who was pale and sweaty, still bent over his own sick.

"Glad to see you are all enjoying yourselves today!" He stepped around Hanley to stand in the middle of our group. "Now. I am keeping my eye on you the next few weeks. Since Bradley graduated, I'm out a captain for the year. So far I've decided to watch Hanley"—he looked over his shoulder at the figure attempting to get to his feet—"Graham"—he looked at Steven, who looked around to see if there was possibly another person with the surname Graham—"and Mattison."

I looked up at Coach, startled myself. I did not expect that.

"Now go shower up. I'll see you all same time tomorrow. Freshmen? Stay back a minute. I've got to weed out the weaklings; can't have all of you on my team."

Steven gaped at me.

We showered and started our way back to the dorms. Steven and I were both surprised that Coach even knew our names.

"It might be cool, being captain," Steve said.

"It wouldn't be much different," I replied. "I couldn't really care less. I was just surprised."

"Yeah, but the fact that Coach thinks I am good enough to be considered is pretty sweet."

"You're a good player, Steve. You should be captain."

Buzz buzz buzz.

My pocket started to vibrate. Surprised, I reached down and

slid my phone out of my pocket. I quickly eyed the caller I.D. and saw that it was a Colorado number. My house number.

Dad.

I looked up at Steven with big eyes.

"What's up man?"

The phone continued to buzz in my hand. *Should I answer it?*

Steven looked over my shoulder and read the number, and his eyes too grew large. "Dude, is that--"

"Yeah," I replied heavily. As we walked, I answered the phone. Steven watched my face for a reaction.

"Hello?"

"Eli? Hi. It's Dad."

He sounded *thrilled* to be on the phone with me. "Um, hey. What's up?"

I heard him click his tongue on the other end. "I just wanted to check and make sure you actually got to the school. You didn't call me."

His voice didn't sound parental at all, just annoyed. I felt my anger slowly start to rise. "I guess I forgot."

"Yeah, guess so," he replied flatly. A silence settled in on the phone.

I looked for something to say, and settled on my most recent news. "So, I am in consideration for lacrosse captain this year."

Still more silence. "It's about time," was all I heard in response.

That was definitely not the response I wanted, but nevertheless, I wasn't surprised. I grit my teeth and sighed.

"Finally you are working yourself hard enough to get noticed a little."

"Captains are usually seniors," I said, not trying to keep the anger out of my voice. "I'm only a junior," I reminded him. *How is it that we can't ever have a normal conversation?*

"Congratulations," he replied sarcastically. I fumed.

"I gotta go," I said, and tried to resist the urge to hang up on him.

"All right," he said, his voice emotionless.

"Bye," I said, and ended the call before I even heard him say it back.

Steven looked sympathetic, but waited a minute before he said anything. "Bad?"

I shrugged. "It was normal."

"Ah," he replied. He didn't bring it up again after that.

5 KERANA

The next morning came quickly, with sunlight washing over my small room that I shared with Ev. She and I had stayed up quite late talking, just getting to know each other.

I woke up quite earlier than she did, finding her sprawled out entirely across her small bed, snoring slightly. As quiet as the whispering wind flowing into the room from the open window, I retreated to the shower rooms, which I found somewhat awkward and intimidating, and then got dressed for the day, choosing a simple pair of jeans again with a wonderful watery blue shirt. I sat on the edge of my bed for a long while, and watched the clouds form in the sky. My first class, English, wasn't until noon, and to my delight, I discovered that Ev had the same class. I waited patiently until she woke up later that morning.

She sat up, ran her fingers through her wild, fiery hair, and opened her vivid blue eyes in my direction.

"You're awake already?" she asked, trying to stifle a yawn that was growing. "And ready, no less."

I smiled. "Yes, I have been since the sun rose."

Ev laughed, a sound that reminded me of a wind chime. "I am pretty sure I won't ever understand you. Why were you up so early?"

"I always woke up with the sun when I lived back home."

"Well, whatever makes you happy, I suppose. You didn't make a peep, though, because I would have known if you did. I sleep very lightly."

I looked back out the window as Ev got up and got ready. She adorned a bright red shirt that exposed her shoulders with a black pair of shorts and high boots. I was sure *I* was never going to understand *her* style of dress, but I had to commend her for her unique ways. She also grabbed a black box with a glass circle on the front, and as I eyed it curiously, she puffed up proudly.

"You like it? This baby cost me almost eight hundred dollars."

"I haven't seen anything like it before," I relayed to her, being perfectly honest. She smirked, pride evident on her gentle face again. She obviously didn't realize that I really didn't know what it was.

"I know. I saved up for two summers in high school for this camera."

A camera—a photo box then? That must be what she means by being a photography major. I will have to do more research on cameras and photography.

She and I made our way down to the dining hall, where we found only a handful of people. She continued to talk on our way to class about her camera and about some of the shooting she had been doing just before she came to school. It sounded contradictory; I wasn't sure how shooting could be beautiful. Wasn't shooting dangerous?

She must mean something entirely different, I decided.

We walked among the tall trees where sunlight filtered through, causing shadows to spread haphazardly across the paved walkways and green lawns.

She was in the middle of a sentence when I lost my concentration on our conversation as a group of other females passed us. All of their eyes were fixated on me, and it made me incredibly uncomfortable. Ev, on the other hand, didn't seem to notice at all. They all stared at me with wide, unblinking eyes, and it made me feel so flustered that I had to look away.

"You all right, there?" Ev asked me, eyeing me suspiciously. I readjusted my focus to her, but I could feel my face falling into a grimace.

"Well, that's not such a pretty look on your pretty face," she laughed. "Seriously, what's bothering you all of the sudden?"

"All these girls walking by are—"

"Ogling at you? Yeah, I've been noticing that. But they have been since you set foot on campus, honey."

I watched as another cluster of females descended from a nearby staircase coming from another building to the center of campus. I caught eye contact with one of them, who essentially gasped, and leaned closer to her friend. I could just hear what she whispered.

"Should we take bets on what she hasn't changed with plastic surgery?" I heard the girl hiss into the other's ear as she made eye contact with me. Instantly I felt a chill run over my arms and down my back, as if ice had been given life and decided to roam over me. The girl hearing the comment mimicked the face of her friend beside her. I felt absolutely no warmth or smiles from either of those girls, or from many of the girls, for that matter.

I couldn't exactly understand what I was doing wrong, only to feel very unhappy about it. I was sure that I was doing an awful job of blending with the rest of the students here. The point was to not draw attention to myself, and here I was, doing just that. I sighed.

"Speak to me, woman!" Ev dramatically said, shaking my arm. My lips curled into a small smile.

"What did you want me to say?" I asked. She rolled her eyes.

"You aren't exactly difficult to read, Kerana."

I frowned. That was disappointing for some reason.

"You are obviously upset about something, and I want you to tell me what that something is!"

I sighed again.

"See? Now, come on." she said.

"I just don't like all this attention that I am getting." I answered, shifting my gaze from yet more girls walking by me. Ev looked sideways at me.

"You never got this reaction from people back home?"

I considered it for a moment. "No, I never did, to be honest."

She seemed somewhat shocked by my answer. "Well, I wouldn't worry too much about it, anyway. They will all get used to being around you eventually."

"Eventually? How long will that be? I don't like being looked at like this."

Ev raised a single eyebrow speculatively at me. "You are one of a kind. This kind of attention is reserved simply for the most elite of the elite."

"I'm not sure I understand. These girls seem to be, well, mad at me."

"Well, they probably are. Mad with jealousy. It makes sense. Girls like you don't happen naturally. Or often. So when perfection crosses the paths of imperfect women, they tend to get a bit—well, feisty."

I still wasn't sure I understood. We walked in silence for a few moments when we came upon a group of young males who were all standing in a group talking before class. As soon as we got close, I relaxed. They weren't females after all, so maybe their reactions wouldn't be quite so potent.

I couldn't have been more wrong.

The nearest one to me let his face slip from a look of awe to a wide grin, his eyes raking over my frame that made me think he wanted to eat me. Another beside him noticed me at about the same time, and whistled between his teeth as his buddies across from him laughed like giddy children.

I bent my head and sped away from them. Ev followed at my heels, glaring over her shoulder at the Human males who had made a scene out of me walking by them.

I felt Ev place a hand on my shoulder, a sign of affection, protection, and comfort. It was much appreciated at the moment. The reaction of the males left me feeling embarrassed and distressed, and I wasn't entirely sure why.

"Well, you just got the attention of half of the school's lacrosse team, that's for sure," Ev said, and she kindly steered me away from another grouping of people congregated near the main doorway to the English Arts and Literature building. We walked through the door together and I couldn't keep my head up to look where I was going. I was afraid of finding more glassy-eyed gazes.

We found our classroom at the end of the western wing, and since we were early, Ev led me to a pair of empty seats behind a small table towards the back of the room. Windows flanked the whole left wall, and worn bookshelves stretched all the way to the ceiling on the wall behind our desks. It smelled like warm coffee and old, yellowing pages of ancient books.

Ev sat beside me, and I felt tears welling up in my eyes, threatening to cascade down my cheeks. I wiped them away with the back of my hand, frustrated with myself for feeling this way, and also frustrated with the way people were reacting towards me. I didn't know how Humans could survive feeling these emotions; they were awful.

Ev just sat there beside me and looked at me with her aquarium hued eyes, a look of concern fixed on her slim face.

"You know, I'm sorry that all of these girls are acting like a bunch of witches to you. Let me fill you in on something that I learned living in Chicago, okay? So listen up."

I looked over at Ev.

"Women are ruthless. Especially jealous women. You are gorgeous. And it still shocks me that you aren't strutting around acting like you are better than everyone else. There's a reason why women are nasty to each other, why they continually stab each other in the back. They usually *do* act like they are better than everyone else. That causes problems."

She leaned closer to me. "You've really never seen any of this before?"

"Never," I responded.

"Well it's probably a good thing for you to remember that. But I can promise you this. It will die down eventually. They'll stop staring eventually, and they'll all go back to their boring, little, petty lives. So not to worry, dear friend."

I smiled weakly at her, wanting to thank her for being so supportive thus far. She seemed to get the hint.

"Don't mention it, sweetie. I know how it feels to be the outcast. I used to go to school in a small town outside of Columbus, Ohio and, man, did people look at me funny for the way I dressed. Everyone avoided me and didn't like me."

I straightened a bit. How could someone not like her?

"That's horrible," I said. I couldn't grasp how anyone couldn't be attracted to Ev's bright personality and contagious smile.

Ev smirked, stretched her arms and let them come to rest behind her head. "You bet. And do you want to know the best thing to do in order to deal with all the unwanted attention?"

I nodded.

"Just ignore it. Like I said, they will relax after a while. Either that or you will just get used to it. Whichever comes first, I suppose."

I shifted uncomfortably. She was right, I figured. But I made a mental note as the classroom began to fill up. *I am definitely going to talk to my mother about this when I go home tonight.*

6 ELI

I was tired already of being cooped up in the dorm. Steve and I had started to plow through homework that night after dinner, and I had made a sizeable dent in mine. As I relaxed in my chair, checking my email lazily, I checked my watch, and it was only eight; I easily had enough time for a short walk. I glanced over at Steven, who was slumped against his pillows. He was eyeing his video games, which had been freshly scattered near the television on his dresser.

I got to my feet and stretched my arms over my head. "Why don't you just play? You aren't doing your homework anyways."

Steven shook his head. "What? Oh. Yeah. All right. I can do it in an hour. Yeah, I'll do it in an hour."

Yeah right. I thought, and laughed at the thought.

"I'm going for a walk, I'll be back later."

"All right, man, later," Steve said. He was already off his bed and picking a game to play.

The night was clear as I stepped outside. The lights scattered across campus, vivid and sterile, accenting the grave features of the landscape. The walkways were awash in the white light, making the shadows long and somewhat ominous. I followed the paths mindlessly, knowing I didn't have to even think in order to get where I was headed. The moon overhead was aglow with speckles of fiery blue stars that pinpricked its surroundings and complemented it.

I came upon the tall building that I had discovered in my freshman year. I realized I had wandered there unintentionally. It was for the most part quiet on campus at the moment, and I figured it was because it was only the first day back. I made my way around to the rear of the building, and found the usual door I used, cloaked in shadows. I reached out and tried the cold, metal handle; as usual, it was unlocked. I sneaked inside, well-practiced from sneaking in for nearly three years.

I fumbled through the dark hallway, my hand grazing the wall for mental clarity and familiarity of the space. I found another heavy door at the end of the hall, and pushed it open too. I felt the nearby wall for a light switch, and flicked it on.

The smell that hit me was like my own personal heaven. Polished wood floors; upholstered rows of ghostly, old, deep burgundy chairs; dusty carpet that was faded from years of feet strolling on it. But the best smell that I recognized immediately was the smell of my passion and my life: the Schimmel grand piano. It was a large, black, beautiful piece, almost a century old, that stood in the very center of a large theater stage. It had been empty all summer, as I could tell by the stillness of everything in the room. I smiled. I was going to be the first to use it.

I strode over to the piano and let my fingers lightly graze across the polished surfaces. They were dusty, of course. I wiped each key with the end of my T-shirt. I had waited all summer to play this wonderful instrument. I sat on the bench at the front of the piano and rested my fingers gently on the ivory. The black and white contrast was comforting, from the ebony and ivory keys, the shimmering lights reflecting off the black glossy surface, and the dark notes dancing and swirling over the old white sheet music—the book was open to the same page. I pushed middle C, and smiled back at the incredible acoustics in this auditorium. I graduated to simple chords and let my mind unwind from all the stress. Pent-up frustration mingled with fresh delight transferred through my fingers, onto the keys, and rang from the strings. The music filled the large hall around me, bouncing off the walls and the floors. It was intoxicating, growing louder, fueled by the tension of the last few months of pretending to live. The sound pierced my soul, cut down deep, tore open my heart and filled it with a tangible peace and a new sense of life. I closed my eyes and let my fingers breathe across the keys. The music reached a crescendo I could feel in my heart, my hands, my head. I lost a sense of time.

I transitioned into one of my oldest songs. I had written it when I was younger, and it was a song of lament and sorrow. My whole heart and soul had been inscribed into the lyrics, so singing it was a release to my spirit. I cried out the lyrics, blending the chords in the piano with the grief in my words. Here, I felt transformed into something more than a lacrosse player, more than the son of Carl Mattison.

Hungry for more, I played every song I had ever written, and relived the ache in my heart since I last played. I sighed deeply. It had been months. The music was both healing and poison, life and death. I played until my fingers numbed.

I slowed the low G bass keys and glanced down at my watch.

Whoa! After midnight. Determined to end the affair with a sweet goodbye, I let my right hand glide down the high keys while my left hand trembled the bass. When I was finished, the bass lingered and I listened. Soft echoes rang from each corner, as though the room was lined with speakers, high and low. Satisfied, I stopped. Only then did I look at my watch again.

I made my way to the light switch. I looked back longingly at the piano, shut off the lights, and made my way back across campus.

The outside air was breezy except it felt good on my sweaty face. Besides, the walk back to the dorm was part of the aura of my secret recitals. I breathed easier now, my thoughts soothed by the music's medicine.

I chuckled a little under my breath. I had worked up a sweat playing piano. Sometimes I didn't sweat a lot at lacrosse practice. That was really kind of sad. Heaven forbid my father ever found out that piece of information.

I was in no hurry to get back to my room. I walked in step with the song I hummed, not exactly paying attention to where I was going. But that was when I heard something that didn't fit my melodic rhythm.

I stopped in my tracks. The place could be creepy-looking at night when you weren't moving. I looked up at the dark buildings and empty, intertwining pathways. I could have sworn I heard footsteps, but I couldn't see anyone. I strained my ears toward the sound again. Nothing. I shrugged it off and hopped back into step towards my dorm. I passed in front of one of the girls' buildings and I heard it again. Footsteps. This time I was sure. I waited to see if whoever it was would show themselves.

I saw a slight-framed, tall girl slide out of the ring of shadows just outside one of the lampposts. I jumped back behind a tree so I could watch her without her finding me. She stepped out into the flood of light. I gasped. It was the girl I had met the day before! Kerana! Everyone was talking about her.

Her long blonde hair billowed gently in the breeze, and her brilliant blue eyes were like beacons in the darkness. She was well dressed, and she looked as if she wasn't heading to bed anytime soon. Actually, she looked like she was heading out for the night. Not entirely uncommon in college, but she was alone, and that was unusual for a girl. But as soon as I had seen her, she disappeared from the light to the darkness on the other side of the path. And like that, she was gone.

I stood rooted to the spot, watching her silhouette vanish from view. I realized I was holding my breath. That thought kind of annoyed me. She had stopped me dead in my tracks twice now. There was something seriously extraordinary about that girl. No one before her had affected me so much. But then, a few of the other guys seemed affected, too. *Is that all this is? A physical attraction to a beautiful girl?*

I shook it off and quietly made my way back to the fourth floor of my dorm. After using the restroom I opened the room door that Steven had kindly left unlocked for me. I slipped out of my jeans and t-shirt and passed out on my bed.

7 KERANA

The darkness was comforting. I wanted the shadows to engulf all sound around me so my footsteps would be muffled, undetected by Human ears. I attempted to avoid the lights so that I wouldn't be discovered. Closer to my dorm, I was almost positive that I had noticed a Human nearby, but didn't stay to investigate. I waited until Ev fell asleep, which took quite a while because she wanted to talk in great detail about our first day at the university. While I was very interested in hearing about her and what she had done, I was also aching to just dash out of the room and back to the Portal a few short miles away. But I was patient, and listened intently to her talk. I also had to admit I enjoyed sharing some of my experiences from the day as well. She was the perfect roommate—incredibly helpful with everything despite not knowing I desperately needed someone to show me how to properly function as a Human.

The still night air did wonders for my throbbing mind. It felt as if a dense cloud settled into my once fluid and clear thoughts. Even walking away from the dorm gave me minutes to relax and

I slid out of my Human pretenses back into my natural self.

It did not take me terribly long to reach the Portal. With a deep breath of anticipation, I slipped through.

It was night on the other side as well, but I couldn't believe how enticing the scent of my own home was; the scent of warm earth, murmuring brooks, and timeless greenery. I could see the stars winking down at me from above, joyfully welcoming me home.

My feet glided over the familiar path. I stood outside the door. It seemed silly to knock, but I didn't want to startle them by just walking in. I knocked on the outside door. Footsteps approached instantaneously from the other side. They were heavier, so I knew it was my father even before he opened the door inward.

His bright eyes smiled at me before he laughed and pulled me into a warm embrace.

"My child, how wonderful it is to see you," he said. I felt the warmth of his breath in my hair. I buried my face into his chest, relishing the earthy, familiar feel. I realized at that moment just how homesick I had been, even in only a matter of hours.

I heard more footsteps behind my father, and saw the exquisite face of my mother peering over his shoulder, her oceanic blue eyes welling up with tears.

"Mother!" My voice caught and I turned to hear, salty tears staining my cheeks. She beamed at me, happiness radiating off of her as she held me tightly.

"I am so glad you have come home." I could hear the earnestness in her voice. She pulled away and looked at me as only my mother could. Wet face, sparkling eyes—both of us. Around my waist I felt little hands, and looked down to see the glittering smiles of my younger siblings. I bent down to their level and let them wrap their arms around my neck. The close proximity of my entire family was like a sedative to my antsy spirit.

They brought me inside and I noticed all of their eyes glanced at me every few moments. Even the younger ones seemed very aware of me, their orb like eyes wide and ever watchful. My father motioned us into the living quarters, and we all naturally found our way to our usual seats; my father in the large chair in the corner, my siblings on either side of me on the large couch, and my mother in the rocking chair beside the fireplace. It felt like an ordinary night at home, where my mother would have just made a fabulous meal, my siblings would be settling down for sleep, and my father would pull an old book off the shelf and read to us all. My heart clenched in my chest when I realized that this was not an ordinary night.

Father leaned forward in his chair. "So please, daughter of mine, tell us about your first two days within the Human realm. We all asked Adonai to keep a close eye on you while you explored and started your learning experience." Father's eyes, like raw emeralds, reflected cheerfully in the glow of the candles and firelight. I smiled, in spite of myself. The younger ones sat in rapt attention, twitching with curiosity, I was sure, about what Humans were actually like. I retold the past few days' events, relishing the details, realizing the fondness with which I spoke of the other realm. I saw relief on my father's face, and joy on my mother's. I told them about my classes, about Ev, and about my new room. I told them about my doubts and fears the first day, and about all the looks people had been giving me. That part of the conversation brought a sinking feeling back to the pit of my stomach. Maybe I wasn't so fond of it after all.

"Kerana, darling, let me share my experiences in the Human realm with you." My father leaned forward on his chair in my direction, his eyes fiery and wise. "As you know, there are many different places assigned to Eldurians to go to for their training in the Human realm. I was placed into a small town in the state of Maine, very far from where you are now." He paused, exchanging a glance with his wife. She smiled and nodded, encouraging him on. "And I'm sure this is the very last thing that you want to hear, but I do truly know what you are going through right now.

I remember exactly how it felt to step through that Portal for the first time into an alien environment. I remember how it felt to try and interact with the Humans, try to get them to believe that you were one of them. I will be very honest, I stood out just as much as you are right now."

"As did I, my dearest," my mother said, her gentle gaze moving from my father to me.

My father smiled. "It is difficult, especially when you are trying so hard not to draw attention to yourself. But let me fill you in on a little secret: it does get easier. That much I do promise you. Especially once you learn where the balance is between being an Eldurian, a guardian to the Humans, and being a friend to them, someone who can learn how to think and act like them. Adonai created us to be very similar to one another, so it is only natural that we find a medium between the two."

"Being an Eldurian is hard, we know. We understand the difficulties of being within that realm. But through us Adonai can save their world, and still shed light on their lives. You will be a shining example of good to their dark and hurting world, and it may be apparent to many of them already. It sounds as if your new friend Evelyn sees something very special in you even now." My mother said reassuringly. I smiled at the thought of my roommate, probably sprawled out across her small bed back in the dormitory, snoring, with her amber hair disheveled across her pillows.

"I think I'm quite fond of her, too," I replied, my heart lightening.

"And there is nothing wrong with that, dear. Don't think that your training is going to exempt you from developing relationships." My mother's face slipped into a smile. "Even though I ended up marrying your father, I had many friends from the Human realm, many of whom I miss dearly. But I know that Adonai is taking good care of them."

I shifted, thinking of Ev again. I realized that after a short year I was going to have to leave her. Was it worth the pain of having to lose someone I could end up very close to if I knew it had to end to create a friendship with her? As if she could read my thoughts, my father's face slipped into a sympathetic expression.

"My sweetheart, you must not let the finish line in that world stop you from moving forward and doing what your heart wants. You can't just bypass that opportunity. We are given it for a reason."

I smiled at him. I was so happy to have been able to come home. It just made everything so much clearer. We sat until the early hours of the morning sharing stories and laughs, and I listened to more advice. I helped my mother carry the young twins to bed, since they had fallen asleep while we were talking in the living space. She and my father kissed me goodnight, and I retreated to my own sleeping quarters. I lay awake for a long while, thinking about what I had seen and heard over and over. I finally fell into an exhausted slumber, and the last thing that floated across my mind's eye was a pair of dusky blue, stormy eyes.

8 ELI

The trees started to make their annual change from sunny noontime green to late afternoon gold to sunset orange. It was one thing that wasn't so bad about this school; at least I could see subtle changes in the seasons. School had been in session for over a month now, and I was already tired of everything. Steve was the only thing that kept me sane.

The sun still had a way of being unbearable during practices in the afternoons. I got back into shape really quick, which was good, I guess. And lucky me, today was drills. I hated doing drills.

"Gentlemen, welcome to the practice from Hell. I need you to run around the field for five or so miles, pretty much until I feel like you've run enough." There was a chorus of groaning all around us. Coach grinned in that nasty way he grinned when we were miserable. "And not jog. I mean run. Then we're doing suicides. Now GO!" Coach Clarkson called to us, his plastic red whistle latched between his teeth. He blew it, filling the air with an ear-splitting shriek. Steve actually rubbed his ears as we took off. He and I got to the front pretty easily, letting the rest of the team fall into step behind us.

"So, who do you think is going to be captain this year?" Steve asked, glancing sideways at me. His breath started to come in pants. I shrugged, pumping my arms, sucking in deep breaths of oxygen.

"I'm not sure, really. And I don't really care." I answered, calculating how many laps I could do in ten minutes.

"Of course you don't care," Steven sneered back at me, a ghost of a smirk crossing his face. "My bet is on Jones or Hanley. They have the biggest heads and have the smallest brains, so to me, it's only natural."

Again, I didn't really care. But I let him ramble, knowing it made the time pass more quickly for him. He knew I was only partially paying attention to what he was saying, but he still appreciated me running beside him.

We finished practice with suicide drills, which left us all like the walking dead when Coach finally decided to end practice after sunset. Most of the team collapsed beside the bench, grabbing for bottles and towels. Steve and I stood back, trying not to give into the temptation of tearing through the rest of the team to reach the bags and water. Waiting would get us our bottles just as quickly.

"All right, ladies," Coach said, slapping his clipboard that he held with the back of his free hand, his whistle still lodged between his teeth. I realized that I almost never saw him without it in or around his mouth. "It's time to announce which of you will have the wonderful privilege of being the captain for this season. Our first game is in two weeks, so I figure the captain should figure out how to fill those shoes between now and then."

He grabbed his pen, scratched something down on the clipboard, and muttered under his breath, making the whistle squeak softly. He glared at each of us, which made some of the new freshmen flinch and shy away. I just laughed. He didn't intimidate me anymore, and never really had.

He gestured towards Steve and myself. "You two. Front and

center."

Steve looked at me with wide eyes and a fearful expression. I just shrugged at him. We stepped forward in front of Coach Clarkson and waited for whatever he had to deal at us.

"Congratulations, ladies. I couldn't decide who I wanted to be captain. So you two now have the honor of splitting the position. Have fun with it. Be ready with your duties divvied up between yourselves for the first game. It's going to be your fault if we lose." He held out his hand, and on two lanyards were two red whistles that looked like the one he held between his teeth; coaches whistles.

And with that, Coach called a wrap up meeting in the locker rooms. Steve, on the other hand, was in such shock that his jaw hung open and didn't move an inch as Coach and the rest of the team walked back into the locker room. I saw some of the seniors give us nasty looks over their shoulders as they followed the tide moving inside. I laughed.

"Wow. I was not expecting that." I said, looking at Steven. I clapped him on the shoulder. "Congrats, partner."

Steve turned his bulbous eyes to me, clenching the whistle in his fingers. I snickered.

"Dude, you look like a bug right now, your eyes are so big."

He shook his head, running his fingers through his hair. "Us? Me?! Why on earth would he pick me?" he exclaimed, his face turning from shock to a look of self-pity. I grabbed his arm and steered him towards the locker room.

"You're a good player, kid. Obviously. Coach only likes good players like us. But you missed the finale to a great show—the looks that Hanley and Jones gave us." I laughed again.

Steve shook his head, extracting himself from my grasp. "No! No no no no! I can't go in there! They're gonna kill me, man! You've seen the size of them! They'll tear me apart and then they'll probably eat me or something."

"Seriously, Steve," I said, laughing at the same time, spinning my own whistle around my fingers. "It's going to be fine."

And it was fine, just like I said it was going to be. The other players were for the most part happy for us, calling out congratulations and well wishes to us as we left. There were a few, who Steve shied away from, that did nothing more than just stare us down from the other side of the room. *Very threatening*, I thought.

Steven finally got excited about the opportunity that we now had as we walked back to our dorm. He assumed his responsible role, going through everything that we were going to need to do.

"Remember to breathe, man," I said. "You're talking at the speed of light here."

He continued to prattle on as we rounded the corner to our building, sliding the lanyard over his neck and letting the whistle hang there in the open.

There! *It's her!*

Her long blonde hair was caught up in the winds that were drifting across the cement path, and her cerulean eyes gazed upwards and mirrored the color of a clear sky on a summer day. There was a faint smile on her gentle face, and she held books against herself in her small arms. Steven's ranting faded to the background as we got closer to her.

She looked up, and a dazzling smile swept across her features.

"Hey... Kerana, right?" I said, and waved at her. I felt stupid, awkward, and out of sorts, but that was the best I could come up with. She slowed her pace, and I fell back from Steve.

"Eli, yes? It is nice to see you."

I watched Steve out of the corner of my eye as he realized he was alone and doubled back to where I stood with Kerana.

"How are you?" I asked, finding that I couldn't look away from her. I had been bumping into her occasionally over the last few weeks; between classes, at meal times and other random places. I always made an attempt to talk to her somehow. The first time seeing her again I apologized for acting like an idiot. Things seemed easier after that.

The simple T-shirt she wore was the exact color of her eyes. They reminded me of the clear blue water in the Bahamas, or the rivers back home, or—

"I'm doing well, thank you. I am discovering that college is very challenging." She smiled at me, and I felt my heart tighten in my chest, almost constricting my breathing. She shifted her eyes to Steven, whose mouth was open and slightly gaping. I nudged him in the arm.

"Kerana, this is my roommate Steven. Steven, this is—" *What exactly is she to me?* "This is Kerana."

Steven's face lit up like the sun peeking out from behind a cloud. "It's nice to meet you officially," he said. She extended her hand to him, and he shook it. He side-glanced over at me, his face incredulous. "We have Algebra II together," he said, in a tone that made me think he was trying to impress me somehow.

"That's right," she said, as she smiled at him. "Yes, you sit in the row beside Evelyn and myself. Now I remember."

She returned her attention to me, which made me fidget again. Her gaze was like ice in a hot bath to me; it caught me off guard. And it really annoyed me. "How are you doing, Eli?"

The way she said my name made the hair on the back of my neck stand up. "I'm doing all right, I guess. Just got out of practice."

"Yeah, and Eli and I are the new captains for the lacrosse team!" Steven added, his chest puffing out proudly, displaying the whistle that hung there. I rolled my eyes. Kerana's face slid into an amused expression.

"Well, congratulations to you both."

I smiled, which was uncommon for me. Even Steven seemed to notice. He nudged me with his foot. I smacked him in the chest. Kerana arched a single thin eyebrow at us.

"Well, I must be going. I have a test in the morning, and I still have studying to do," Kerana said, her voice singing. I would have been able to listen to it all day.

Wait, I really need to get my head on straight, I scolded myself.

I nodded, and hoped my facial features guarded my crazy thoughts that seemed to direct themselves. "We should go too. After a long practice and everything, a hot shower and getting to bed sounds good."

Steve started to protest, but I led him along with a hard, steely look. He dropped it. Kerana flashed me a pearly smile, her hair golden in the lights beside the path. And then she was off.

Steven and I turned away, and I shoved my hands in my pockets, feeling really drained. Not because of practice, no. But because of a female.

I glanced over my shoulder, just to steal one last glance of her. To my surprise, I saw her mirroring me, with her sparkling eyes watching me. As soon as she knew I had spotted her, she flushed, and quickly looked to her feet. I grinned as I turned back around.

"Dude. She has to be the hottest girl I have ever seen." Steve said, letting his thoughts just come out like they normally did. That kid had no brain-to-mouth filter. Or maybe he just didn't have a brain. Then he looked at me. "Seriously, where do girls like that come from?"

I glared at him again, and he shrunk back. "What?" Then he grinned at me. "You two seemed kind of into each other, huh?" he joked, shoving me. I smacked him full force upside the head. "No."

Steve laughed, not even upset that he got hit. "You are never one to lose your cool, man. But you just totally didn't know how to act back there. I've never seen you like that."

I all but snarled at him. He was right, and I totally hated him for it.

9 KERANA

School was far more difficult than I initially expected. When I was an Eldun, we sat outside by the stream and our teachers shared stories and read to us from other Eldurians' times in the Human world. We practiced greeting each other in French and German, wrote in Greek and Hebrew, and sang in Italian and Icelandic. But I never had work to bring home, nor did I struggle with what I was learning.

On Earth, I frequently visited the library in an attempt to stay on top of my studies. I felt frustration, an annoying emotion, when I felt forced to spend many hours away from classes doing work. Humans wanted students to do more than learn, they wanted them to perform. It was a forced performance that sometimes seemed to be for the teacher's benefit rather than the student's. I found myself resentful at times. Father checked me on my attitude, but I spent less time visiting my parents than at first. In time, I found a balance between my life at school and my life with the Eldurians.

I found myself enjoying the Human month of October. The

northern California air was crisp and the leaves began to change. I was just leaving the library late one night, having lost track of time. I had even missed dinner. *Ev must wonder where I am.* She had an odd tendency to worry about me sometimes, if not all the time.

I slowed my descent down the library steps and looked into the heavens. The night was clear, with pinpricks of fiery stars up above that cast an atmosphere of infinite beauty upon the world.

Adonai, your creations are your reflections, and they show us that you are amazing. Thank you for even the stars up above, that those that look upon them may enjoy their majesty and splendor.

I stopped completely on the white steps of the library and stared at the stars. The wind swept through the light sweater I wore. I wrapped it more tightly around me. I heard the faint sound of a piano song that matched the melody my soul was feeling. If stars could be turned to music, this was certainly it.

I strained to hear. I wasn't imagining the music. It was coming from somewhere on the campus. It was breathtaking, soft, a wide range of fluttering notes. I couldn't believe I hadn't heard it before. For one of the few times since I had entered the Human realm, I used my Eldurian sense of hearing to track down where the music was coming from. I found myself standing in front of a tall brick building, one of the oldest on campus. I had walked by this building dozens of times, knowing it was the music hall, but never hearing anything quite like what I was hearing presently coming out of it. And who would be allowed in here at such an hour?

I meandered around the building, looking for a way in. I wasn't quite sure why, but I had to see the face of the person playing the piano, to relish in their passion and gift. I knew that Humans were all blessed with certain gifts, and music was certainly the gift given to this musician. The main entrance was locked. Looking up, I saw a window open on the second floor. I smiled to myself. It had been a while since I had taken a leap like this. I put my books on the ground, checked over my shoulder to make sure that no one would see me, and lightly leapt up to the window sill.

I ducked inside and sat on the sill, looking inward. I was sitting on the ledge of one of the windows in the foyer, the marble floor and main doors below me. I let go of the sill and landed easily on my feet. My boots made a soft thud sound as they struck the marble. I straightened up and listened. The music was just beyond the door to my right.

It was open halfway, so I slipped inside without disturbing it. I discovered a large music hall, with a long, expansive balcony over my head and rows and rows of burgundy chairs and sconces on the walls that were dark. I was stood in the shadows of the back of the auditorium in awe of the beauty of the room.

My eyes followed the music to the stage where a single spot-light shone on the person playing the sleek black piano in the very center. I inched around to the side of the auditorium to get a better look at the person's face, making sure I stayed in the shadows.

The music was still soft, almost whimsical now. My heart felt light and my soul filled with abandon. The musician was male. His dark hair covered his face, but I could tell in the way he was sitting that he was completely engrossed in playing. I was sure that even if I was sitting in the first row directly in front of him that he wouldn't even notice.

I took a seat on the floor, leaned my back against the wall, and watched the piano player. I felt the emotions thrumming from him, through his fingers, to the keys, and into the night in a melody that could melt any heart. I listened as he played, as it changed from light to dark, then to sorrow, and finally to pure desperation. It was when the music reached a crescendo that the player lifted his head to the night, singing beautiful and poetic lyrics, that I realized who I was looking at.

It was Eli.

I sat in stunned silence. My mind whirled through all of the times I had run into him since I had met him, and this profile didn't seem to match up with what I had seen. The Eli I was associated with was cool, dark, and reserved. The Eli that was playing right now was singing with such strength and fervor that he was completely vulnerable and uninhibited.

But I stayed and listened; something held me there in that room. I took in his lyrics, most of which spoke of freedom and pain, wanting to find the right path, and being alone. My heart ached as if the pain he felt was no longer just his own. I learned so much about him just by listening to his voice, to his songs. I knew I was intruding, but the music that he created was like nothing I had ever heard, and I was attracted to it. I was mesmerized by the way he played, by the way his face showed the emotions it invoked, by the way his fingers knew exactly where to fall even if he wasn't looking at the ivory keys.

I was startled when he finished. The song he played was one that left a hole in my chest, a feeling of emptiness that I couldn't quite explain. I saw Eli hang his head, affectionately run his fingers across the keys one more time before he closed the cover and slowly made his way off the stage. I decided then that it was my turn to leave as well.

I softly landed on the ground outside the windows and picked up my books. The music still played inside me, as though part of it somehow belonged to me. I felt connected to Eli in some way, sharing in his unique world at the piano.

As I walked back to my dorm, I finally realized why Adonai chose and created my people to help protect His people, the Human race. They needed *someone* to look into their hearts and souls and recognize them for who they really are, and Adonai was giving me the opportunity to see Eli as he was intended to be.

All I knew was I wanted to return. I wanted to listen to his music again.

The moon outside was full, and the clouds were thinly spanned across the darkness. *I wonder if they heard? I wonder if they heard the music Eli played?*

I hugged my arms around myself to preserve body heat. But I didn't want to lose the music, so I walked slowly and let the melody that Eli played repeat itself over and over in my mind. I found myself humming it softly.

It wasn't until I was out of the flood of light from the large lamp posts that I heard some voices. They were distinctly male, and I heard them approaching me from ahead. I didn't stop to consider who was coming, but walked on. A sense of foreboding descended over me and my skin began to itch. *What is this? Is this what it feels like to be in the presence of evil?*

No! This can't be evil.

I contemplated running, but something kept me walking in that direction, towards the voices, even though my inward spirit warned me against it.

A group of three males stood around the next lamp post beside the Athletic Center, shadows drowning out their features. I kept my head down and looked at my tennis shoes. Even though I didn't look at them, I felt their stares. They were watching me.

"Well, look at this pretty little thing," one of them sneered. He leaned against the lamp post, and his red hair was cut short against his scalp. It had obviously been some days since he had shaved, and he had a very glassy look in his eyes. I only looked at him for a quick moment before attempting to continue on and ignore him. One of the other males, tall and scrawny with dirty-looking long blonde hair, stepped in front of me and blocked my direct path. I gasped softly, and tried to step around him, but his other friend stood beside him and blocked me. I couldn't see him well in the shadows, but he was taller and smelled of something very potent and bitter. I heard the redheaded boy laugh, and he shrugged himself away from the post, slowly approaching me. His movements were sluggish, and he stumbled a bit. They made a circle around me, and I realized that I really didn't have a way out. They surrounded me and backed me closer into the shadows of the wall of the Athletic Center. I was blocked in.

"Where did you think you were going, Beautiful? You should stay and talk to us for a little while." The redhead spoke softly, but there was something frightening in his tone. His friends sneered and chuckled; the sound made me afraid. I began to shudder.

"I—I don't have anything to talk to you about," I said, my hands beginning to shake as well as my voice. I looked at the ground, and lifted my heart to Adonai.

Please! Please help me! I need help!

The boys began to come even closer to me, though they were already very close, as if I were dying in a desert and they were vultures. I couldn't help but feel powerless against them, and I wanted to curse myself for coming to this world in the first place. I decided to just keep my mouth shut and wait for some form of help. I had no clue how to react to these Humans.

Run! I can't! I can't move my legs!

I screamed inside, but found no voice. There was no opening between any of them big enough for me to get through. I reprimanded myself, and tried to calm down. I knew that if I wanted to, I could run away, get away from these guys. I could use my Eldurian strength to get away from them. But could I bring myself to hurt one of them, even if my life were being threatened? Should I expose myself and therefore my entire race and raise questions, revealing part of my identity to these Humans, even if it was in protection of myself? *I don't know! I can't think!*

"What? Nothing to say?" said the tall one.

"I—I don't have anything to talk to you about," I said.

"Well, that's not very polite of you. We are just trying to make friends with you," the red-haired male said.

I didn't believe him.

His words were slurred, and the same odor came from the mouth of the third tall boy as he leaned down to me. I held my breath so I didn't have to smell it again. He lifted his hand to my face and grazed his rough fingers across the skin of my cheek. I had every mental urge to shove him away and make a run for it, but fear paralyzed me, which made me even more afraid. I felt my chest seizing up, and tears began to form in my eyes. I tried not to let them see I was afraid, but I knew it was useless; they were trying to make me afraid. Why, though, I couldn't understand. *How can people be this terrible?*

These Humans, these boys, were people I came to Earth to protect. I despised the situation for a moment, the fear now drawing a hot anger in me. They were a fallen race, yes, but I never knew exactly what fallen was until this very moment.

The blond boy stood directly in front of me, and the smirk on his face was full of something I didn't recognize, but he looked at me as if I was something far lesser than himself, and I feared for my very being. I took a step backwards, and ended up bumping into the chest of the redhead. His arms wrapped around my waist and spun me around to face him. His eyes, still glassy, couldn't focus on me exactly, but I knew just by what was on his face that he had no intention of being nice to me. I closed my eyes, nearly defeated. I heard them all laugh. The red head leaned down to me, grasping my shoulders with his big hands, squeezing until it actually hurt.

"There, now. That's better. We don't like a lady who is too vocal. I would much rather have you doing something else with your mouth..." he whispered in my ear. I opened my mouth to scream, hoping that someone, anyone, would hear me.

But when I did, I heard another voice hollering towards us.

"Hey!"

I recognized that voice instantly: Eli.

Adonai, thank you!

I opened my eyes, hope flooding my expended body. I felt the redheaded male drop his hands and turn to face the voice.

"Who are you?" The redhead stammered, turning away from me. His allies turned around as well, seeming to intentionally shield me away from the voice. I backed up a few steps and stood cowering against the wall, but I could just see through a gap between their shoulders. Eli slowly approached.

"Well, well." He said coolly. I couldn't see him between their shoulders. He must have been standing too close.

"What's going on here, boys?" Eli asked casually. I imagined him standing there with his hands in his pockets. *He must have not seen me yet!* I had to let him know I was here, that I needed help!

"Eli!" I shouted over their shoulders. All three of the males standing in front of me turned to look at me and growled like wild animals. Their faces were angry and it frightened me even more, and I clawed at the wall behind me, hoping it would fall through and I could escape.

"Kerana?" I heard from in front of the boys. His tone had completely changed: the casual question was now only fear.

"Mattison," said the redhead. He snickered. "Nice to see ya."

Now I was even more confused. *They know each other?*

"Yeah," Eli said dismissively. "I'm glad you found her, I've been looking for her." He said, and I heard him take a step towards us. *He was looking for me?*

The three guys in front of me all made a closer-knit circle around me and put up their hands. "Easy there, buddy, you aren't going anywhere with her. We were spending some time with her."

"Now, fellas," he said, an obviously fake laugh under his words, "I don't want to cause any trouble. So if you don't mind, I will just take Kerana and get out of your hair."

"See, Mattison, that's where you're wrong. I don't think that's gonna happen," the redhead said thickly. He kept shifting his weight back and forth on his legs, and I was wondering how he was even standing up straight with how much he was swaying.

"Seriously, Hanley. Let it go. You're taking this a little too far," Eli replied, a note of anger in his deep voice. The other three laughed at this. "Nobody needs to get hurt."

"Who said anyone was gonna get hurt?"

"Let her go, Hanley." Eli's voice was serious and strong.

"We were actually having a *great* time until you came and interrupted us."

"I'm warning you, Hanley. Either you let her go willingly or I'll make sure you can't walk tomorrow."

The males around me laughed in unison at Eli. "You seriously think you could hurt us? Let alone fight us in the first place?" Hanley asked. They broke out in laughter again.

"You are all completely smashed. I'd be able to do more damage with my hands tied behind my back than you three combined right now."

"You want me to prove you wrong?" Hanley's voice became frosty, the maniacal laughter gone and a dangerous growling came out of his throat. The volume of his voice made me cringe. I stood on my toes again and finally was able to see Eli. He looked up at the same moment I did, and we locked eyes. I silently pleaded with him to help me.

10 ELI

The look on her face—she was utterly terrified. I figured she was going to be afraid, but I didn't realize how much until she peeked over Hanley's shoulder and I saw her.

I sighed and shook my head. I tried to play it off like I wasn't afraid of this guy, but in all reality, I was a little afraid, especially when he was drunk. He was known to be the violent type any day, but way more so when intoxicated. That was why I came over to see what was going on in the first place, assuming they were harassing someone, but I wasn't sure if it was just one of his booty calls or not. I heard once that he beat up a girl for looking at him the wrong way at a club a few blocks from the college when he was drunk. That was two years ago, and he got off clean with the police. Not sure how, but it always seems like the ones who cause problems don't get punished.

Now they were toying with Kerana. I had to get her away from them. I realized that trying to take on three guys by myself was not smart, even if I was sober and would have much better reaction time. Hanley alone was twice my weight.

So I had to stall until I came up with something that was going to save her and myself.

Hanley took a step towards me, the smell of alcohol heavily clinging to him. I tried as best as I could to hold my ground, to look unintimidated by him. I knew if he thought I didn't care he'd be even madder. But I could handle him and his anger; I dealt with it all the time on the lacrosse field. I just wanted Kerana out of danger.

"You feelin' lucky, punk?" He spat in my face. I felt saliva spatter my face, but I didn't give him the satisfaction of wiping if off.

"No, I just know I'm right."

Hanley and his boys came up to my face, though kind of slowly and clumsily. I knew they were far enough away from Kerana now that she had room to get away from them. I glanced over at her for half of a second. I saw her wide eyes were glued to me. I looked back at Hanley, but I nodded my head to the side slightly, telling Kerana that now was her chance to get out of here.

I realized that I was willingly calling violence upon myself, and even though I felt the fear making the tips of my fingers go numb and my chest was starting to hurt, I willed it to come. I looked over at Kerana quickly and noticed she was still standing there like a deer immobile in front of a speeding car. I mouthed *Run!* in her direction. It seemed to register, and she looked around her like she came back to her senses.

"But you know what I think it really is?" I said finally, steeling myself. I leaned closer to Hanley, breathing through my mouth instead of my nose to avoid gagging on the smell of whiskey. "You're just mad because you *know* I'm right."

He looked like he was going to explode, his already blotchy face turning an interesting shade of purple. I saw Kerana quietly sneaking along the building, her eyes snapping back to me every few seconds, making sure she was getting away without them knowing.

Relief loosened my tight throat when I realized she was going to be safe.

Before I even knew what was happening, I saw a curled fist flying at my face before I even thought about a way to counter it.

The pain bloomed white-hot around my left eye as I heard his fist come into contact with me, and I grabbed at my face, stumbling backwards and swearing loudly. It was awful, and what was worse was that I had made this happen. I hollered out loud in agony, and I heard Hanley and the other two idiots laugh at me. Their hands grabbed my shirt roughly and threw me to the ground.

"Wait, wait!" I cried. They hesitated for half a second. "Hanley, it's Coach!" I hollered, cradling my left eye with one hand and pointed over their shoulders with the other in the opposite direction that Kerana had run; I didn't want them to notice she was gone in case she was still nearby. Like the gullible, drunken idiots I knew they were, they all three turned around and looked where I had pointed.

I scrambled to my feet and took off, adrenaline pumping and helping ease the pain on my face. I didn't need my left eye to run; I still had one perfectly good right one. I heard Hanley react from behind me, angrier than a bear, but I had already taken off down the path at a full sprint towards the center of campus and a good distance away from them. If I could run around enough, I could lose them somewhere and then loop back around.

I knew Hanley was slow, but he was even slower with alcohol in his system. I was grateful for the cluster of academic buildings in the center of campus. I weaved in and out of them, stopping to check every once in a while to see if they were still following me. They pursued me around the Athletic Center, the Music building, and the English Arts and Literature department. I hid in the shadows of the building for Administration a while later and peered back around the corner at them. They were wheezing and came to a halt under the light of one of the lamp posts. I tried to breathe as quietly as I could and listened to them.

"I'm gonna kill that scrawny little worm when I find him," Hanley said. He gasped for breath, his hands on his knees. "You see him?"

His blonde friend shook his head, panting. "No, man. He's gone."

"Whatever. Let's get out of here," Hanley said. "I'll see him at practice on Monday."

Yeah, well I'll let Coach know about this, and you'll be arrested. I thought. *Have fun playing in your fresh, new orange jumpsuit.*

I watched them sluggishly make their way back up the path, and I then collapsed against the wall, the pain overcoming me. I grit my teeth and put my hand over my eye. Hanley was good at one thing, I guess.

I slid down to the dew covered grass and sighed heavily.

"Wasn't expecting that tonight," I murmured to myself. I tenderly held my face, knowing I had to go find ice somewhere before it got too much worse. The adrenaline started to burn out of my bloodstream, and the pain started to grow. But I didn't really care at that moment. I rested my head again the brick of the building behind me and just closed my good eye; the other was already swollen shut.

I hoped Kerana was safe.

I didn't even know which dorm she was living in, so I had no way of knowing. I could only hope that she was safe, and that had to be good enough for right now. I still couldn't believe what had happened, or even what could have happened if I hadn't been there.

Don't go there, Mattison. That is just going to drive you to murder those idiots.

I sat there for a long time, in total silence, the only sound was the dull throbbing behind my eye. I couldn't move, nor did I want to. I just wanted to sit there and not to do anything for a few minutes. I was startled when I my phone vibrated in my pocket. It was a text message from Steve.

Hey man, where are you?

I closed my phone without answering him. I didn't feel like explaining any of this right now, especially since I still was dazed from it. I checked the time out of habit. It was nearly one in the morning. I sighed. *Come on. Ice, now.*

I dragged myself through the darkness and occasional pools of light to the restaurant called Frankie's on the other end of campus that stayed open all night. I walked inside the small diner and made my way to a table in the very back corner. The waitress was a young woman who had dated Steve once our freshman year. Marietta, I think her name was. She saw me and she gasped.

"Oh my gosh! Eli! Are you okay?"

I was surprised she remembered my name, in all honesty.

Wanting to avoid the questions, I just asked her for a glass of water and a bag of ice. With a worried expression and a quick nod yes, she dashed away from my table to the kitchen without even scratching my request down on the little pad of paper in her hands. I made sure to sit with my back to the few others in the restaurant. I was grateful I didn't know a single one of them.

The red tablecloth in front of me was well worn. There was a set of silverware and a paper placemat. Everything seemed dull, lifeless. I grabbed the spoon and decided to check out the damage on my face. I turned it over and was met with the upside down image if myself, and I looked really distorted. Not to mention I had a huge red ring around my eye that was now turning a lovely shade of blue. My entire eye was puffy and tender, which I already knew since I could feel that, but it really looked a lot worse than what I had thought. From the looks of it, I was surprised Hanley hadn't broken my nose. He wasn't far off.

Oh well, dear old dad would be proud of me, huh? I sat there reminded of when my father had taken a swing at me when I was younger.

Eli, get over here. Now! He had hollered at me.

My little, nine-year-old self cautiously went up to him. He had that scary look in his eyes that I saw far too often as a kid, the cause of a drunken stupor.

What is it, Dad?

You've been digging in the side yard again, haven't you?

No! I haven't! I swear!

Didn't your mother used to tell you not to swear? And didn't she tell you not to lie?

Daddy, I'm not! It had been the neighbor's dog digging in that patch of dirt that used to be my mother's flowerbed.

Boy, I'm gonna count to three, and you better tell me the truth! One...

Daddy, please, no!

Two...

Daddy! Please, I am telling the truth!

Three!

Maybe that's partially why I let Hanley do it; in a weird, twisted way, I already knew I could handle it.

Marietta came back with my water and my ice, and to my surprise, she set everything down and left me in peace. Relief spread through me as I lifted the bag to my eye. The chill of the ice instantly erased the stinging and I no longer felt like my eye was going to pop out of my skull. I sat back in my chair and just let the ice do its job. Occasionally I would sip the water she brought me, but for the most part I just sat there.

My thoughts kept returning to Kerana and that horrified look on her face. I smiled, a sick sort of satisfaction spreading through me as I felt a glimmer of pride rise in me at having been able to help her. I didn't know why, but even though I was the one that got socked, I was the one who walked away on top. Kerana was safe. I kept repeating it in my head. *She's safe. She's safe.*

I couldn't be quite sure how long I sat there. Every fifteen minutes or so Marietta would be kind enough to come refill my drink, and she even offered to replace my bag of ice, which I accepted since I was getting more of it on the front of my shirt than on my eye. She returned with a new bag in hand, and handed it to me.

"I didn't know if you wanted to know or not, Eli, but it is about three-thirty."

"Thanks, Marietta. I actually was wondering."

She smiled at me, and I wondered why Steve hadn't stayed with her. She gently rested her hand on my shoulder, and then left me alone again. I decided that I should get going. Even though I knew I wasn't tired and wouldn't be able to find a comfortable way to sleep to save my life, I decided I should head back to the dorm. I really had nowhere else to go. I left a ten-dollar bill on the table and started to walk out with my bag of ice.

"Eli, you didn't need to pay for some ice and water!" She called after me. I waved over my shoulder.

"Don't worry about it. You gave me more than enough, so thanks for your help, Marietta." I replied. I then walked back out into the night.

I wandered back to my dorm building, passing by the girl's dorm. I stopped in front of it and looked up at all the dark windows. I wondered which one Kerana was in, and if she was sleeping. I really hoped she was. She needed her rest. I hoped that when she woke up she wouldn't be afraid anymore.

11 KERANA

The morning brought a new form of hope that I had never before experienced.

I felt the sunlight before I saw it. The thought of waking up and having to move was upsetting, especially after what had happened the night before. My mind was restless, though I was grateful for what had been a good night's sleep.

Thank you, Adonai. You saved me through Eli and allowed my heart peace long enough to rest. Help me to overcome this fear that is building in my heart. Protect me.

I rolled over, away from the window, and eased my eyes open. I found that the room was very comfortable, more comfortable than I had been able to understand any time prior. This world had always felt foreign, but for the first time, I almost felt like it could pass for home. But then I felt my heart constrict; it certainly was not home. I sighed, brushing a strand of hair out of my eyes. I wondered if Humans often felt these horrible emotions so strongly all the time. Fear, frustration, confusion, stress—I never understood the depth of them until I arrived. I now saw why we were required to spend so much time in this realm: in order to know how to protect, one must understand who exactly they are protecting.

I heard a rustling, and looked over across the room to Ev's bed. I saw her small body wrestle halfheartedly with the blankets she was cocooned underneath, and then she violently rolled over until she was facing me. I laughed silently.

Her big aqua eyes opened as she yawned widely. She smiled, her eyes still glassy from sleep. "Good morning," she said, trying to fight back another yawn.

"Hello, Ev. Did you sleep well?" I asked her. She nodded back at me, the expression on her face like an innocent child who was completely at peace with the world. I almost envied her. Yet another new emotion that I still didn't understand or like much.

She propped herself up on her elbow, her gaze sharpening. The sunlight made her eyes look like sea water, and her tousled red hair looked like licks of flames. "When did you get back last night? I didn't even hear you come in."

I shifted uncomfortably, turning my gaze to the ceiling. "Well..." I began.

Before I realized what was happening, I felt the mattress sink with the weight of a body. I slid over a bit, and Ev casually pulled her knees up to her chest and fixed her eyes on me.

"Was it a guy?" she asked, her eyes bright and excited. Why, though, I wasn't sure. I shook my head.

"Well, yes, it was. It was four males, actually, three of whom I pray I will never see again."

Ev cocked her head to the side, confusion etched into her gentle face. "What happened, Kerana?"

I looked at Ev for a moment, studied her face. I could see that I could trust her, that I indeed had been blessed with a wonderful girl to be able to call a friend. I knew that if I could trust anyone in this realm, I could trust Ev. So I began to tell her what had occurred the night before. I decided to leave out the part about watching Eli play, but I left in everything else. I didn't look at her the entire time I was speaking; instead I stared at the ceiling. After I finished my story, I lay there, silent. I knew Ev would speak if she wanted to, so I left her that option. It was quiet for a minute or so, with the only sound being the morning birds out our window and the rise and fall of our chests.

"I—I am so sorry, Kerana," she finally said. She reached out a hand and intertwined her fingers in my own. I sighed heavily, nodding in return. I didn't realize how hard it would be to retell that story. Her eyes were sad pools now, and a terror lay behind them. I appreciated the genuine nature of this girl and her willingness to understand.

"I am sorry as well. I wish that it hadn't happened. But..." I trailed off, realizing that my heart was beginning to break for people like Ev; Humans who had to live with horrors like what had happened to me every day, and I had been blessed to get away unharmed. I was seeing more and more why it was Adonai's desire for the Eldurians to help protect the Humans, and to aid them.

Ev squeezed my fingers affectionately. She smiled at me with a look that said she was sorry. It didn't make the ache go away, but it loosened its grip on me.

I showered and let the hot water ease the weariness in my bones. I felt like I hadn't slept in weeks, and I still checked to see if my hands were still shaking every few minutes. I knew that I needed to get home; I was desperate to make sense of it all. As I stood there and let the constant stream of the burning water create steam and fog up the room, I decided that my father could help me figure this out after I spoke with Adonai. It was time I made it back to my own realm.

Ev didn't ask any questions when I told her I was going to be gone for a few days. She gave me a big hug, telling me that she hoped I could find some peace, and helped me pack up some of my clothes. I took a look at her over my shoulder, and thanked her. All she did was smile while she gently closed the door behind me as I stepped into the hall.

I strode outside and made my way to the edge of campus and saw the vast forest where the portal awaited into the Eldurian realm. I shifted the weight of the backpack on my shoulder as I passed under the shade of the trees. Somehow, I felt safer now that I was under the cover of the branches and the bark. I took a deep breath and picked up my pace, wanting to feel the rush of the wind on my cheeks and the pounding of my feet on the earth. I could have taken my shoes off and ran the way I was used to, but I knew that I would be happier doing that once I crossed the portal.

I finally reached the end of this world and the portal to my own. It was bizarre, standing in the space between the two. I now resided in both, but I wasn't sure where I belonged at this point in my life. Too much had happened to me in my first few months already in the mortal realm, so I felt that a part of me would always belong there. And yet, my heart and soul obviously were Eldurian. I smiled as I thought of the lush green trees and the fragrant flowers, and stepped through the archway of branches.

I felt a rush of joy as I stepped into the familiar territory. The air here was crisp and clear, like it had just rained. I didn't even stop to look around; I took off at a full sprint for my home.

I arrived there in good time, and each time my feet pounded against the ground my heart grew lighter and lighter. I was glad to arrive at midday and not in the evening. The daylight in this realm was far more energizing. I soon saw my lovely tree where I knew my family was, and I picked up my pace. I called as I walked inside.

"Kerana, dear!" she exclaimed. "What a pleasant surprise! What are you doing home so soon?"

I smiled a little at her, and I threw my arms around her. It was wonderful for me to be able to hug her again, to know that here with her, I was safe. "Some pretty serious stuff happened last night. I needed to come home and talk to you and Father and go to the Fountain."

I felt my mom stiffen at my words, and she pulled away from me to look me in the eye. She searched my face. "Kerana, what on earth happened to make you need to go to the Fountain?"

I looked past her inside, and down the stairs. "Is Father home?" I asked. My mother shook her head.

"No, he is at the Council Hall with the Elders. They are discussing the new mortal realm travelers like yourself. He had only good things to say about your travels, but I worry that might be inaccurate now."

I shrugged a little bit. "You can see what you think once I've told you. But Father should be here too."

My mother nodded. "Very well. They should be finishing their meeting just about now, so if you run down to Eden, you will be able to find him."

I kissed her on the cheek and ran farther down the narrow path through the trees. I met a few other Eldurians and some young Elduns on the way, all of them elated to see me and to pass a blessing along to me. I didn't have time to talk though; I needed to find my father.

Shortly enough, I came to the epicenter of the entire realm, and it had been so long since I had seen it, I had to stop and stare at its beauty.

I saw the luscious garden that was the most central area in all of Eden. I could see the four regions of the realm were clearly defined, with each area parted into equal and perfect boundaries that represented each of the four different seasons on Earth: a region covered in snow and ice; a region where the trees were all shades of gold and ruby with their leaves scattered across the ground; a region where the flowers were all in bloom and new life was brimming; and the region where I stood and lived in, where it was perpetually summertime. In the very center, where the four corners of the regions met, there was a large white stone fountain, with a single tiered pedestal where water cascaded down, pure and perfectly clean. Surrounding the fountain were hundreds of newly bloomed pink roses.

The trees here were bigger in this part of the realm

Elduns played in the snow and threw balls of it at each other. Their shrieks echoed off the tall trees. Some of the elderly women sat under the shade of the newly formed trees in the spring region. Several others gathered around the Fountain in the center, and I watched with a smile on my face as one older Eldurian took a single petal from one of the roses, placed it between the palms of his hands, and raised his hands to his mouth. Then I watched as he whispered into his hands, and then gently released the petal onto the water of the Fountain. It danced around on the surface of the water, and the elder gentleman smiled and walked away. I knew that those whispered words upon that petal were a prayer lying on the heart of that Eldurian.

I strolled more into the clear space, and let the sheer size of what was around me rush over me. People that I had known my whole life came right up to me, embraced me, and warmed my heart with their smiles.

The biggest and oldest tree was the Council Hall of the Elders, nestled perfectly between the spring and the summer regions. Inside, I remembered, the rooms were beautiful and large, with the purpose of holding many Eldurians at once. The halls were lined with the rich wood of the entwined trees, and grand windows that overlooked all four of the separate seasoned realms.

A large set of solid doors stood opened to the warm air of the Spring and Summer climates, and welcomed those who passed through them. As I approached, I saw him.

"Kerana!"

"Father!" Dressed in the custom long white robe that every Eldurian wore, Father smiled at me from the threshold of the door. We crossed the distance between us, and my father embraced me.

"This is an unexpected surprise, Dear One. Why have you returned so soon?"

"That is something I must speak with you about soon, and with mother. I came to find you here when you were not at home."

He nodded his head; the sunlight from the spring realm made his blonde hair look like the bright embers in a fire. "Yes, we had a follow-up meeting about all of you students on Earth, to make sure everything was running smoothly."

A man stepped up beside my father. His face was older and held far more wisdom than any other I had known. He was an elder, like my father, though he had been one for as long as I could remember. I wasn't even sure exactly how old he was; hundreds if not thousands of years old, I assumed.

"Your daughter is growing more beautiful and pure every time I see her, Erez," he said. My father beamed.

"Thank you, Dru. She is certainly turning out well, inside and out."

Dru smiled at me, reached out and touched my shoulder, and looked me straight in the eyes. "Adonai has great things in store for you. Always follow Him, and He will never lead you astray."

With that, he bid myself and my father goodbye, and set off down through the snowy paths of the winter realm. My father turned his attention back to myself; concern creased his gentle face.

"Now what was it you had to talk to me about?" he asked. I shook my head.

"Not here, let us talk at home so Mother can hear it too."

It only took us a few minutes to reach home again. We walked back through the summer realm and found my mother and my two younger siblings outside, playing with some of the neighbor Elduns.

"Kerana!" the twins shrieked. Each flung his small arms around my middle. I hugged their heads, felt the softness of their young hair and caught the faint, sunny scent of their clothing. Oh, how I had missed them.

They soon lost interest in me, however, and went back to play with the other children down the path.

Father pointed to a grassy spot near the outside of our home and the three of us sat down together. "All right, Kerana, talk to us. Tell us what happened."

So I took a deep breath, and I told them all about Eli, about his incredible gift of playing piano and how he rescued me from the three Human males who acted strangely.

"The fear became so great that I wasn't sure what would happen, and that was when Eli showed up."

They watched with quiet and still expressions as I shared that Eli stood up for me, and how he had saved me. I felt drained. My mother spoke first.

"My daughter, you have certainly experienced something I can say I never did. It is extraordinary that nothing happened to you. I had heard of such evils when I spent my term in the Human realm, but I had never known it to happen to anyone I knew, certainly not my own child."

My father's reactions were similar. "I am simply glad that you are safe. Fear is an ugly emotion, and it can paralyze us, as you have now seen. But now that you have felt it, you cannot let it dominate you next time. You are what is good and pure that Adonai offers the world; you cannot let the Fallen world change that."

I was silent. I knew what my father said was true. I knew what I was, and who I was. I wasn't going to let the world that the Humans lived in change me.

"They are a fallen race; it is our job to help protect them and provide them with opportunities for Adonai to heal them."

I nodded. *He is right.* As I opened my mouth to speak, I saw the wind rustled through the tree tops above our heads.

I knew that Adonai was calling me.

"I must go to the Clearing."

Mother and Father nodded. "Then go on, my child, and see what Adonai has to say."

And so I set off. The Clearing was in a place that was separated from all of the four realms, in a place of seclusion. The only way to find it was to wander deeper and farther away from the joining of the realms and eventually it would be found. Adonai wanted us to seek Him, and His promise was that He would always appear when we did.

I heard a melody somewhere overhead, a song that was neither voice nor instrument. It danced through the air like a ripple through a stream. No more than a mile later, I found the Clearing. It was the precise setting of the gardens of Eden, but the fountain, the shops and homes, and the Eldurians had all disappeared. The realms of the seasons still met at the very center, but all that was there was a single stump of a tree. The music filled the meadow, coming from no particular place.

I approached the humble tree at the center and bent to my knees, my head bent in reverence and humility. "Your Majesty," I murmured, and waited on Him.

"Kerana, I've been waiting for you," I heard in a response that was both strong and loving. I looked up and saw the stump had transformed into a glorious white throne that seemed to glow. Adonai sat upon the throne, adorned in a white robe. His face was gentle, strong, and powerful. His smile was comforting, and his eyes were loving and affectionate. To see Adonai was to see goodness itself.

I looked up and smiled. In the presence of the greatest Love, any and all fear dissipated immediately. Without hesitation, I stood and embraced Him, as a child would her mother or father. To know Adonai was to feel a love that surpassed all others.

Once our embrace was over, he leaned back and took a good look at me. He smiled at me like a proud father. I could see so much of my own father, of all Eldurians for that matter, in Him. And as I looked closer, I could see how the Humans resembled Him as well.

"You had an interesting night last night," He said now more

seriously, as He sat back as I settled myself at His feet.

"I did."

He smiled gently, but his manner was still somewhat sober. "Well, tell me what you think of it."

"I felt—fear. For the first time."

Adonai nodded. His loving eyes never left mine. "Yes, you did. It is something that, unfortunately, the Humans feel often."

I shuddered visibly. "I can't imagine feeling that all the time."

"Well, they don't feel it all the time. But it is very real for them. I don't want them to feel this way. I want them to be prosperous and to be happy. It breaks my heart to see them hurt."

"But, why do they live in fear? Why does it even exist?"

He sighed, and affectionately placed His hand on my shoulder. "That, my dear, is a very long story, and one that you already know." When I was silent, He continued on. "Long ago, when I first created the Human race, I created them to be in my image." I nodded. "It all was going well at first, and they were much like the Eldurians. I loved them, and they loved me. I gave them joy and peace, and they knew no wrong. But then came the day when Eden no longer knew the work of the Humans," He trailed off. I could see the sadness in His eyes.

"Since that day, evil has plagued the hearts of the Humans. It is the evil that instills fear, and anger, and sadness, and pain. They must somehow find a way to live amongst these very real horrors. Sometimes, these evils consume them, and they are lost to them."

We sat in silence for a moment.

I looked up at His face again, and His eyes met mine. "But this is not what you have come to speak with me about. You have come to speak with me about Eli and what happened last night with the other three Humans."

"Yes, it is what I wanted to ask you about. I wondered why it was Eli that helped me, why it was Eli that stood up to those other Humans, and why those three Humans frightened me so much."

Adonai's gaze skimmed the trees around us before He looked back at me. "There are some questions that you ask, Kerana, that I cannot answer. The question of why I sent Eli is one of them."

I frowned. I hoped He would have answered that. "But what about why he stood up for me the way he did? He got hurt! It could have been worse."

"Yes, it could have been. But Eli has a soul that longs to do good. He wants to do what is right, even if he can't always know what that is. Last night, it was very obvious to him. He knew the right thing to do and he did it."

"Protect me?"

"It was more than protect you, even though that was his dominant desire," Adonai replied. "He stood up for himself as well. He rarely does that."

"What do you mean?"

"Again, another question for another time."

I realized I wasn't going to get all of the answers I wanted now, so I decided to move on. "Why was I frightened?"

He placed His hand on my shoulder again. "I was there with you. I was not going to let harm come to you. But I did need you to see how Humans feel. My plan for you requires you to know how to better protect them."

"You need me to protect them, but you had one of them protect me."

"It is sometimes a way in which one learns. You must experience it in order to understand it. The process is more important than the end result."

"What do you mean by that?"

"I mean that your term on Earth is a process, and the end result is being able to serve me by better understanding them. You need to understand them."

I frowned.

But He smiled, and gestured at the woods around us. "Look around you, Kerana."

I did. I glanced at all four of the seasons, from the spring to summer, from fall to winter.

"Do you see the change from the winter to the spring?" He asked, and I nodded. "The spring can only come if the winter occurs. There would be no spring without it. The new life that the spring brings can only be if the winter's time makes it lie dormant. It is the same with learning. As one of my servants, you must go through the rough, difficult times of winter in order to experience the new life and understanding of the spring."

I smiled up at Him. He clasped my shoulder gently, and beamed at me.

"Go forth, then," He added. "You have much to learn."

I stood and turned to leave when I added over my shoulder "Please watch over Eli. Keep him safe."

Adonai smiled. "I have a plan for Eli; a plan to nurture him and not to harm him. A plan to give him hope and a future."

I smiled at Him in response. "Thank you, for all you do." And I left the Clearing.

As I left, I started to hear the delighted cries and shrieks of children from a short ways ahead. I looked over my shoulder and the Clearing had disappeared. Only the extensive forest remained.

I smiled, and set off back towards home to spend the rest of the evening with my family.

12 ELI

I used sunglasses to and from classes that morning. I sat in the cafeteria at the back corner against the window, exhausted. Steve found me as I drowned in the late afternoon sunlight. I ignored my plate and cup of coffee.

"Whoa! Where'd you get that shiner?" Steven asked me, his blue eyes wide. He was peering at me like I had a third eye, but my eye was so swollen it almost looked like I did.

"A couple of—" I let the profanity pass in my mind. "Idiots."

Steve's face was blank.

"Eli, someone took a swing at you? Why?"

"It's no big deal." I just wanted to be out of eyesight.

I had sat forward out of the sunshine that put the spotlight on my black eye.

"Well it certainly looks like a big deal," he said as he leaned across the table and looked me square in the eye. "Come on, man, tell me what happened."

I sighed and glanced back out the window at the toy-sized people that walked by a few floors down. "Fine. I was walking last night..."

"Why were you walking at night?" Steven interrupted. I tried hard not to let that annoy me; this was Steve being a friend to me. The look on my face, even with the black eye, must have told him what I wanted to say.

"Sorry," he uttered. "Go on."

"I was walking when I heard a bunch of drunken guys near the Athletic Center. Hanley and his guys. But I also heard a female voice. So, just to make sure everything was okay, I walked over. Found out they were harassing a girl, and I knew who it was."

Steve's face lit up. "Wait a second. Dude! Was it that girl you know?"

"Yes, Steve. It was Kerana."

His eyes were wide. I tried to roll my eyes, which hurt more than I had anticipated. So I just reached out and shoved his shoulder.

"Shut up."

"I'm just saying," he said, amused. "So let me guess. You played Ethan Hunt and saved the girl?"

"It wasn't *Mission Impossible*, Steve. I just told them to knock it off."

Steve smirked, his initial worry gone, apparently. "I take it they didn't take *that* too well."

I scowled.

"Oh come on, Eli, cut it out. What'd you do to tick 'em off so much?" I hesitated, and looked down at the cheap ceramic mug that had to have been washed in an economy sized dishwasher thousands of times.

"I just," I paused. "I just kept threatening them and stuff. I wasn't actually planning to start a fight. Hanley was completely wasted. I don't know, it wasn't really any one thing I said. I just wanted her to get away without getting hurt. They were all over her, and I could see," I said, looking away from Steve, back across the rest of the cafeteria. "I could see she was really afraid."

I sighed.

"So I was afraid for her, realizing that these—" I held my tongue again. "Guys, idiots, whatever—that they were serious. You know Hanley. I mean, you have to agree, it probably wouldn't be the first time that he forced a girl into something. And I wasn't about to let that happen."

"Bravo," Steve said, mock applauding me. "That was great! Say it again, but with more disdain! You should sign up for the play, with skills like that!"

"Steven, this is serious."

"I know, I know, I'm just kidding. Keep your pants on."

I looked back out the window. My whole head hurt, begging me to lie down and rest.

Steve still looked at me intently, and I knew his jokes were an attempt to cheer me up. Strange kid, but he was a good kid. That was one of the only reasons I didn't sock him for sitting with me.

"Dude, I just can't believe it was Hanley."

"I knew I didn't like him," I replied, looking out the window.

He was quiet for a minute, but his fingers drummed on the table.

"I'm glad you're okay, man."

"Me too," I answered.

"You look exhausted. Why don't you get some sleep? I won't let anybody bother you."

I nodded. "Maybe you're right." I took one last sip of my now cold coffee, got to my feet, and followed him out. The sun was hot at this time of day, even in November, and I could feel beads of sweat rising on the back of my neck and my forehead. Steve was quiet as we walked. I was glad. My headed pounded—probably more from the overdose of caffeine and the lack of food. But my brain kept rehearsing Kerana's face, full of fear, over and over. Sleep sounded like an amazing way to just let go of that image—and the rest of reality while I was at it.

"It's nice this new building has AC, huh? Good for these weird warm days that feel like the middle of August."

I nodded. Steven wanted to distract me. I didn't care to stop him. My legs felt like tree trunks. I just wanted to sleep.

"I have to admit, I wasn't so sure a brand-new building was such a great idea. But I think they did a pretty decent job."

A conversation we had already had in the past, but again, I didn't stop him. It helped my mind from wandering.

We hopped onto the elevator to the fourth floor, and were silent again. Steve tapped his foot to a song in his head. I just stared at the glowing buttons. They reminded me of stars, or the ivory keys of a piano as the stage lights reflected off of them. The elevator dinged and the doors slid open in front of us. Something ground underneath us, and it didn't sound quite right to me, but I was too tired to care.

"I'm just gonna grab my gym bag and then get out of your way, all right?" Steve said as he fumbled for his room key. I beat him to it and pushed the door open. He followed me in and grabbed his Nike bag at the foot of his bed as I collapsed onto my own. I popped a couple of ibuprofen and took a swig of an old bottle of water on my bedside table. Steve patted the end of my bed on his way out and my last coherent thought was the sound of the door clicking shut.

The next time I woke up, hours had passed. I glanced at the clock near my bed and it read 6:56pm. I felt like I had only slept five minutes, and my head throbbed dully. It took me a minute to realize that the throbbing wasn't just in my head; there was an alarm going off outside in the hallway. It was the fire alarm. Thoroughly disgusted that it had woken me up from my nap, I rolled over and pulled the blankets over my head, still only partially awake. My head felt like lead and my good eye refused to open anymore. The alarm blared out in the hallway. I just hoped it would shut off eventually. I knew it was a drill. Real fires never happened; they were always just drills. I added my pillows to the pile of blankets over my head.

After a while, the alarm started to fade into the background, almost where I could ignore it. Satisfied and on the verge of sleep, I tried to imagine myself elsewhere. I thought of home, for some reason, as my friends and I sat out on a summer night by a campfire and roasted marshmallows. We laughed. I was happy; those days were some of the best I could remember. It was almost as if I could smell the smoke from the campfire.

And that was when I realized that I actually *could* smell smoke.

I leapt out of my bed like a rabbit would out of his hole, and I sniffed the air hesitantly. *Yep, that's smoke. Figures. For once it's not a drill and I ignore it.*

I tried not to let fear bubble up. I crossed to the window, but with only one usable eye, my depth perception was way off and I ran into everything. The alarm out in the hall had given me a headache. Or was it the smoke?

The sun had started to graze the top of the trees. I could see people littered across the grounds out in front of the dorm with my good right eye, but I couldn't see any serious flames outside. But I could see smoke, all right, and that meant I probably didn't have very long to get out. My heart pounded. My throat went dry.

They always say that you should never stop to grab anything if there is a fire, just get out. But I have to make sure that I can live without it all.

I really wished that I had both eyes to be able to navigate my way around.

"Come on, Eli, you're fine. Just take a quick look and get outta here," I muttered under my breath, and hoped that getting angry with myself would keep the fear away. It didn't work.

I looked through my closet, and didn't find anything. I rummaged through my dresser, my desk, and then my school bag, and found nothing. The only thing I found that I really wanted was my wallet, which I had stuck on my bedside table when I came into the room with Steve.

Steve.

Steve hadn't been here at all since he left me after lunch; I would have heard him come in. *He has to be safe. If I don't want to end up like a pig roast, I'd better get out of here.* I felt the door. It was warm.

Smoke crept in and it was hard to breathe. I pulled my T-shirt up over my face in order to help me breathe. I grabbed the handle.

"Yaaaaah!"

The handle was sizzling. Terror went up my throat. I ran back to the window and looked out; it was a four-story drop, and there was no way I would ever make it if I jumped. I didn't see any flashing lights or guys in fire retardant suits, so I knew the firemen wouldn't be at the base of my window for a while with their little trampoline I always wanted to try when I was a kid. I felt like an animal caught in a trap. I couldn't get out the door; the fire was directly on the other side and would eventually eat through the plywood. I couldn't jump out the window because I would kill myself doing it.

Allow myself to be engulfed in flames, or die by jumping out a window?

The window seemed like a better choice at this point.

Today is just really *not my day!*

I found the strength to move legs that felt like lead, and started to cross back over to the window.

CRACK!

It sounded like a tree falling down, except it was underneath my feet. The building was beginning to collapse, and I was still inside!

Never in a hundred, thousand years did I think I was going to die trapped in a building with a huge black eye from some idiot the night before. I was just on a roll.

I was dizzy and my lungs hurt. I staggered towards the window, still listening with some small instinctive part of me that was still rational for the floorboards beneath my feet. I really, really hoped that they would hold out just a little bit longer. Before I reached the window, I went into a coughing fit, and doubled over. My lungs couldn't handle any more of that black sooty smoke that piled into the room from under the door. I coughed and coughed, unable to stand upright again. I felt blindly for the window, and was surprised when I saw flames licked the outside of it out of the corner of my eye. I knew that if that glass broke, I would be dead.

I staggered back into the room and tried to put distance between myself and the window. But it was useless.

The flames licked the outside of the window again.

CRASH!

Glass shattered inward. Whoosh! I flew backward against the wall beside the door. I could feel the heat of the fire right on the other side.

"Help! Help!"

My lap was full of glass, but I couldn't move. My body was full of little stings.

I'm about to die—alone and scared stiff, in this stupid college I didn't even want to go to.

Did anyone hear my scream?

I watched through muddied vision. The fire fanned under the doorway and slowly slipped into the room like a dog that sniffed out its prey.

13 KERANA

I had just stepped back through the Portal when I heard the scream from a voice I recognized immediately.

It was Eli.

Without hesitation, I sprinted towards campus and arrived in less than a minute, far faster than any Human would be able to. It was the first time that I had pushed myself as fast as I could go in many years.

Huge, black clouds formed in the sky over one of the buildings. I had never seen that much smoke. I rounded the corner and couldn't believe my eyes. Amber flames roared on top of the building and black smoke poured out of nearly every window in the brand new boys' dorm. People stood out in front, like bugs drawn to a light. The only good news was that no one had seemed to notice me arrive.

I just stood there, uncertain what to do next. I knew I heard Eli scream, so obviously he was in danger. Was he still in the building?

Ev was in the crowd. Near her was Eli's roommate, Steven.

He'll know where Eli is! I dashed over to him, gently pushing through huddles of people.

"Steven!" I shouted over people's heads. He looked around wildly before making eye contact with me and attempted to make his way to me. It was hot standing this close to the flames, but it didn't matter; the Humans continued to stand there.

"Kerana!" Steven finally reached me.

I could barely think. "Have you seen Eli?" I questioned, very much afraid of the answer.

Steven's face was as white as an Eldurian's robe. "Kerana, I haven't. I'm freakin' out. He was in there, taking a nap earlier. I told him to because he didn't sleep at all last night."

"No!" My heart leapt and I did not wait to hear anymore. Steven's face told me all I needed to know. I scanned the crowd as I made my way toward the front. Maybe he was standing among them? *No. He wouldn't scream like that if he was safe.*

Steven called me again, but I ignored him. If Eli was in the building, every minute would count. I had to get him out. I whispered a prayer as I ran. "Adonai, let him be okay until I get there."

Since everyone's attention seemed to be on the glow at the front of the building, I met no obstacles reaching the back of it. From the looks of it all, the fire had started below the ground floor. That was where the most heat was coming from and where the most damage appeared to be. Not wanting to dwell on the how or the why, I searched for a fire escape door to get inside.

There was no time to play Human anymore; I had to become full Eldurian to finish this job and find him.

The door was at the very back of the building, and down a set of stairs. I took a deep breath and grabbed the metal handle. It was hot, but fire could not burn me. I pulled on the handle, and the door flew open and completely off the hinges. I stepped back and it crashed to the ground. Smoke poured out of the hole I made. I looked inside at the basement—I'd have to be careful the building wouldn't collapse on me. Even if I would most likely be able to make it out safely myself, I didn't want to endanger Eli or anyone else possibly trapped in this blaze. I forced myself to calm down. I stepped into the inferno.

It was stuffy in the basement, but I could handle it. I was in some sort of storage room. Everything that could burn was inflamed. I tried not to let my fear for Eli prevent me from moving. I quickly navigated my way towards the collapsing door frame at the back of the room. The air was so hot that it was uncomfortable to breathe.

I stepped through the doorway and discovered a hole in the wall of the next room. Another storage room, probably. On the other side of the hole I found a long hallway that probably mirrored the hallways on the floors above it. I knew the elevator would be entirely useless at this point.

Where are the stairs?

I ran down the hallway. Flames lashed out at me, as if to warn me that they intended to take this structure down. I wasn't going to let it happen, not with an innocent Human inside.

The staircase! It appeared to go all the way up the side of the building, an alternate route between the floor levels. I tore up the flight of stairs and skipped the steps three at a time. Suddenly, it dawned on me that I had no clue where Eli's room was located or, if he'd tried to get out of it, where else he might be in the building. I halted midway up the third floor staircase.

I pushed out everything from my mind and listened as closely as I could to my surroundings. I strained to hear the sound of breathing, coughing, or movement. The roar of the flames sounded like a constant storm of explosions, and the split-crack of the break-down of the building like giant hammers pounding the hard earth. I winced, but continued to listen at this level. At first, I could hear nothing past the inferno and the creaking framework. On the verge of tears, I was about to run through the halls and inspect every room in the time I had left, but then I heard it.

Breathing. It was faint, extremely faint, but it was there. It was raspy and raw. I knew that I had found him. *Higher—he's on another floor!* I ran up to the fourth floor. The breathing sound intensified. I focused as hard as I could on that noise, and tried to ignore the roaring flames. They whipped out at me, as if with a mind of their own, and raced up the walls and into the surrounding rooms. I came to the hallway of the fourth floor and stopped. Yes! I was close—very close. I dashed down to the end of the hall. The breathing came from behind the door on the second to last room on the left. I was surprised the fire hadn't eaten through the door yet. I pulled the handle until it fell back off its hinges. I laid the door on its side in the hallway and looked inside the room.

There, slumped against the wall beside the door, was Eli, unconscious.

Relieved tears sprang to my eyes. I bent to inspect him. He was still breathing, but just barely so. I pulled a few shards of glass out of his hair. He had scratches all over his face and a gash over his left eye. His shirt was bloodstained in a few places. Blood streamed down his arms, black jagged streaks in the firelight. His left eye was black and blue, swollen shut, and it brought back a whole wave of new emotion from just the night before, which felt like eons ago.

Without a moment to lose, I scooped him up in my arms like he was a child. I spun in circles, and inspected my surroundings.

I heard the floor hiss underneath me, as loud as a waterfall, and for the first time I noticed a giant crack across the room. *The floor's going to cave in!* Out in the hallway was the death trap, and the room was about to fall to pieces.

I closed my eyes and willed my prayers to escape me to reach Adonai. "Adonai, help!" I cried.

Suddenly, the flames behind me in the hallway seemed to part down the middle, leaving a clear path for me to pass through with Eli safely. "Thank you Adonai!" I shouted loudly into the walls of fire on both sides of us. Fearless, I ran with ease back to the stairs, the fire continuing to part before me. Looking up, I heard a series of crashes; the floors above were falling in on themselves. "Adonai! Help!" Just then, a wall right beside me broke and created a convenient passage out of the rubble. I dove out of it, Eli in my arms still, and made it outside just as the rest of the building fell in on itself. I ran and ran, Eli flopping in my arms. I ran toward the hill beside the dorm. Dust and shards of metal and glass exploded into the sky. *Just a little farther. I can do this.*

Finally, I reached the top and fell to the ground. *BOOM!*

I quickly covered Eli as best as I could with my body.

Moments passed.

The roar of the collapse subsided, and I lifted my head. I could now hear sirens in the distance and saw men in big yellow suits running toward the fiery ruins, a long hose in their hands. They must have been the firemen; they were obviously too late.

They immediately roped off the front of the building and pushed the crowds backward, away from the danger. Still, the people continued to look on, mouths open in shock and horror. One thing I would never understand about Humans was their fascination with destruction.

The firemen lined up and turned their big hose toward the wall. Water shot out, a late attempt to extinguish the living blaze. It all seemed unreal to me, sitting up high on the hill, away from all the chaos.

I looked down and saw that Eli and I were both covered in soot and ash, and I sat up on my knees in front of him. He looked like he was made of stone, with the thick layer plastered on his face and hands.

I'm not sure why I did it, but I touched his face, gently. I wiped away some of the soot, enough to reveal the sun tanned skin underneath. His dark hair was grey as well, and I brushed the strands hanging in his eyes away. I was gentle around his swollen eye. My heart hurt to see him in such a state.

As my fingers left his face, he suddenly convulsed and sputtered. He doubled over to his side and coughed out a lungful of ash and smoke.

I can't let him see me!

I fought the urge to stay with him and make sure he was really all right. But how could I stay? I stood. He was safe, after all. Out of the building. Slowly it dawned on me, the seriousness of the act that I had just performed. Eldurians were never supposed to show themselves when they perform miraculous acts. So I had to leave, now, before Eli realized what had happened to him, before he realized that I had rescued him. It would cause far too many problems and questions. Eli coughed again. I turned to our left and ran toward the nearby building to escape before he knew I was there.

14 ELI

I thought I had just passed from the living to the dead, and back to the living again. If that is what death felt like, I thought, it wasn't so bad. It felt like falling into a deep, comfortable sleep. It was quiet, death was. I didn't remember the fire trying to eat the flesh off of me, or the smoke slowly and painfully killing me. All I remembered was the darkness, and the quiet.

What sucked was coming back from death. Sirens. Heat all around me but I couldn't see the sun.

My vision was all blurred in my only good eye, and my lungs felt like they were being ripped apart every time I drew a breath. I laid there for a moment or two before I was able to stop sputtering and open my eyes. Black smoke hurled skyward. Horns. Shouting. More sputtering.

My eyes burned and I wiped them with the inside of my T-shirt. I smelled like soot and smoke. I spit into the sooty grass. I rubbed my good eye again and stared at my hands. They were an odd shade of grey-white, like a corpse that had been dead for a few hours. My whole body was grey-white, with streaks of pasty grey stuck where I knew I was cut and bloody.

Shouts.

Between coughs, I looked down the hill at the dorm building I had been living in all year—the dorm I'd been sleeping in just two hours earlier. A pile of stone and heaps of ash spread across the grounds. Flames shot up here and there and reached for the open, blue sky. I shuddered despite the heat.

Something moved in the grass behind me.

I turned to see long blonde hair disappear behind the Center for the Sciences. Footprints through the soot created a pathway.

What on earth? Was that—Kerana?

"Hey!" I shouted after the girl running away. I went into another coughing fit as I struggled to my feet. *Is that who saved me?* There was no other explanation. I did not get myself out of the building. Someone else must have gotten me out. But there were no firefighters around, and I doubted that one would have rescued me and then dumped me on the hilltop alone with no medical help.

"Hey! Wait up!" I hollered again. I ran up the hill, around the Science Center, with still enough soot to mark the way. I sprinted after them right to the edge of campus. There was a busy intersection, and across the street was a large forest. I had rarely been to this side of campus; it was more for the graduate students. There! The blonde hair disappeared into the trees.

I ran after her. I felt air fill my lungs and I had to stop. I sputtered and coughed repeatedly until I caught my breath. I knew I should go back and seek out a medic, but not before I found Kerana. I was sure it was her who had saved me, but how? There was no way she could have picked me up, a guy twice her size, and walked through a burning building. That was just ridiculous.

I made my way through the trees, which were hundreds of feet tall, and my entire arm span wide.

"Wait up!" I hollered again. I lost sight of her and there was no longer a path to follow—anywhere. I wandered aimlessly, unsure where to look. Hopelessly lost, I started to feel fatigued. I leaned my back on one of the ancient trees and tried to get my bearings. No water. No pathway. My arms burned now from sweat and soot in my scrapes and cuts.

A squirrel scampered up a tree. *What's that?* A smudge of chalky white on a tree? Soot! She passed this way! Two trees ahead were shorter than the rest, and stood side by side, about shoulders-width apart. Their branches intertwined with each other and created a natural doorway. They must have been new trees. The ground between them looked pushed down a little.

I walked between the trees.

What the—where in the world am I? As soon as I had crossed between the two young trees, everything around me had completely changed. The trees were thicker, more lush, and even, if possible, more alive. The air smelled of the richest soil, something I only had a memory of from when I was young and my mother used to garden. I froze. Flowers that were completely unknown to me were blooming along a new path, and everything seemed so much more alive than I had ever seen it. Sunlight glinted through the trees, but now it was coming from a different direction.

I touched my eye. It didn't hurt! *This is weird.* All of my injuries were gone! I could see with both of my eyes and all the cuts and scrapes had disappeared. Only the blood spots on my shirt and the soot remained. The trees were quiet and reverent and I wondered if they could see me. *I must be dreaming.*

I pinched myself. *Okay, I felt that.* I breathed deeply. My lungs no longer felt congested.

"What are you doing here?" I whirled toward the voice and saw Kerana standing a few feet up a path that looked well used. And by the tone of her voice, she was *not* happy with me. She was covered in a layer of dust.

I stared.

She shouted. I never knew that this woman *could* shout.

"How in the *world* did you get through there? There is no

way—it can't be! You are a *Human!*"

Confused, I finally found my voice. "And you aren't? What the—"

She drew closer to me and stared at me with such fire in her eyes that I almost cowered. Not too many women could say that they made me do that. That close, I was able to take a better look at her. I always knew she was breathtaking, but for some reason, she seemed to be--glowing? All the way around her, and especially in her eyes, a golden light seemed to trace her frame, as if the sun was shimmering behind her. I had never seen anything like it except in the movies.

"Why did you follow me?" she asked, cutting me off, pointing a thin, delicate finger in my face, level with my nose. I put up my hands defensively.

"Whoa, whoa, easy with that thing, girl," I said. "Can you explain what is going on here?"

She glared at me, her hands on her hips. Man, this girl was unhappy with me. That didn't so much bother me; it was the fact that I didn't know *why* she was unhappy with me.

Kerana sighed heavily. "This is bad. Very, very bad." Her eyes were cast down, and her hand knotted in her hair. I smiled a bit, in spite of myself; she looked beautiful all flustered this way. I shook my head, allowing that thought to pass.

"Can you tell me what happened? Or where I am?" I asked.

"I'm sorry, that's impossible." She took my arm and pushed me back towards the trees I had just walked through.

"Hey, what are you doing? Wait, will you please tell me what is going on?" I asked, becoming more and more confused. She didn't answer, but she let go of my arm right in front of the two trees.

"Walk back through," was all she said. She wouldn't look at me either; she was looking right past me, at something in the distance over my left shoulder. When I just stood there, staring at her, she became irritated, and repeated herself.

"Walk back through," with more force.

For once, I did what I was told. I looked at the new trees in front of me, the ones that I had passed through before, and I stepped between them. I didn't know what I expected. I thought maybe I would feel the change this time, now that it had happened once before. I even closed my eyes as I passed through, but when I took the step and came out on the other side, I felt nothing.

I also heard Kerana's voice, which did not sound pleased, and knew I hadn't gone anywhere.

I opened my eyes and looked around; nope, I was still in this weird place. I looked back around to Kerana, and shrugged. "I guess I am not going out the way I came in. Is there a back door?"

She made a strange noise, a snarl maybe? Whatever it was, it made me laugh a little.

"This is not funny, Eli."

"Sorry, but it is to me. You at least seem to have some clue as to what's going on right now. So since it seems that I am not going to be leaving right now, or whatever you were trying to get me to do, would you *please* fill me in?"

"You are in the realm called Eden," she replied hastily, not looking at me. Her head was bent, a hand to her face, eyes closed. She was obviously *really* upset about this. I considered continuing with my questions since my curiosity was going wild, but the look on Kerana's face made me hold my tongue for a second.

"You can't go through the Portal! I have no idea how to get you back to Earth--"

"Wait a minute—I'm on another planet?" I asked, the idea of it boggling my mind.

So wait—is she an alien of some sort?

Yeah, it would make sense that I'd be attracted to an alien.

She stopped her musings and looked at me. "No, Eli. You are not on another planet," she replied, very exasperated. She looked nearly on the edge of hysterics. "You're in a different realm connected to Earth, another dimension." She grew quiet again. I let her be.

I tried to wrap my head around the fact that I wasn't on Earth. How was that even possible? I was sure that *some* places on Earth had to be this beautiful, but then that left the thought of why my injuries healed, why I was suddenly feeling better than I ever had and...

Well, how did I end up here?

"Okay," Kerana said suddenly. I looked back over at her. She seemed to have regained her composure, yet her eyes were on something on the ground at my feet. I looked down to see what it could have been. Her voice drew my attention back up again.

"I'm going to take you to my father."

15 KERANA

Eli looked bewildered; the ash in his hair and on his face made him look far older.

Oh, I could kick myself for letting this happen. "Come on," I said, and reached out to him. I grabbed his hand, then dragged him with me up the path that wound out of sight.

Yes, Father will be able to make some semblance of sense out of this. If I just bring Eli there, Father will have the answer and we can find a way to send Eli back.

That thought then led to another.

But how did he get through in the first place? I thought it was impossible for Humans to come to this realm! The Portal was supposed to be sealed! My mind continued to whirl as we walked. I heard Eli exclaim small things out loud in surprise when we would pass certain elements that were entirely new to him along the way.

What was my father going to say?

I wasn't careful enough. Why, oh why, did I let myself admire him as closely as I had?

Oh, Adonai, what a royal mess I have created.

"You okay?" I heard from beside me.

I looked over at him. "Me? Oh, yes, I'm fine." I replied half-heartedly. He looked at me a little closer.

For a few moments, the only sound was our feet as they scuffed the dirt. The wind whispered through the trees around us. His hand started to fidget in mine.

"Oh, I'm sorry. I guess I don't need to pull you along like a child," I murmured, and let go of his hand.

I was surprised Eli wasn't bombarding me with questions, or going into some sort of shock. But then I remembered he was not one to show his true thoughts or feelings on the outside. I had learned that when I saw the difference between his piano playing and then his actions and behaviors away from the piano.

I looked over at him. His hands were in his pockets, a familiar stance. But his eyes were not downcast or cloudy; they were open, bright, and took in everything around him. I would have been too, if I had just entered a new world. It reminded me of when I had gone to Earth for the first time. At least I had forewarning and preparation for being in the new world.

After some time, we came to the populated areas of the realm, and the fear that ate at my insides grew more violent. I had not anticipated for any other Eldurians to appear along the way. I stopped around the bend where the homes began.

They would surely know he was Human. He and I would both stand out because of our clothes and the layers of soot on them, but he was also too rough around the edges, too tall, and too muscular to blend in here.

"Are you well enough to run for a few minutes?" I asked him. My question was received with a very peculiar look.

"Yeah, I feel great, actually. Not at all like I just escaped from a fire or got punched in the face last night. But why are we gonna have to run?"

"My people should not see you, Eli. They will anyway, I realize, but we need to get you to my home, quickly. They will obviously know you are from Earth but I would rather have my family's help in figuring out what exactly is going on first."

He considered me for a moment. "Well, I'm glad I'm not the only one who is really confused. I can't tell if I'm having a really vivid dream, or if I'm just on some crazy drugs the medics gave me when they saved me from the dorm."

Somewhat hurt by his statement and also infuriated, I said very seriously, "This is real, Eli, you are not dreaming. Nor are you under any influence of drugs from anyone. You are awake and alive."

He gave me a quizzical and amused look, and shook his head. "All right, Kerana. But I hope I can get answers to some of my questions before any real problems with my rational thinking starts. Or my sanity."

"You will have your questions answered, I'm sure." I said, even though I wasn't so sure. *What if my father simply found a way to send him back to Earth, and somehow caused Eli to forget ever have being here in the first place?* I didn't know, and didn't want to think on it now. *One thing at a time.*

"Come on; just follow me as closely as you can."

He nodded. I set off at a steady pace that Eli could easily match. He was a good runner, and I was glad he was on the athletic teams at the college. I knew the path to home well, but I think it was the first time I was ever nervous to go there.

As we ran, we saw several Eldurians outside their homes beneath the trees and their children playing. They recognized me, and stared at my appearance, and then they noticed Eli. I saw many of them gasp, some stare with their mouths open, and even a child or two run off of the path away from us. It hurt my heart to see these reactions.

I saw my mother in the garden as we approached, and I slowed until I came to a stop beside the large, graceful tree I called home. She had a small shovel in her hand with which she turned the fresh earth up to the surface, and small pouches of seeds lay beside her. My mother saw me and rose to her feet. Her mouth opened immediately upon seeing my state. "Kerana, dear, what has happened to you—?"

And then she saw Eli who slowed to a halt beside me.

The shovel in her hand fell to the earth, and her eyes widened more than I had ever seen them.

"My dear girl—what is going on?" she said; her words trembled. I crossed over to her and put my hands on her arms.

"Mother, please, we must go inside, and I must find Father."

Father emerged from the other side of our tree home. He stopped instantly. His eyes were on Eli.

"Follow me inside. Now." was all he said, and passed by us towards the door leading down beneath the tree. My mother stood very still, which was something I was not accustomed to, her eyes on Eli and I as we followed Father.

He opened the door, looking around to see if anyone was watching us. We walked down the stairs that I had thousands of times before, but not ever the way I walked down them now; slow, cautious, and hesitant. We reached the bottom and I waited until Eli and Father had come to stand in front of me. My father said not a word, just looked at us and walked down the hall to the living area.

I looked up at Eli, whose face was very white. I could only imagine what was going through his mind right now. I saw a glimmer of fear in his eyes for the first time since coming here.

My father stood beside our round table made from roots wound together from the tree above. His eyes were steady, and he gestured to one of the chairs. "Come sit, both of you."

Eli and I exchanged hesitant glances. "What is your name, young man?" he asked, his voice calm. I was confused by my father's reactions, since I could not understand what he was thinking.

Eli cleared his throat and fidgeted in his chair. "I'm Eli, sir."

He replied. I sat helpless beside him, unsure of my father's questions.

"Hmm." Father said.

Then he turned his attention to me. "Kerana, I understand your urgency. I'm sure your grand entrance has already attracted the attention of the rest of the Elders." A small shadow of a smile lightened his features, and therefore lightened the mood. I was thankful for the insight into his feelings; he was not furious at us.

"My name is Erez. I am Kerana's father, as I am sure you know."

We heard footsteps in the hallway, and looked up a moment later to see my mother appear in the room. Her arms were wrapped around herself in a protective stance, yet her face was calm. "Aonani, I'm glad you are here. Please sit with us. We have much to discuss."

She nodded, and a smile appeared on her face. It eased my heart. I wanted to reach over to Eli, to promise we were going to work things out.

"My parents are here now, so they will fix everything," I heard myself saying to him in my head. And I realized, in that same second that it didn't seem incredibly likely anymore.

My father sighed and looked at my mother, and then back at Eli and I. "Well, first of all, did you try to send Eli back?"

He and I both nodded. "I told him to walk back through, and when he walked through the gap in the trees, he just came out on the other side of them like he had stepped through ordinary trees."

Father's eyebrows furrowed. "Interesting."

"Did you try everything?" Mother asked.

"I didn't know what else to do besides pushing him back through. When that didn't work, well," I paused, looking at Eli whose eyes were on his hands that were folded on the table. "I thought maybe you would have an answer."

My father sat back and looked at Eli. "I'm sorry we are not addressing you, Eli, it is not as if we have forgotten you. I would like to retain as much of your clarity and state of mind at this point as possible."

"It's okay, because I really have no idea what is going on right now," he responded. His voice held a note of defeat in it. I felt my heart ache for him for a moment.

"I am sure you have many questions for us, and I fear that we have just as many for you. So let us try to figure out the best way to solve this problem. Adonai will show it to us, one way or another." Father said and nodded confidently.

"Adonai? Is that one of the Elders?" Eli asked, his eyes on my father now.

"That we can explain later," I cut in.

"Well I first want to know what happened, *exactly* what happened." Father said.

I looked over at Eli. "Would you like to start?" He sat back in his chair, returned his eyes to his hands now in his lap, and nodded, his face hidden by most of his long, disheveled hair.

16 ELI

I knew that these people sitting across from me were not human, or at least that is how Kerana made it seem. I trusted Kerana, but that didn't mean I trusted her family. Kerana's mother reminded me of my own before she died: her eyes were gentle, and soft, just like Mom's; her hair was the exact length of Mom's, and not much darker; and she had this way of looking at me like Mom used to when she knew I was in trouble and it wasn't my fault. I choked down those thoughts.

"There was a fire back on *Earth*, at the college," I said, trying to sound calm. "I remember being in my room, and I ignored the fire alarm, because I thought it was just a fire drill, so I ended up right in the middle of it. Then I passed out."

Kerana shifted uncomfortably as if she itched to interrupt, and her parents' eyes were on her for a brief moment. I went on.

"I woke up—I have no idea how long afterward—on a hill near the dorm. It was in ruins and still on fire, and I was covered in soot." I gestured down at myself, the remnants of the ashes still in the folds of my shirt and jeans. "I saw Kerana dash behind a building, so I chased after her. I got to a point where I had lost her, and I found two smaller trees in the middle of all of these tall and ancient ones. It looked like there was a path between them, and I thought I saw footsteps. And then, well," I looked around. "I ended up here."

"Is that all?" Erez asked.

I nodded my head. "Nothing really miraculous happened. One minute I was there, and then I was here, staring at Kerana." I looked over at her, and she seemed to only want to chew the inside of her lip. "There were no flashing lights, no magical noises, nothing. It just happened."

Erez and Aonani exchanged hesitant looks. "Okay. Well, then. Kerana? Anything you wish to add?"

She sat up straighter and stopped biting her bottom lip. "He told you almost everything. I knew he was in the building, so I went in after him. I was lucky I found him when I did, or otherwise he might not have survived."

Erez inclined his head and inspected the wood grain of the table. "So you went in, retrieved him, and then what?"

She fidgeted again, crossed and uncrossed her legs. "I set him out on the hill and attempted to get away before he was able to see me."

"Which he did," He said to her.

I couldn't hold it in any longer.

"I'm sorry, but you don't seem too concerned about the fact that your daughter went into a *burning building* to save me." I emphasized the words just in case they had missed them somehow in the midst of this conversation.

Erez and Aonani and Kerana all exchanged a nervous glance. "No, actually, it isn't a surprise at all." Erez replied.

"Why?" I said indignantly. "She should have been burned alive, and there was no way that she would have been able to make it up all those stairs, and then somehow magically carry me out, someone who is easily twice her weight."

Kerana looked afraid. "Father, we have to do something."

"I know. I just never thought we would have to do this."

"Have to do what?" I said, and looked between them.

"Have to tell a Human what we are."

I made a noise of disgust, which I instantly regretted because it was rude, even if I was angry. "'A human!' Yeah, *sure* you aren't human. Good luck convincing me of that."

An elite race of human, maybe, but still human, was all I could think.

Kerana hung her head, her perfectly straight hair hiding her face. I felt my heart tighten in my chest. I certainly was lost, but I did know Kerana. She was real, even if the rest of this didn't seem to be.

"Eli, I don't expect you to believe any of what I will soon tell you, but I nevertheless ask that you listen to me—and listen well. We have never encountered this sort of problem, with a Human crossing over our borders. There is much to discuss and decide, and in order for any of that to happen, we need you to understand where you are and who we are. On top of that, we still need to see if we can determine how or why any of this has happened. So do not fear; you are not alone in being confused and frustrated," Erez said, his tone calm but his face serious. I felt less alone, strangely, and so I let it go for the moment and nodded.

Kerana spoke up. "I just wanted to check and make sure he was all right when we got out of the building, so I stayed with him for a few more minutes. I should have just walked away, let the medics or the firemen find him, but for some reason, I just had to make sure." Kerana continued on with her story.

"We understand," Aonani said suddenly. Her voice was just as captivating as Kerana's. "It is perfectly natural to want to make sure that the Humans are safe. I remember the first Humans that I had to protect and how much I wanted to continue to care for them. But you know that we are asked to not reveal ourselves;

otherwise, things like this happen," and she gestured to me. Kerana made a noise that sounded like a whimper.

"I know, and it is all my fault because I wasn't careful enough."

"That is not it at all, my dear," Erez said to her, and he reached across the table for her hand. "We are not blaming this on you. You did what you thought was right. There is a reason for everything. Adonai has a plan, remember that."

There was that *Adonai* name again.

She paused for a moment. "Well, then he started to cough, and I knew he was coming around. At that point, I knew I had to leave him alone, otherwise he would see me, covered in ashes just like him, and it would raise questions..." She trailed off. "But as I ran, I could hear him following me. He actually kept up with me quite well."

Erez looked at me with a new form of respect. "You could keep up with an Eldurian? I am impressed."

"Eldurian?" I questioned, as more questions stemmed in my brain.

"It is what we are called," Kerana added, finally looking up at me. But then her eyes left mine and returned across the table. "It is one of our many strengths and blessings."

"Oh, you mean like walking through fire?" I replied, somewhat sarcastically. I felt bad for being so rude to these people, to Kerana. But I didn't know how else to handle it. She looked at me in a way that made my heart stop; she was neither mad, nor upset, nor serious. She almost seemed relieved.

"Yes, actually. That is one of them as well."

"Why did you decide to come back here in the first place?" Aonani asked.

Kerana was silent for a moment. "Because it was the first time I had rescued a Human. I don't know, it must have been instinct. I didn't know what else to do! I had no idea he would be able to follow me through the *Portal*!"

If I ever believed any of this stuff at any point that night, it was at this point. I don't even know why, but that was when I started to think maybe it wasn't so crazy after all. Maybe it was the desperation in Kerana's voice.

Erez stood to his feet. "Well, I think I should go inspect the Portal and see if there is anything there worth looking at, Kerana. You can point everything out to me and we can decide what to do from there."

"And what about Eli, dear?" Aonani asked him as she rose to her feet as well.

"Perhaps we should get the boy cleaned up and out of those bloody clothes. He would probably be in favor of a bath as well as some rest."

Aonani smiled at me for the first time. "Erez has some clothes somewhere that he wore while he was in the Human realm. They might be a bit small, but I think they should do the job well enough." And with that, she turned to go.

Erez followed Aonani out of the room, which left Kerana and I alone. She still sat in the chair beside me, but she wouldn't look at me.

"I'm sorry."

I looked over at her.

"Sorry for what exactly?"

"For bringing you here." She replied.

"You didn't bring me here. I brought myself here."

"Just out of curiosity, why did you follow me?" She asked me as she looked up at me. She still glowed faintly, and it made it that much harder to talk to her without stumbling over my words.

"Because I figured you had something to do with me getting out of there alive. And by the fact that you were running, you wanted to hide something. I'm a curious guy, and running is the international sign of guilt."

She looked at me in a faintly puzzled way.

I smiled at her a little. "But seriously, I wanted to know what just happened, and I recognized you by your hair."

She looked at me very closely. "You are handling this extremely well."

"I never said I believed it—"

She sighed.

"I was going to say that I never said I believed it *yet.*"

Aonani and Erez returned to the room. Erez has an armful of clothing and I stood when he approached me, and Aonani lingered by the entrance to the room. "Here you are. I hope that these will fit you. At the very least, they will be better than bloody and torn clothes, right?"

I nodded. "Thank you." I wanted to say more, but what? I didn't know them, they didn't know me, and apparently we weren't even the same species. I looked at Kerana again quickly.

Erez smiled at me, and then turned to Kerana. "Let's go and see what we can make of this."

So he and Kerana walked out of the room side by side, leaving me alone with her mother. Kerana gave me one last long glance over her shoulder. Aonani ushered me out of the room and down to the very end of the hall. There was a door at the end, and she told me to go through and take as much time as I needed. She handed me an incredibly large but soft cloth for a towel and an armful of clothes. "Thank you, Aonani. I really don't know what else to say."

She smiled up at me. "I believe you have a good heart, Eli. We will get this worked out for you, I know it." And with that, she turned and walked back down the hall to the common area.

I sighed. Well, if I was really stuck on another dimension or whatever it was, I could at least enjoy the pampering I was getting. I opened the door and found a decent-sized bathroom, with two sinks made from the roots of the tree above my head. Clear water trickled into the bowl-shaped indentations. There was another root that looked an awful lot like a toilet in the back left corner, and in the very middle of the room, sunken into the floor, was a large, full and steaming wooden tub. It smelled flowery and sweet in the room, but I didn't care; I had left some of my dignity back on Earth. I set the new clothes off to the side, the sponge, towel, and soap beside the tub, and I cast off my clothes. I slid easily into the tub, and I forgot about my predicament entirely for a moment. I shut my eyes, subconsciously grateful that I could see out of both of them again so soon, and allowed the hot and heavily scented water to soak deep into my skin.

17 KERANA

Father was outside a moment or so before me. The sky had darkened to the dark amethyst of twilight, and pinpricks of stars were beginning to show their faces. Everything was quiet and still. My father looked at me. His eyes were very dark in this evening light, the color of the shadowed grass at our feet.

"I'm sorry," I muttered, not able to look him in the eyes when I said it. I looked down the path where Eli and I had run just a short time ago, and felt a stone-like weight in my stomach. I heard my father take a step towards me.

He cupped my face in his hands and made me look at him. "Kerana, you need not be sorry. I am not entirely convinced that this is a bad thing. You know that nothing happens by chance."

"I know. Adonai doesn't make mistakes. But why this? Why send everything that we've ever known into chaos?"

"This is not quite chaos, dear," he said, and gestured for me to follow him up the path. I fell into a steady stride beside him. "When we bring him before the rest of the Elders tomorrow—well, that may be chaos."

"The Elders must know by now. Enough people saw us run by to know that something is going on. I'm surprised everyone is this calm."

Father looked at me out of the corner of his eye. "When have you ever known an Eldurian to not be calm?"

"This has never happened before!" I said. "And it is entirely my fault. I wasn't careful enough, and I didn't follow the rules."

"Our job isn't about rules, Kerana," he responded. "Adonai created us to help Him. That is why He uses us, to help shape the world into a better place where He can be found."

I nodded. "But why would He allow this when it has never happened before?"

He shrugged his shoulders. "I do not know, Kerana. But it is also not my job to know. We will need to seek Adonai's counsel; He is the only one who really knows what's going on anyway."

By now we had reached the Portal. It looked just as it had an hour or so ago when Eli had followed me through it. We looked at the scene; I was frustrated, since nothing seemed different to me at all. The Portal was exactly the same as it had always been. None of the trees were out of place, it was just as clear as always; nothing seemed wrong.

Father decided to take a look at it himself. He circled the Portal and paid attention to every aspect of it, up and down. He scrutinized it for several minutes before he stood in front of it.

"Kerana, did you try to go back through it?... Or was it just Eli who tried to re-enter?"

I hesitated for a moment. "No, I didn't even think of that. Do you think it would have sealed itself for Eldurians, too?"

"I suppose there is only one sure way to discover that." And so he walked through the Portal. He, unlike Eli, had stepped through the Portal onto Earth, and a moment later, he appeared in front of me again, and turned back to look at the Portal.

"Very peculiar. I can't understand why we can go through,

but the Human can't."

"Is there any other way that we can send him back?"

My father looked at me. "Well, I suppose we could try one of the other three Portals, but my guess is that if he can't go back through the one he came through, it is even less likely that he would be able to go through any of those."

I sighed. "So what do we do now?" I asked. I looked around and hoped that something, *anything*, would jump out at me and give us the answer we were looking for.

"Our best choice I think is to take him to the Elders first thing in the morning."

"I don't know how they will take this."

"Neither do I, my dear. That is why we will go in with our best intentions, and pray that Adonai will give us the answers to our questions."

The sky had turned to a silky black, and shimmered with stars overhead as we walked back. I would have loved to entertain the thought of the stars that night, but other things required my attention.

As I followed my father inside, I realized that Adonai had brought Eli to us for some purpose, for some reason. I just was very confused as to what it was.

My mother stood near the sofa in the living quarters. She spread blankets across it to make what I assumed was a bed for Eli. The fire in the fireplace crackled softly, and created a warm glow across the wooden floors and tables. She turned around to look at us as we walked in.

"Any success?" She asked as she unfolded another blanket. I crossed across the room to help her tuck in the blankets between the cushions.

"Not yet, no," my father said. He followed me to her and stood behind the couch.

"Where are Hani and Oni?" I asked, as I realized it was incredibly quiet in the house.

"I sent them to Feren's house for the evening. I figured that we didn't need all that noise tonight too. Eli can meet them tomorrow, but I didn't want to overwhelm him any more by having those boys staring at him all night. He is uncomfortable enough."

She finished tucking in the last blanket, and began to pick up some fluffy pillows from the floor, and positioned them at the end of the couch.

"Where is Eli, by the way?" I asked.

"I sent him off to take a bath. I suspect he is taking advantage of the solitude, for now." She replied, and sat on the bed she had just made. "So you didn't find anything at all to help you understand what is going on?"

My father shook his head. "We did not. The only thing that was interesting is that when I stepped through the Portal, I crossed back over to Earth. So the Portal isn't closed entirely; it is simply closed to Eli."

"And do you think any of the other Elders will have any idea what this means?"

"I don't know, but I doubt it. I think what they will have the most problem getting past is the fact that he is here in the first place."

"That is a given," I cut in, and sat down beside my mother.

"And how are you feeling?" she asked.

"I think I am better now that I have brought him here and it is no longer my own burden. It's comforting to know that I am not alone in this, and that Adonai has a place in His plan for this crazy, bizarre thing that is happening."

My mother and my father both nodded at me. "But what do you both think about this? I mean really think of it?" I asked them.

They exchanged glances, and my mother decided to start. "I find this whole thing very strange."

Father agreed with a nod. "I suspect Eli feels very much of what we felt going to Earth for the first time, except that he gets to experience the power of a world that is still pure and alive."

"I like him," Mother continued. "I met some Humans during my term on Earth that he reminds me of—Humans with good hearts. Eli is eager for acceptance, though afraid to show it. I am anticipating the great things that Adonai will bring about with all of this."

I looked down the hall in the direction of the bathroom. "What will Adonai say?"

"We will talk with Him tomorrow at the Council Hall, but He may not respond to us; He likes to make us wait sometimes on His answers. Just because we are His servants and His workers, it does not mean that He will always fill us in about the workings of everything."

I nodded. "I do know that. Do you think Eli will meet Adonai while he is here?"

"I doubt Adonai would bring Eli here without giving him the opportunity to do so." Father replied.

Just as my father finished his statement, Eli walked back into the room. He wore a dark pair of blue pajama bottoms and a loose, grey T-shirt. His eyes were bright and clear, and his shaggy hair stuck out at odd angles and to the back of his neck in some places. He silently padded into the room with bare feet, and stood just inside in the open doorway, unsure if he should come in any farther.

"Eli, come in here. We made a bed for you," Mother said as she got to her feet and gestured to the sofa. I stood too, and looked at Eli. There was something that captivated me about him, the way he stood there, vulnerable and quiet.

"Thank you, for letting me clean up."

"The clothes fit you well, Eli," my Father commented. Eli smiled a very small smile.

"Yeah." He crossed the room over to where we were, and looked down at the couch.

"I hope this will be all right," my mother said. "I know it isn't a real bed, but I think it will do for now."

"Don't worry; I've slept on plenty of couches before. This won't be anything new. Well, not entirely new, I guess." He added.

My father and mother looked from each other to him and I. "I think it is time that we went to bed ourselves. Eli, we will wake you up in the morning and we can go speak to the Elders."

He nodded, and thanked my parents as they left the room.

"Good night, both of you. May Adonai watch you and keep you," my father said, and they disappeared.

Eli, obviously uncomfortable and uneasy, stood beside the couch. He looked as if he had not slept in days. I smiled at him, hoping to encourage him, and he just simply looked back at me. It made me feel slightly flustered, so I made to leave the room.

"Kerana?" He said quietly as I turned to walk away. I glanced over my shoulder at him.

"Are you still upset with me?" he asked, a subdued playful look on his gentle, handsome face. I returned to the couch, and motioned for him to sit beside me.

"No, Eli. I am not angry with you," I replied, and smiled. "I just want you to be safe. And I'm confused, but not upset."

He smiled back. "I keep thinking I must be dreaming, but then I pinch myself—and it hurts."

He sat very straight-backed on the edge of the sofa.

"It must seem like a dream, Eli. And yes, a lot has happened. And I am sure that I have not yet had an opportunity to thank you for protecting me last night," I said quietly as I examined the soot in my finger nails; I had yet to clean up myself. "I don't know what would have happened if you had not arrived when you had."

He looked at me very seriously, and turned his whole body toward me.

"Kerana, I knew those guys, and they're bad news. They would have—" he drifted off. "Well they could have hurt you pretty badly. I've known them to do that."

I nodded. "They frightened me."

Then the silence fell back over us.

"I'm sorry about your eye."

"Hey, it's no problem."

"Well, I think we should be getting to bed," I said as a silence fell again for a few more moments. I rose to my feet and his eyes followed me.

"I guess," he said, as a sigh escaped him. I could almost see the weight draped around his shoulders.

I smiled to encourage him. "You should get some rest. The Elders will want to see you well and attentive. They will have many questions, I'm sure."

"What will they be like?" he asked.

"Well, my father is an Elder, though he is one of the youngest. The others," I hesitated. "Well it has been a while since any of them have been to Earth, or been with Humans."

"Will they judge me? Is it going to be like a trial or something?"

"No, not at all. I am sure all they will do is simply question you. My father hopes that with many minds coming together and seeking Adonai's wisdom, we will be able to determine how to make sense of it. I am sorry that we cannot give you the answers you seek. We are just going through it step by step, like you."

He nodded at me. I saw him try and stifle a yawn. "But you really should get to sleep, Eli. There will be plenty of time to talk tomorrow."

"You're probably right. I can't believe how tired I am."

His face slowly slipped into a smile as his eyes met mine. It made my heart skip a beat. "Tomorrow you can show me how you are different from the *Humans*."

I went to my room and collapsed onto my bed. I looked up out of the window above me at the darkest blue sky. It was the exact shade of Eli's eyes.

18 ELI

I woke up to the smell of something very sweet.

I begrudgingly opened my eyes. Sunshine streamed in through the windows tucked in the corners between the ceiling and the wall of bark and tree roots, and the room was bright with the light of dawn. I yawned. I must have kicked that fantastic blanket to the floor in the middle of the night, since I felt cool and somewhat exposed. I then closed my eyes again for a moment to feel the comfort from the couch and pillows sink in. I hadn't been this comfortable, or slept as well for that matter, in a really, really long time.

I heard footsteps enter the kitchen and then heard voices that spoke in hushed tones.

"He's still asleep, then?" I heard Aonani whisper. There was the chink of silverware on a plate.

"Yes, he hasn't made a sound since I came in. He must have really needed to sleep."

"When do you plan on going down to the Council Hall?" she

asked.

"I was hoping before the morning rush in an hour or so, but we'll have to see; I don't want to wake him."

I heard water run, and peeked out of the corner of my eye.

"Good morning, Eli," I heard Aonani say.

"How'd you sleep?" Erez asked me.

Aonani had come closer to the couch, a bright smile on her beautiful face. Erez stood in the kitchen with a bowl in his hands and a small cloth over his shoulder. They both wore white robes.

"My sleep was incredible, actually. Thanks," I replied, and returned Aonani's smile.

Just as I stood, Kerana walked into the room. I was in mid-stretch, and I froze. She wore the same robe as her parents, which was very striking on her, as it hugged her frame just slightly. Her long hair was as beautiful as I had ever known it to be, and her big blue eyes had instantly fallen on me, like some sort of heat-seeking missile. She and her parents glowed faintly. I must have looked like an idiot, and it brought back memories of the day that I met her when I babbled and stumbled over myself.

"Good morning, my daughter," Erez said.

"Good morning," she said pleasantly. The way everyone was acting, it was as if last night never happened and everything was fine and normal. Not like I was in some alternate dimension or something. But after I slept here, the idea didn't seem too bad anymore, as if sleeping had made it sink into my brain. Maybe I would learn to accept it one day. And maybe coming to that point would require therapy when I got back to Earth.

"Would anyone care for some breakfast?" called Erez, who was watching me inspect the table with a look of amusement.

"No need to fear the food, Eli. It is very similar to the foods you have on Earth, but these are far better for you, all natural."

I looked more closely at the bowl of what looked like berries on the table in front of me. They were dark blues and vibrant reds and pinks and oranges. They looked like many of the berries I knew. There were breads, and something that looked like oatmeal. So I grabbed a spoonful and put some of everything on my plate. Erez also explained that they did not eat meat and didn't kill animals. I found that really weird, and felt bad for the Eldurians. What was life without a big, juicy burger?

But the food sure made up for the lack of meat and I soon changed my mind on that matter. It was delicious, every last bit. I was sure that I could eat and eat and never get tired of any of it.

After a hearty breakfast and some casual and normal table conversation, which I was thankful for, Erez showed me to their room and his collection of Human's clothing. The bedroom he shared with Aonani was very large, with a large bed that I would have loved to jump on as a kid, and bookshelves and another overstuffed couch. Erez crossed to a large armoire and pulled aside several more white robes to a few articles of colored clothing. He pulled them out and showed them to me.

"You may use these while you are here. Put on something you will look best in; let the Elders see your true self."

So he sent me off to the bathroom to change. I chose a white button-up and dark jeans and hoped the sneakers I was wearing in the first place were good enough. I didn't have anything else.

Seeing everything in daylight was so much different than the night before.

It was all fresh, so alive. I had never seen anything quite so magnificent in my life.

The trees, though just like trees on Earth, were somehow more alive. They were what I imagined the trees on Earth looked like when the planet first began. The people here were all as beautiful as Kerana's family. Along with being stunning, the Eldurians were all incredibly graceful. It was like only ballet dancers were allowed there. I felt clumsy, unattractive, and out of place. And compared to everyone there, I was.

As we walked, Kerana pointed out plants and trees and grasses to me. Their names sounded extraordinary and beautiful, just like the living things they represented. We stopped a few minutes away from the Council Hall and she showed me these huge turquoise flowers along the path that sparkled and hummed. She told me they were called Astrums, since they looked like miniature stars. I asked how those two words related, and she laughed.

"I forget that you do not know all the languages I do. It is the Latin word for 'star' and we have called these flowers Astrums for many centuries."

We then continued up the path through the trees. "So how do you know so many languages?" I asked her. "I know English, and a little bit of Spanish. But that's nothing compared to you." She smiled shyly.

"We are all taught all of the languages of mankind. It is part of our upbringing, part of our studies as Elduns."

"Elduns?" I asked.

"Elduns are what we call Eldurians that have not come of age yet."

"So like on Earth we call someone a minor if they are not eighteen."

"Yes, very similar. But one becomes an Eldurian when they are old enough to travel to Earth. That can be anywhere between the ages of eighteen and twenty-five, depending on their education level."

"You came to Earth, so you obviously are now an Eldurian. How old are you exactly?"

She looked at me in a playful way, which surprised me coming from her. She answered softly. "I'm twenty."

"How old are you?" She asked.

"I'm twenty-two."

Two Eldurians walked towards us with two young Elduns, all of them dressed in white. The younger boys were bright and excited, and wore a simple white shirt and white shorts, and they were barefoot.

As they came closer to us, the boys, who I now realized were twins, ran towards Erez and Aonani, their ecstatic shrieks filling the air. The couple who walked with them, however, had their eyes on me.

Aonani bent to the little boys, and I guessed then that they were Kerana's little brothers. They looked a lot like her. She hugged them both, and they then ran back to Kerana, who was still beside me. They ignored me as they wrapped their arms around her waist, and buried their faces in the folds of her robe.

I heard tiny gasps around my middle and shifted my gaze to the twins. Their green eyes were bulbous and glued to me, as if they were looking at some sort of alien creature. Well, I guess to them, I was an alien.

"Boys, this is Eli. He is our new guest, so treat him as such."

They continued to stare at me as if she hadn't said anything.

The one on the right opened his mouth and his eyes squinted. "But he's *Human!*"

"Oni!" Kerana exclaimed. "That was not very nice way to say it."

"But he is!" The other one piped up. I smiled at them bemusedly.

"There's nothing wrong with telling me what I am." I added. These kids were funny. Kerana looked over at me.

"I'm sorry. Hani and Oni can be very vocal." She said, as she placed a hand on Hani's shoulder.

"Why would it matter to me? If they called me stupid or ugly, then I might have an issue with it," I replied playfully.

"He sounds funny," said Hani, and he peered up at me, obviously unable to resist opening his mouth again. Oni nodded fervently in reply as he stared at me.

"He does not sound funny," Kerana added, while I laughed out loud.

"Does so!" Oni continued. "It's all deep and raspy. And he looks funny too."

I just chuckled.

She let out an exasperated sigh. "Well, when you two are old enough to go to Earth, then you will see Eli is a fine example of a Human and does not sound funny or look funny. Am I understood?"

A fine example of a Human, huh?

They shrugged in unison, looking at each other. "Sure, but we have to go now. Feren and Tyrin are taking us to the city square this afternoon to play in the Winter Realm with the rest of our class while you all go to the Council Hall."

And without another word, they scampered off down the path behind us.

"They're something else," I said and tried to stop laughing.

"I'm sorry—" Kerana started to reply sincerely. I held up a hand.

"Not at all. How could they know what to say, anyway? Besides, I've heard far worse things from kids half their age."

"What do you mean?" she asked me.

"I worked at a summer camp for one summer. The kids were horrible. I never went back."

She was quiet for a moment. Then the couple who were talking with Aonani and Erez walked towards us.

"Good morning, Feren and Tyrin. I trust that you are well this morning?"

The woman, who had silvery, short hair and big grey eyes, smiled at Kerana. Did all of the people here have to be incredibly attractive? She smiled at Kerana and me, and then she and the man beside her, who had a shaved head and dark eyebrows, ushered the twins up the path again.

"Come, Kerana and Eli. We must go to the Council Hall." Erez called to us from up the path. She and I glanced at one another and then continued up the path, this time in silence.

We walked for a few more minutes before I noticed the trees starting to thin out. Kerana's eyes lit up. I looked around me and tried to see what excited her so much. She quickened her pace to her parents, so I followed her.

Before I saw what excited her so much, I heard it. There was what sounded like tambourines, violins, and guitars floating in the air. Then I heard the voices along with the sound of rushing water.

There was a clearing or something up ahead, and as we came to the end of the path, it widened out and forked.

"Whoa," I murmured, and Kerana turned to me. She beamed.

I saw a huge stone fountain right in the middle of the clearing; it had to be as big as a two-story house and just as wide around. The clearing itself was as big as four football fields, and there were trees all around. The fountain bubbled merrily, and I saw something that floated on the surface. *Rose petals?*

The clearing was split evenly into four different sections that met at the fountain, and they all looked like seasons. We stood in the summer section, it seemed, and to our left was the fall, and to our right was the spring. I noticed that even some trees were part way between the divisions and therefore a part of two different seasons. It was amazing, like something out of a sci-fi movie or video game.

And then there were the people, the Eldurians. There were hundreds of them; they walked and laughed together. As Kerana linked her arm through mine and pulled me out into the open, I saw people that sat playing guitars and singing in a language I didn't understand; I saw people place more of the rose petals into the water of the fountain; I saw Elduns race around and weave in between the adults. It was like a city back on Earth in regards to the number of people, except here everyone was happy and got along. The perfect world.

Kerana pulled me towards one of the biggest trees in sight, with a huge set of doors carved right into the trunk of the tree that were two stories tall, with intricate carvings on them.

"Kerana," I said, "This is astounding."

She smiled at me and eased her grip. "I'm so glad you think

so."

"So that's the Council Hall?" I questioned, looking over at the tall, enormously wide tree. She nodded.

"Yes. That is where we are taking you."

We got closer to it, with stares from many Eldurians along the way. Each of them was different, but they were all phenomenally gorgeous. The women were all thin and delicate and graceful, whereas the men were lean and handsome. I continued to feel horribly out of place, even if I was in awe of everything around me.

The large doors opened outward as we got closer, as if they knew we were coming. There was a long hallway with tall ceilings and lots of windows. The main hallway branched out into more hallways along both walls. There was also another large set of doors at the opposite end.

It was quieter in here, but we could still hear the music and the laughter from outside. As the doors closed us in, I was really nervous again. Up and down, up and down. My feelings were just all over the board.

Kerana patted my arm gently in an attempt to reassure me. She probably felt me tense up.

Erez and Aonani turned down the left hallway, and we followed them in silence. There were several doors along this new corridor, and I tried to swallow my dread as Erez stopped at a door at the very end. Kerana and I caught up and he and Aonani looked around at us.

"Now Eli, I can't promise you that this will go smoothly, or that it will be easy. But I can promise you one thing; you are in no danger here."

That's reassuring, I thought sarcastically.

"Let me go in first, explain what is going on, and then come retrieve you."

So he slipped in the door and closed it behind him. Aonani sighed. "I pray that this goes well."

In silence, we all waited out in front of that door for nearly twenty minutes. I could barely hear what was being said on the other side, but I heard voices raise and some shouts. It didn't sound angry, just that they all tried to talk over one another.

"There are twelve Elders?" I asked. Kerana looked up at me in surprise, maybe since she wanted to listen in on what they were saying.

"Yes. Adonai chose twelve to follow Him and to continue his works here just like He chose twelve on Earth."

"I thought Adonai was an Elder." I replied. Kerana and Aonani shook their heads.

"He is far above the Elders, dear one." Aonani replied. Before any more could be said, the door opened and Erez stepped out. The room behind him was silent as death.

"Come inside."

Kerana and Aonani stepped through before me, and then I made eye contact with Erez as I walked through. "Have faith, child," he said.

The room was oval, with a large circular table in the middle. The ceilings were tall just like in the hallway. Eleven older looking men in white robes awaited. Kerana and Aonani seated themselves opposite the men, which left a spot in between them for me. Erez went across to the other side and sat amongst the Elders.

Erez spoke first. "We are the Elders, chosen by Adonai Himself. We each bring unique ways and skills to this table, creating a diverse and well-rounded collaboration of leaders. I am Erez, which you know, Eli. I want to introduce you to my fellow Elders and I will begin to my right and continue down all the way around the table."

And so he did. Their names were Conan, Ovid, Tedros, Teom, Dru, Eneas, Kimo, Seoras, Faris, Kobe, and Keon. Each of them was as handsome and strong-looking as the next, yet all looked entirely different from each other. Some were tall and thin, others broad, and one was even short.

One of the men nearest me cleared his throat. He was bald,

with dark brown eyes and a very angular face. He might have been a professional wrestlers if he was Human. "My name is Kobe, Eli. I am one of the eldest Eldurians sitting before you. Erez explained to you that this has never happened before in the history of Eden, correct?

"Correct, sir," I replied, nodding my head. He folded his hands in front of himself on the table. "We knew you were here the moment you came last night. Nothing remains secret in Eden to us."

"Eli, tell them everything you told me last night," Erez instructed.

After I was done, they all started to talk over one another.

"Perhaps she passed some of her gift to him while she carried him out," a man with white hair and eyes almost the same color said to the man on his left.

"Not possible. It would have happened before. Other Eldurians have saved Humans from fires," the man replied back.

I heard another trio straight across the table, "—just a mistake? Maybe he is part Eldurian? There were those who never came back, or what if he is another prophet that Adonai just never…"

"We would have known," Kobe said loud enough to cut off everyone else's conversations. They all looked at him. A second or two passed before anyone talked again.

"Not always, Kobe. He often times does things without our consent. You of all of us should know this." Erez replied. Other men around the table nodded.

A man two down from me spoke up. "Well then answer me this; why is the Human here in the first place?" He hadn't spoken at all since we came in. His long, red hair fell over his shoulders, and he had small, piercing blue eyes. He gave me the same vibe as Kobe did, and he was talking about me like I wasn't even there. I didn't like the way he said *Human.*

"The peace has vanished since the Fallen One entered," mumbled Dru, a man with jet black hair and bright eyes. All eyes looked at him, and were silent.

And Dru looked at me. "Once a Fallen One of Adonai enters an Eldurian's midst, the Eldurian then is exposed to the world in which the Fallen One lives. He still brings the sins of Earth with him. He brings the hurt, the hate, and the contamination of that wretched place."

"Come over here, boy. I want to see you more closely."

"Why?" I asked. There was something wrong with his voice.

Dru's eyes slid over my face and down my shoulders. "I need to see something. Now please. Stand over here on this dais." He said and pointed towards the floor to ceiling windows on the wall behind Erez and Conan.

I didn't move.

"If you wonder why I ask you to put yourself on display, it is merely because I have a theory, and wish to see if I am right. Now," he bent lower to me. "I wish to understand this as much as you do. If I can just see you in the light."

"Why can't you just see me from here?" I was already sitting in a patch of sunlight; I could feel the heat against the crown of my head. "What do you want to see?"

"Your hand, please."

I looked up at him, maybe even more perplexed now than when I came into the room. Slowly, I lifted my hand up away from the table, and Dru took it in his own and bathed it in the sunlight over my head.

"Tell me. Did you have injuries from the fire?" Dru asked me as he inspected my hand.

"Well, yeah. I had smoke in my lungs, cuts and scrapes, but nothing fatal." Then I remembered the black eye I had that had disappeared. "And I had a black eye from a different incident the night before."

Dru stopped and stood in front of me. "Interesting."

"I suppose that makes sense, though," one of the other men said. He looked gentle.

"What does, Keon?" Dru asked him.

"Being this close to Adonai Himself would cure a Human of their physical ailments; just being near Adonai would do such miracles."

"But if the physical problems are gone, the emotional and mental tarnishes and cracks would have to be gone too," Conan added. "They are ailments just like physical ones."

Dru then continued to pace around me. "And those are not gone yet."

"But those are things that are at the mercy of the man himself," Kobe said. I looked up at him. His arms were folded across his broad chest, and his eyes looked all over me as if he searched for something.

"I see Adonai written all over him," Dru added offhandedly as he inspected the left side of my face closely. Did he know it was my left eye that had been injured? I didn't say it was, did I? And what the heck did he mean that Adonai was written all over me?

"But I thought Humans weren't allowed in Eden; they were banished at the Beginning," Keon added. Dru held up a hand to silence him.

"They aren't allowed here." He turned to me in explanation. "Adonai created the Portals to only allow Eldurians to pass through. That way, if a Human did accidentally walk where a Portal was, they would pass through it and continue through on Earth."

Dru stared at my hand and turned it over and over in his. It looked like he was tracing my veins with his forefinger. It was strange, because it looked to me like my veins stood out a little today. I figured it was the adrenaline that pumped through me because I had been so nervous.

"Adonai said that they would never come here. They aren't like us. They are just fleshy bodies that are broken on the inside." Kimo carried on.

"He doesn't even look whole!" Kobe exclaimed.

A harsh silence settled in the room.

"And that, my brothers," Dru cut in, "is where our problem lies."

He released my hand and stepped back away from me. And that was when I noticed that Kobe was right.

I looked down at the hand that Dru just let go of. I held it up to my face and let the sunlight wash over it. I saw that my skin looked vaguely transparent. I held it away from me, towards the window, and thought I was going crazy when I thought I could see the sunlight through my hand. It was like I looked through the murky water of a pond I had growing up when I tried to swim to the surface. I was solid, but not entirely.

That was when I began to panic.

"Oh my God, what's happening to me?" I asked as I jumped out of my chair, and looked wildly around. "Tell me what's happening to me." I hollered. I clutched my hand like it was going to fall off.

I saw Kerana out of the corner of my eye. She looked like she was ready to dash over to me, but I didn't want her near me either. She was tied to this place—this place that was doing weird things to my body.

"What's happening!?" I shouted again, my back up against the wall opposite the windows.

"What do you mean, that's where our problem lies?" Erez asked Dru, one hand extended towards me, the other pointing at Dru.

"Kobe was very close when he said Eli didn't look whole. I said it was our problem because he *isn't* whole anymore. He lives in a Fallen world, and that is where his body is built to be. Here, in a world that isn't Fallen, I suspect the parts of him that were tied to his Fallen nature are being 'purified.'"

"Purified meaning what?" I sputtered angrily.

"Purified meaning disappearing, in general terms."

Disappearing?!

"How did you determine that?" Erez asked. He looked as if he wanted to come closer to me, but fought the urge. I'm glad he did; I was so freaked out I wasn't sure what I would do in self-defense.

"Well, judging by the fact that what Keon said about being close to Adonai would heal him of his physical injuries, I figured that being this close to Adonai would have other effects as well. Even if man is in control of the emotional and mental parts of himself, Adonai's control supersedes the man's control, and therefore the broken and filthy parts of the man will eventually begin to ebb away, to disappear."

"Literally?" I butted in. Dru looked at me from across the room.

"You were born in a Fallen world. The Fallen parts of you make up your very being. So yes, literally."

I looked down at my trembling hands. If I looked hard enough, I could see the edges of my skin were transparent. "He's been here for how long, would you say?" Dru asked Erez calmly. Erez, who had been looking at me with a face that held just enough fear for me to notice, looked back at him.

"About eighteen hours."

"Then if what I have assumed is correct, his body will entirely disappear in a matter of," he hesitated.

"Six days."

19 KERANA

Eli's face went from pale to ghost white.

"Dru, what do you mean he will entirely disappear?" Father questioned.

"I mean just what I say. If we can't figure out how to stop it, his body will continue to gradually disappear. He will, like I said, at the end of six days, just be gone."

"Gone to where?" Erez asked.

"That is a good question. I do not know the answer to that," Dru responded.

"So basically I'm gonna just die?" Eli exclaimed. I looked back over at him.

"Death has not even been spoken of, Eli," My father chimed in. He took a hesitant step toward Eli.

"What else would you consider completely disappearing?" he cried as he threw his hands into the air. My mother's hand was on my arm, gentle but I recognized the warning.

"This is all we have determined; we now have to decide what our next step is." Dru said.

"Our next step is to find a way to get him out of Eden!" I looked over at Kobe. My inside's burned. In Eli's time of need, it was not right for Kobe to be so determined to get rid of him.

"Is this ever going to stop?" Eli asked quietly. He looked like he inspected something on the ground at his feet, like he was sleep-walking. He went from furious to stoic in a matter of moments, and it worried me.

"No, this shouldn't have even happened. Just because I am not one of you doesn't give your king any right to put a spell on me."

"It's not a spell, you foolish Human! You know nothing of which you speak!" Kimo spat.

"Kimo, this is not the way we should handle this. Please," Eneas murmured for the first time since this meeting began. "Let's all address the King and hope for His wisdom."

"I am not meeting your king. Tell him to fix me first, and then *maybe* I'll talk to him!" Eli cried.

"If you need information, and if you need someone to speak to Adonai, I will," I cried, before I really even knew what I was doing. My heart beat painfully against my ribcage. "Eli has been through enough. I will speak to Adonai on Eli's behalf."

They all turned and glanced at one another. And to my surprise, my father smiled ever so softly, and my mother's grip on my arm was gone.

I crossed over to Eli who looked as if his spirit had aged fifty years in the last half hour, and I slipped my arm through his and led him from the room without another word.

He simply turned his head towards me as we walked out into the hall, and his eyes fell onto mine. He held my gaze for a moment or two, and all I could see was a storm in his twilight eyes. His countenance was unsettled—the peace gone from him. I hated this. He was looking at an all-consuming flame that he could not run from. It was fire that I had no power to save him from.

The rest of the day and the evening were filled with awkward silences and little to no joy. We allowed him to stay in my room so he wouldn't be disturbed as he slept. I stood at the very inside of the door as I made sure he was comfortable. He crawled into the bed and continued to sit up, his hands cradled on his legs.

"If you need anything," I had said, "I'll be out in the living quarters the rest of the day. If you want to go for a walk, or if you want something to eat, please don't hesitate to come ask me."

"Thank you, Kerana." he mumbled. His shaggy hair hung over his eyes so I couldn't see them. His bare back was tense, though, and I could see his muscles tense in his arms. He tried to contain his anger and his sorrow. My heart ached.

"You're welcome. Is there anything else you need, then?" I asked softly.

"No," he simply replied.

I went to shut the door when I heard him speak again.

"Wait."

It brought me back to the very first time I ever saw him. I remembered how strange I thought Humans to be, how bizarre and different. Yet as I looked at Eli, at this man who had become so important to me, I realized I felt like I had known all about him and his race for as long as I could remember, almost as if we were one and the same.

"Yes?"

He slowly lifted his head to me, and I was able to see his eyes. They were still dark and stormy blue, but there was some sort of light there mixed in with the angry waves and the steely emotions.

"Can you stay with me a little while?"

Such a simple request, but one that made my heart constrict.

"Of course I can."

I sat down on the chair beside my bed so I could see Eli. He didn't say any more to me as he nestled down into the blankets and the pillows, except he didn't turn away from me. For a while he just simply gazed at me, and I gazed right back. He was beginning to disappear. His Human body was being rejected by the realm of Eden.

Eventually he fell into a restless sleep. I sat there for several hours watching him toss and turn, but I couldn't leave him. He had asked me to stay, and I was going to. I fought the urge to brush the hair from his eyes as he lay there, and fought the urge to bring the covers up to his shoulders when they slipped down. I couldn't bear the thought of him waking up alone in a place that was as confused by him as he was by it.

I heard my father, and after much consideration, decided it was all right if I slipped out just for a moment to ask him what was found out.

"Nothing. Adonai has asked us simply to wait."

"To wait? To wait on what?" I asked.

Mother came out of the kitchen to the hallway where we talked. "Lower your voices, Eli is resting."

Father looked at the closed door to my room and dropped his voice. "He has asked us to wait for His answer."

"Well that is not what we hoped for," Mother sighed. "But He does know what He is doing," she added. Mother, with her faith as solid and firm as the ground she stood upon.

"Yes, He does. He just asks us to trust Him."

Even though I agreed with everything they said, my heart sank. I hoped that Adonai would give us the answer right away. "In the morning, I would like to take him to see the Portal, to see if anything has changed." There was little confidence in my father's voice. I knew if Eli could leave, it would be more obvious than simply trying the Portal again.

Mother asked me to bring him a plate of food before we all went to sleep. I peeked inside the room and saw that he was sprawled on his stomach, his arms spread out across the width of the bed, and his legs hung out of the blankets. His breathing was steady, and it looked as if he finally slept peacefully. I leaned against the doorframe and simply watched the steady rise and fall of his back. I quietly crossed the room, placed the plate on the nightstand beside the bed, and hoped he would wake up and find it.

As I went to leave again, I heard the blankets rustle. I looked over my shoulder at him, and realized he was just shifting his legs. I smiled a little. As I went to close the door behind me, I heard him mutter something. To Human ears, it could have easily been missed. But I heard it.

"Kerana."

And I stopped. I felt that strange knot in my chest again, and a spark of joy and hope tinged with fear flickered deep inside of me. *He called my name in his sleep.*

I slept on the couch where he had been the night prior. There was a strange scent attached to the blankets now, one that I realized I noticed frequently since I met Eli; it was an earthy smell, like rain water and summer sky and lush fields. It was unique, and as I laid my head against the pillow he had slept on, I found myself breathing in the scent, even memorizing it.

Morning came and went, and still Eli didn't come out to see us. Father woke him early and escorted him to the Portal. Still nothing happened when he passed through. When he and my father came home, he simply returned to my room.

"But why does he want to be alone like this?" I asked in the early afternoon.

Father glanced at the entrance to the hallway, and I suspect he half expected Eli to walk in. "Humans have arrived at a point where they believe being alone with their thoughts will be beneficial somehow. Often times, other Humans are far too selfish to really care for one another's problems. They are consumed in their own. And when they cannot handle even those, they break."

"Have you ever seen a Human break, Father?"

"I have. And it isn't pretty."

"Is it hard to put them back together?"

He thought in silence for a moment. "It takes time, that is for sure. But it isn't impossible. Humans' hearts, like ours, are very complex. But the difference is they have the darkness in theirs.

So they struggle with the light and the darkness. Sadly one cannot exist without the other in their hearts."

Then I asked the question I dreaded. "Do you think Eli is broken?"

He looked at me very seriously. "No, I don't think he is. I think he is very close to being broken, and we must take care of him until we can figure out how to get him back to Earth, if that is Adonai's plan."

"You don't think that Adonai would have allowed him here to just let him disappear?"

"No. You and I both know that Adonai's plan is far bigger than that. And we are very blessed; we get to see something very new and what I assume is very big unfold."

Finally, when the sun had begun to set, I heard the door to my bedroom open. Mother, Father, Hani, Oni, and I all sat at the table in the kitchen. He appeared in the entrance, and his eyes looked tired and heavy.

"Eli!" My mother said, and she got to her feet immediately. She put an arm around his shoulders and brought him to the table. "We made you a plate. Eat something, please, you must be famished."

He looked up at me and smiled slightly. I returned it.

"The Human guy is still here?" Hani asked with fork in hand. Oni's nose was wrinkled.

"Hani," I said warningly.

"It's okay, Kerana. And thank you, Aonani, for the food."

She smiled at him. "You are most welcome, young man."

Eli sat in silence, listening, but not responding to my brothers' chatter.

"Can we go for a walk, Kerana?" he asked me. He hadn't touched his food.

"Certainly we can," I replied, and I stood. He quickly followed suit. The twins asked where we were going, but my parents hushed them. I led Eli out into the hallway and up the stairs, out into the evening air. The sun danced through the tree branches and turned everything to shades of gold and copper. This was my favorite time at night.

As soon as he stepped outside, he took a deep breath. His hands were in the pockets of the jeans he wore. "I can't believe how long I slept."

"You obviously needed it, didn't you?"

He nodded.

"Would you like to just walk? Or would you like me to show you one of my favorite places in Eden?" I had momentarily considered taking him back to the Portal, to see if he could go back to Earth, but I decided quickly that it would just upset him, and Eli needed comfort, not pressure, at the moment.

He looked over at me. His eyes looked mossy green in the light of the setting sun. "I think I would like to see your favorite spot."

So I led him back up the path we had run two days before, and took a smaller path that meandered through the trees. The path gave way to a hilltop that was completely free of trees or bushes. It looked over the summer realm and gave a good vantage point of the great Fountain at the center of Eden.

"This is one of the hilltops in this realm. Each realm only boasts a few of them, but this one is my favorite because it looks right into Eden."

"This is amazing up here." Eli murmured. I smiled. I was glad he was happy up here. "I've never seen such a beautiful sunset in all my life."

The colors were alive and moved, and each one could be felt in the core of my soul.

"I'm speechless. I don't know what to say."

"You don't have to say anything. Just sit and enjoy it."

So we sat on the sun-warmed grass and watched the sun set for a few moments together.

"So how are you feeling, Eli?"

He didn't turn towards me; his eyes remained on the view

and the setting sun. The colors turned his dark hair a deep shade of ruby and his face gleamed with a golden tone. Eli himself was breathtaking right now.

"I'm not sure, honestly. Being here makes me feel better than I ever had on Earth physically. But mentally? I'm pretty screwed up."

"I'm sorry the Elders could not give you any more answers yesterday," I said, turning to look back at the sun. "I had hoped so much that they would know what to do right away. But since this has never happened before... " I trailed off.

He pondered my thought for a moment. "Have they found anything out since I spoke to them?"

Now it was my turn to be lost for words. "They spoke with Adonai, yes."

"And?" He asked as he moved his gaze to me now. The hurt and anxiety in his eyes made me want to wrap my arms around his neck and try to alleviate some of that pain.

"He has asked us to wait for His answer and His time."

Eli let out a long, slow, heavy sigh. He looked away from me, and I feared if he ever would look at me again.

"And what," he muttered softly, "does that mean?"

"It just means that we have to trust Him and what He will do. He knows the answers, and we will get them soon enough. Just not right now. It's not the right time right now."

"Why not? This Adonai knows I'm slowly fading away into nothing, correct?"

His words pierced my heart. He was mad; I could hear the intentional sting in his words. He had every reason to be upset. But he didn't need to be mad at me. "Yes, He knows. He knows everything."

"So then why doesn't he just fix this and send me back? If he knows everything, then why can't he just give the Elders the answers so we can be done with this?"

"I don't know, Eli. I don't. He does know what's best, and it is not for us to question His judgment."

"His judgment. Oh, okay. Fine then...So he doesn't care that he's letting me waste away into nothing?"

"That is not it at all, Eli. Adonai cares about you so much; that is why He sends us Eldurians to protect you!"

"How can he care about me? He doesn't even know who I am!" he said spitefully. At this point, he had turned back to me, and I saw darkness written on his face and it frightened me. "Who is this guy, anyway? Some sort of sorcerer or something? How can he 'know' all of this stuff? I know that Eldurians are pretty incredible and can do more than Humans, but your mom even said that he is above the Eldurians. So who is he?"

"There is no easy answer to that question, Eli," I answered him honestly. "He is so many things. He is everything."

"Now you sound like some kind of crazy cultist or something," he huffed. "Like some brainwashed worshipper of a power-hungry ruler."

"A cultist? Brainwashed? No, Eli, it's nothing like that. We are Adonai's servants, His loyal messengers. He created us to serve and protect the Human race who are His own. But you were right about one thing; He is a King, the only King, and we do worship Him."

He laughed out loud, but the sound grated on me. I didn't like the way it sounded. It was fake and hollow. "Okay, okay. So now it sounds like you are worshipping some kind of god or deity. Is that a little closer than a sorcerer?" He added. His words didn't match his tone. I started to see a side of Eli that I was not accustomed to.

"The only way that I could ever explain Adonai is that He created everything. He made every Eldurian, and every Human. He made every tree, every blade of grass, all of the seasons and everything that inhabits and lives in them. He created the world and He created Eden. He is the reason why the sun sets the way it does," I said indicating the sun that now rested on the horizon, the sky filled with rubies and violets. "He made the moon and the stars. He made the forests and the oceans. He made every flower, every rock, every grain of sand. He made me, and he made you, Eli."

Eli stared into the sun. I could have gone on and on, but I realized Eli was either not listening to me or he was trying to pretend like he wasn't.

"Eli?" I asked.

"I heard you. I heard everything you said. And you know what? I don't believe you."

"How, what do you mean?" I questioned.

"My mother believed in this stuff. She believed in your Adonai, I think. And do you know what I learned? I learned that he doesn't care for us Humans."

He turned to me, and I saw so much pain embedded on his face that I was sure he was about to break clean in two. My mouth opened wordlessly.

"You know what I learned?" he cried, and his voice grew in volume as he stood. I just watched him helplessly.

"What?" I finally answered.

"I learned that he can't care about those who he kills off or those who are left to pick up the pieces. He killed my mother. He took her away from me when I was six years old. How on earth could I believe that someone cares for me who took my own mother away from me?"

I could only look intently up at him, my heart being wrenched from my chest as he spoke.

"And you know what else? How could Adonai care when he let my dad beat me as a child? How can I believe that he cared when he let my dad send me to the hospital and made me lie to the nurses saying that all the bruises and gashes on my body were from a bicycling accident? Answer me that! How could Adonai really care about me when he let my life go to hell when I was just a kid, and I've had to fight ever since just to be able to stand on my own two feet?"

"Eli, I—I'm so sorry." I replied in a whisper. I bent my head down and saw two teardrops splash onto the dirt below me.

"Don't be sorry for me. Just understand me when I say I don't believe you."

20 ELI

"I'm going back," I said flatly, looking at the path behind us rather than at Kerana.

"You don't know the way." She replied as she stared at the ground. The tone in her voice made a knot form in my throat.

"I can find it." And with that, I left her on the hilltop to watch the rest of the colors fade away into the sky. I didn't even turn around to see if she watched me leave.

I knocked tree branches out of my way that I had gently pushed aside on our way up the hill. I sat down heavily on a rock, and closed my eyes to calm myself. I was upset and conflicted. These superior people with their fairytale god had belittled me and seemed unconcerned that I would vanish like a wisp of morning dew. Not even Kerana stood by me.

I opened my eyes behind my hands and gasped when I was able to see some of the leafy greens and the deep maroons from the sky through the flesh of my fingers. I jumped and jerked my hands away. They really were starting to just fade away, like a watercolor painting left outside during a thunderstorm.

The anger spiked again, and this time I let it come.

"You wanna play things this way?" I screamed at the top of my lungs to the sky and trees above me. "You really think that I am going to listen to you after everything you've done? Is this really what you want?"

No answer. Not like I expected one in the first place.

It wasn't the first time I had called out to the Creator my mom had believed in.

I sighed heavily, totally spent.

I shoved my hands deep into my pockets and I continued to follow the path back down the hill. I thought things would have been different when she passed away, like maybe the guy she prayed to every day would come through for my dad and me. But I never saw him, nor did I ever hear from him. He never answered me, and I dropped it eventually. I just didn't care. I believed in my mom and the goodness of her golden heart, but I didn't believe in the being she prayed to with me every night as she tucked me into bed.

I saw a small kitchen table with a man sitting at it as he read the paper. He had a blue mug full of steaming tea. He always had his tea with his paper in the mornings.

I sat at a simple oak piano with a faded red velvet topped bench. My feet barely reached the pedals. There was an extraordinary woman seated beside me on the bench, with chocolate-colored hair and bright blue eyes. Her smile was a million-dollar smile. Her red turtleneck reminded me that it was winter.

Carl, don't you think that Eli will be ready by the time the church musical comes around? He could do a number or two, what do you think?

The man at the table looked over the top of his paper. He had short, dark hair like his son's, but his eyes were a rich green color. He smiled at his wife, subtle signs of aging appearing at the corners of his eyes. When she was around, nothing in the world could upset him.

"I think he would do a fine job at the musical."

I remembered being elated at their words. In all honesty, I was rotten.

My dad had put his paper down and walked across the room to where we were seated.

"Let's hear 'O Holy Night' again, kiddo."

"I'm still not all that great at it, you know," I had mumbled sheepishly.

My dad laughed. Back then, I liked the sound of it. "I heard you practice that song at least ten times last night before you went to bed. Let's hear it one more time."

I couldn't get that last part down.

My mother smiled at me, but softly. It always made all the fear disappear the moment I saw it. I really wished I could see it right now.

"Eli, you can do this. I know you can. I believe in you. Just stick with it; you'll make it through this."

Even though she said those words over a decade ago, I still recalled them and heard them as if she had just spoken them to me. And I recalled them whenever I had a hard time believing in myself or things were just plain rotten.

I brushed aside a tear before it fell.

I had arrived at Kerana's house at that moment. I knocked on the door and looked around me one last time.

Erez opened the door. "Eli," he said, and smiled at me. It just made me uncomfortable now instead of making me feel welcome. "Where's Kerana?" he added as he peered over my shoulder.

"She's still up at the hill. I needed to come back," I responded, and tried not to look him in the eye. I could feel him examining me suspiciously.

"All right, well come in," he replied, and stepped aside to let me in. I thanked him quickly and went down the stairs. Now that I was here, what was I going to do?

"Eli?" I heard from down the hall. I looked up to see Hani

standing at the door to the bathroom. His little white outfit was a stark contrast to all of the woody roots around us. His hair was wet and disheveled. Must have been bath time.

"Hey, kiddo," I mumbled as I ran my hands through my hair.

"What's wrong?" he questioned. He stared up at me with wide green eyes as he walked towards me. There was a sadness in them that bothered me.

"Nothing, I'm fine."

"Adonai says not to lie, Eli," Hani retorted. My stomach and my teeth clenched at the mention of that name. "So don't lie to me."

Such attitude and conviction from such a little man. I sighed and bent down to his eye-level.

"It's nothing you would understand, Buddy."

He furrowed his little brow and folded his arms across his chest.

"Tell me."

I couldn't help but chuckle a bit at his words. "Look, I'm just having a hard time adjusting to everything. All of these new things, this new place, new people. It's a lot to take in."

His face fell a little, and he let his guard down. "You mean you don't like it here? You don't like me and Oni?"

"No, that's not what I meant." How was I supposed to explain this to a six year-old? "All I am saying is that it's hard to be the only Human here, and the only Human to have ever been here."

He looked at me skeptically. He and his brother were awfully expressive for being so young. "Okay." Then he smiled, and it caught me off guard. "Don't worry, Adonai will fix it."

And without another word, he turned his little self around and scooted back to the bathroom where I assumed his brother to be. I rubbed my arm nervously. This was way too much for me to take in, that's for sure.

I slipped into Kerana's room and closed the door behind me. I hoped she didn't mind me being in here again tonight.

I pulled on the pajama bottoms Erez had graciously given me, but now I just felt unworthy wearing them. I didn't know what I wanted at this point. I couldn't keep any of my emotions or thoughts straight. They all just kept bumping into each other.

I lay on my back and stared at the ceiling for what seemed like hours, but I knew it was only a matter of minutes. I eventually just buried my face in the pillow and just focused on breathing.

But the more I breathed in, the more I realized that I could only smell Kerana. Stupid me, I was lying on her bed. Of course it smelled like her.

I let out an exasperated moan and slammed my fist into the soft, feathery mattress. I just couldn't escape any of it, could I?

I thought I heard the door open slightly and I instantly recognized Kerana. She must have thought I was sleeping. I decided to keep up that act because I didn't feel much like talking to her. Now that the anger was gone, I just felt hollow inside.

"Eli?" she whispered softly. My heart seized up. I debated answering her.

When I didn't answer she stepped fully into the room and crossed over to where I lay. I heard the rustle of fabric and her fingers gently touch my cheek. I had to force myself to keep my breathing consistent and steady. The touch had sent a shock straight to my gut. She brushed the hair from my eyes, and traced the entire shape of the exposed part of my face.

I stayed perfectly still until she slowly removed her hand from my cheek. I wished she hadn't, though.

Stop it, I reprimanded myself.

I heard her get back to her feet, and the next moment I was alone in her room again. I took the time to roll onto my back and sigh heavily. What the heck was going on with me?

I rolled from side to side for the next however long, and eventually fell into a light, fitful sleep. I finally felt like I was slipping into dreams when I began to hear this soft, entrancing music. It was a piano melody, slow and steady. There was no way any person in the world could play that sort of music. I was sure I made it up in my mind, that I dreamt it.

But as I listened to it more closely, I realized I was more and more conscious of myself and my surroundings. I was awake and heard this incredibly rich and decadent music. If I could have ever found music that represented me as a person, this was it; this was definitely it.

The keys fluttered from the low end up to the soprano-sounding notes. It all glided and flowed right into the next part, smoothly and without flaw. I felt captured by it, completely and utterly at its disposal.

A thought then possessed me: *I have to see where this is coming from.*

I slowly got out of Kerana's bed and listened hard. It was faint, but I was sure I heard music. Sweet music that made everything else in my head seem insignificant. I followed it out into the hallway, and knew without a doubt that it was coming from outside. Everything was dark, but the only thing that mattered was discovering where this music was coming from that was so alluring.

I stepped out into the night air. It was cool, just like a summer's night in early July on Earth. I looked around to try to decide which direction to go. I listened hard and realized the music wasn't coming from any of the paths. It was coming from straight ahead of me, right through the trees.

So I followed it.

I forgot my shoes, but I didn't really mind. I had even forgotten a shirt; I was wandering around in nothing but my pajama pants. I just had to find where this soul-wrenching music was coming from, who was playing it.

I walked past many houses similar to Kerana's in parts of the realm I had not seen yet. I walked over paths and around them, but I didn't follow one. I pressed on. With each step I took, the music grew just a little louder and more intense. I started my search by walking; after about ten minutes in pursuit of it, I began to jog. Before I knew it, I sprinted towards it. I had no idea what was going to meet me, but I had to find out. I felt as if I had no choice.

It didn't take me long to realize that the trees were beginning to thicken, and it was getting harder and harder to navigate my way. I pushed on.

Without any warning, I found myself in an oddly circular clearing. I saw no sign of it as I came close to it, but here I was. I looked around me. There was a single tree stump in the very center. Above me was the cloudless and flawlessly clear night sky, with stars that winked and glistened. The branches shuttered in the tall trees around me, and wind began to blow this way and that. But I couldn't see where the music was coming from. I hadn't really known what to expect; an Eldurian playing a piano? I had expected to find the source of it, and all I found was this clearing.

The wind picked up and swirled around me. This was the first time I had felt wind since I came to Eden, and it took my breath away. It was strong, and it whipped around me and the clearing. Autumn leaves stirred and circled skyward, transported on music as much as the wind.

The swirl of wind crested the center of the meadow and hovered over the lonely tree stump. It expanded and created a tornado around it, and caused all of the leaves to form a pillar. The leaves spun, gathered, and separated. And just as the wind had come, it disappeared.

Only the leaves stayed where they were.

I took a few hesitant steps towards the tree stump where the leaves hovered in midair. As I got closer, I saw that the leaves had formed into a silhouette of a person.

I was in such shock all I could do was stand there and stare at the shape, at the phantom that hung in front of me.

The music ceased. I swallowed hard and took a step back from the leaves.

"Who—what are you?" I asked, my voice raspy in my throat.

"I've been waiting for you, Eli." The voice didn't seem to come from the shape. It came from everything around me. It echoed around me and made me spin around anxiously. It sounded like thousands of voices in unison. I felt as if I stood in a huge auditorium all by myself listening to speaker in surround sound.

I looked back at the silhouette.

The shape sat down on the stump and crossed its leg; one hand rested on the knee. I could tell that the head looked in my direction, but there were no eyes, no mouth, no expression. Just a bunch of leaves that looked like a person.

I blinked twice, lost for words.

"I have been waiting for you for such a long time, Eli."

"Who are you?"

"I think you already know the answer to that question," it replied to me. It was deep, but calmed me and sounded peaceful.

"No, I don't," I replied, but my voice sounded braver than I actually felt.

"Do not be afraid," the voice said, as if I had just shouted out loud how terrified I was. But it had been quiet.

I could feel my heart rate increase, and my hands balled into fists. It wasn't like this thing could hurt me. It was just a bunch of leaves after all.

"Eli," the voice said. "Eli you do know who I am. And you don't have to be afraid anymore."

It was too hard to imagine. Too many things had happened in the last few days for this to make any sense. But then again, too much had happened for this *not* to make sense.

All of the Elders, Erez, Aonani, and Kerana; everything they talked about pointed back to one thing.

To one person.

This is Adonai.

"Yes, Eli. I am Adonai."

"How did you—"

"Read your thoughts? Eli, I know all about you. I did create you, after all."

I could only stare at this phantom. "So you are real."

I heard the voice chuckle softly. It reminded me of the music. "Of course I am. And you have known it all along. You just stayed mad at me for a long time. And I understand that."

I took an even closer step. It was weird to think I was talking to an empty tree stump, but impossible and unpredictable things had happened ever since I stumbled into Eden.

I gulped. "I—I don't even know what to say."

"Well then just listen, my child. Let me tell you the things I have longed to tell you."

All I could do was nod. What else was I supposed to do?

"Eli, first I want to tell you that even though you never believed I answered your prayers or your requests, and even though you believed that you never heard me, I want you to know that I never left you. I was always right there beside you. Even when you turned your back on me, I still held onto you and kept you. You are my own child, and I love you very dearly."

He paused. "Yes, your life has not been easy, but that is not what life is about. Life is about living out your purpose, your duty. And I created you to someday step through that Portal into Eden. You are here for a reason, Eli, a reason that will be revealed in due time. But that time is not right now. If I told you right now, it wouldn't even make any sense. It will all unfold at the given time."

The shape of Adonai leaned closer to me. "Your mother's accident is not something I would ever want to dismiss, for I know it weighs heavy on your heart. Though it was painful for you and your father, it was part of my plans, part of the big picture. Even if I tried to explain it to you, I would never be able to. Your life is just a piece of it, but a piece nevertheless. And Eli, please try to understand that I love your mother so very much. It was simply her time to come home to me."

"But why?" I asked Him. I felt the hot tears come down my

cheeks, but I didn't care to stop them. The Adonai I so wrongly dismissed earlier sat right before me. Who was I to speak to Him, yet how could I not? I could feel anger and peace, hatred and longing, sorrow and hope, all wash together and crash against the caves of my soul.

He looked down at me; or rather the head looked down in my direction. "Come sit beside me, Eli."

Hesitantly, I watched the leaves shift and whisper, yet felt drawn to the shape, pulled to it. I walked right up to the silhouette, and stared at it. "Why can't I see you?"

It was almost as if I could feel Him smile. "No Human can see me, Son. You may very well be a child of mine, and I created the heart that beats in your chest, but there is something that resides in you that I did not place there."

"What's that?"

"That is the darkness that lives within you, the Fallen nature. I cannot be in its presence, for it is what keeps me away from those whom I created. But there is way that I have remedied that, a way that has made it possible for us to sit here and talk the way we are. Do you know what that reason is, Eli?"

"I don't, no."

"It is because I sent my Son, my only Son, to Earth to save you all. I sent Him, and allowed Him to die by the hands of my own creation, in order that He may save the world."

"How would letting your son die solve the problem with the darkness in me?" I asked.

"He renewed the connection that I once had with my people, my creation. His death washed all of the darkness from the hearts of those who come to know me and love me. His final heartbeat completed my plan to reclaim my lost children. He alone stood in the gap between life and death."

"When did you send him?" I questioned.

"I sent Him many years ago. He knew who He was and what His job was. He did what He had to do, though I can promise you that He felt much of what you have felt since you stepped through the barrier here. He saw it all, and faced it all."

"I bet you didn't abuse him like my father did to me."

"You think that sending my own son to die was not difficult for me? But I did it because I loved my people too much to have them be permanently separated from me. I did it because I loved *you* too much, Eli. And let me tell you something," The shape bent closer to me. If there had been eyes, they would have been searing right into me. "Your father loves you, even if he doesn't show it."

"I don't believe you."

"Well, I am also your father, and I love you as well. You believe that I have never been around or there for you for your whole life. You believe I have neglected you, taken advantage of you, toyed with you, and yes, you even think I abused you. And these things are what prevent you from believing that I love you."

I looked up at the starry sky above me. I remembered looking at those stars every night as a kid, praying that Mom would somehow miraculously show up.

"She always taught me to believe in miracles."

"She was right. You just gave up on me when I didn't perform that one miracle."

I felt a lump rising in my throat.

"And you think, like your father, that I didn't care about you at all because I took her away from you?"

I could feel the tears start. I wasn't sad, I wasn't mad, I just felt raw truth gush out of me. This Adonai, everything He said, I knew was the truth. I couldn't deny any of it. He knew everything. Every detail, every aspect, every part of me that ever was.

How could He not be who He said He was?

"I believed that for so long."

"Even until you heard me calling for you, you believed that. Deep down, every time Kerana and her family mentioned me, you knew exactly who I was. You always knew I was real, that I existed. I just felt too far away to you, too powerful to actually be involved in your life, to care."

"That was you calling to me? How did you do that?" I breathed.

I heard a loud, hearty laugh. It was as amazing as the music had been that brought me here. "My dear Eli, I created the whole world and everything in it. It is nothing to create some music to pull at your heartstrings." He laughed again for a moment. "See, my boy, since I created you, I know exactly what makes you tick. I know that music is your love. I put that love in you for a reason. You feel most alive when you play, when you hear it. It is what moves you. Your mother encouraged that trait in you, realizing at a young age that you had a talent."

"And my dad quickly deflated it." The anger spiked in my chest.

"Don't you understand why, Eli?" He asked. Some of the leaves detached themselves from the rest of the shape and came to rest on my shoulders. His hands. "Seeing you play and love music only reminded him of your mother. It pained him. It wasn't that he didn't want you to play, he just couldn't bear to be reminded of your mother."

"Why did you let us fall apart, Adonai? Why did you let everything I knew fall to pieces?"

"It may have certainly seemed that way, Eli. But take a closer look at your life, has really everything gone wrong?"

My first thought jumped to Kerana, her family, Eden, and then Steven's laughing face crossed my mind's eye, as well as that piano in the music hall.

"I thought not," he said, and I could hear a smile in His voice. "I do not want to seem negative, or as if I am making you any less than what you are. If I were to answer your question about why I let you experience all of the trials in your life, you wouldn't be able to understand the answers. In fact, it might make you even more upset with me."

"I've heard that before; that I don't understand something."

"It is not like that, Eli. When I say you wouldn't understand, you honestly would not be able to comprehend it, to wrap your mind around it. Each and every life fits into the plan I have for Earth. Each life is a piece of the puzzle, and each situation, each decision, each turning point, affects all of the rest of them. If I were to try and explain why your mother's death affected someone else's life, I would never be able to tell you all of the chain reactions. They were endless, and are still going on. Your mind is finite, while the answers are not."

I let that sink in a bit. He was the creator of everything, which meant He knew everything. I did not. I was only aware of myself most of the time.

"As I have said, I am not trying to make you sound ignorant or incapable. If Human minds were limitless, they wouldn't last very long. If you knew even a small portion of what I knew, you would wish to have a more limited ability to think."

I remained silent.

"Let me tell you a story, Eli, and see if I can help you understand a little better. There was a police officer at your mother's accident scene that had been having trouble with his wife. He was about to put his own pistol to his head and end it all, but just before he pulled the trigger, he got a call on his radio. It scared him. He answered it, and decided he could put off his suicide just a little bit longer. He figured, what was a few more hours? He got to the scene, and he was the man who pulled her from the wreck. He was the one who attempted to save her life."

"The one who met us in the hospital room the next day," I remembered. The officer had come in with a bouquet of flowers, dressed in his uniform that still had rips and tears in it from the night before. He had apologized, and I remembered how sorry he had been. I could still see his stoic face as he shook my dad's hand and then clapped me on the shoulder before he left.

"That very same one. When they transported her by helicopter to the hospital, he got back in his car and sat there, his hands on the steering wheel. He looked over at his passenger seat and saw his pistol sitting there, taunting him. And at that very moment, I met him where he was. He realized that everything happens for a reason. From that day on, he chose to let me lead his life. He worked things out with his wife, and they just recently introduced a baby boy into their life, their third child."

I was torn at that moment. The story was incredible. I never would have known that if Adonai had not told me. But something nagged at the back of my mind. "Did my mom have to die to make that happen?"

The hands on my shoulders gripped tightly, affectionately. "Like I said earlier, my son, if I could explain them all to you I would. But I cannot. It may never make sense to you, since you loved your mother and knew her, so therefore you would have wished that anything else could have happened rather than losing her. But she is with me now, Eli. She knew me, so when she left Earth, she came to me. When she left, she was able to then allow someone else to find me as well."

"She's really with you?" I felt the tears pool in my eyes again.

"Yes, she is. She is far better with me than she would be on Earth."

I had wished more than anything to know if she was okay, that she had made it to the Heaven she always talked so much about. The tears came out now in a waterfall. I let my head fall into my hands and I just let it all out.

Adonai sat there beside me, His hands on my back. I needed nothing more than to know that He was there with me, that He had always been with me.

After about twenty minutes later, when I was exhausted and spent, I looked back up at Him.

"It really is you."

"It is, Eli. You can trust me. I will never fail you, I will never leave you. I love you more than anyone ever could, and I won't ever take that promise back. That will never change. If you want me to be the lead and the light in your life, if you want me to take that darkness from your heart and get rid of it so you can live and breathe through me instead of the hurt and pain of the world, then just ask me. I promise you that nothing can ever change the fact that I love you and that I always will love you."

How could I say no? Especially when I knew what He said was the truth, and it was the only truth that I ever believed with my whole heart.

"I am sorry, Adonai, for everything," I murmured. I couldn't look at Him when I said it. "I don't deserve any of what you just said. It took me meeting you face to face, in a way, for me to believe in you, and I have screwed up so much in my life. Why should you love someone who questions you—you who made my entire world, who made everything?"

"Because you were mine first, and I am yours always. That is the way it works. It doesn't matter how far you think you are away from me, I will never walk away from you. I won't ever give up on you."

"But why? You should. If I ever turn my back on you, because Humans tend to do that to each other—"

"I am not Human, Eli. Remember that. I do not act or behave in the way that Humans do. It is the Humans who should act and behave as I do."

I nodded. Unsure of what to do now, I just looked up at Him. He was my father, my real, true Father, the one who did love me. I knew it in my bones now.

"You need your rest, my child."

"But I want to stay with you!" I cried, and felt fear rise in me. If He left, how would I ever find Him again?

"Don't fear, Eli. I am always with you. I live in your heart now, in the place of the darkness. Remember that whenever you need me, or you just want to talk, all you have to do is do it."

I nodded to Him.

"I will show you the way back. I will walk with you, but to-morrow is yet another day. There is so much I have planned for you, Eli. So much that I want to show you and do for you. All you have to do is trust me."

And so I did.

21 KERANA

I tossed and turned on the couch all night and fought the desire to go and wake Eli, to try and console him or try and make amends with him. I was not sure what he thought of me now, or how he might react when he saw me next. I wondered if I had hurt Eli by what I said. The things he shared in his anger; I wasn't even sure if he had meant to let me know those things about his family. They were incredibly personal, and incredibly painful things. I remembered the pain that had burned white-hot in his eyes, and remembered clearly seeing he had never been able to find any sort of relief from it. My heart ached as I thought of his words again, and I sighed.

Mother and I looked up to see Eli coming towards us. He looked well.

"Good afternoon, Kerana, Aonani," he said, a shadow of a smile on his strong face. I was transfixed by a change in him, a change that was not there the night before when he had stormed off from me.

"Good afternoon, Eli," my mother replied, a broad smile on

her face.

"May I join you?" he asked. There was a sweetness in his tone and a brightness in his eyes that caught me off guard. From the next room, the boys were making noise.

"I remember being their age," Eli softly said. "That was the year that my mom died."

I held my breath for a moment. It had been this topic that had set him off so badly last night. The last thing I wanted was for him to be mad at me again. There was no trace of anger in his voice. It was more of a sad realization, like he had never said it out loud to himself, as if to speak those words somehow had a healing effect. He turned to look at me, and his eyes instantly found mine. It was never a hard thing to do; they always managed to connect, even when I wasn't ready for them to.

"Kerana, I feel absolutely terrible about last night."

"No, Eli. I should apologize. I never should have pressed you the way I did."

"No, it was good you did. It was really good." his voice trailed off. "I should have never let my anger get the better of me. I usually am a pretty calm person. I have a long fuse."

He looked at me for a moment, hard. He studied my face, studied everything about me. I could feel his eyes taking in everything. "I'm a fool for what I did, for what I have done. Up until last night, I was just living with that. I realized it, and I knew that I was a wreck on the inside. I just chose to ignore all of it." He paused, and took a deep breath. He looked down at his hands in his lap before he continued.

"Then everything you said really hit home with me. You dug up something in me, Kerana. I know it was for a reason. Until you dragged it out of me, surprisingly if you want to know the truth, I had it locked up and sealed tight. But you," His eyes met mine again. "You just have a way with making me open up. Even if I don't want to."

As hard as it was for me to admit it, I felt color rise in my cheeks. It was a nice sensation, but I was totally unprepared for it. He bent closer to me. He was less than a foot away from me. "Kerana, what you did last night, I now see you are the only one who could ever have gotten that out of me, and I thank you for it. Without you and without the way you make me go crazy, I never would have—"

And then it all made so much sense.

The brightness in his eyes, the change in his face and his attitude—it all made sense.

He had met Adonai.

And as I looked closer, I saw evidence of it surrounding him like a halo that covered his whole body. There was a faint glow that came from him and his clothes. He literally beamed, but it was because the darkness in his heart had been wiped clean. He was now a true child of Adonai.

He opened his mouth to continue on, but I grabbed his hand and laced my fingers through his. I couldn't explain why I did it, or why it felt so natural, as if his hands belonged in my own, but I did it.

Eli didn't seem to mind, either. A shocked expression crossed over his face when I had reached out to him, but as I sat there quietly and contentedly with our folded hands resting on my lap, he didn't say a word

Adonai, you are absolutely astounding.

We sat there for some time and just watched the boys, when my father came out into the garden.

"There is a celebration going on in Eden today," he said, and sat on the bench on the other side of me.

"A celebration!" I cried. Eli's face looked a bit blank.

"A celebration for what?"

"Well, today an infant Eldun is being introduced to the Eldurian population!"

"So it's like a huge birthday party?" Eli questioned. My father and I laughed.

"Yes, in a sense, it is. But birthday parties here are far more entertaining than birthday parties on Earth. I can promise you that much." He said to Eli.

Father then peered very closely at Eli. "Son, there is something different about you."

Eli looked down, and tightened his hand on mine.

Father jumped in front of Eli. "Ah ha! I knew you would meet Him!" And without further notice, he pulled Eli to his feet and gave him a brisk hug.

Eli smiled sheepishly as my father let him free.

"When did you meet with Him?" Father questioned. I had to admit, I was interested myself to know the details.

"Last night. He called to me, I guess you could say."

"Very interesting." Father said. I agreed with him.

"What is interesting, sir?" Eli asked.

"You see Eli, we as Eldurians are not called to Adonai. We are born straight into His house. Humans are the only ones who are born separated from Him. So for one to be called, as you say, in Eden, is great indeed."

"I am still in shock from meeting Him last night."

"Don't worry. Once the change becomes familiar to you, you won't even remember when you didn't feel this way."

"It's like I feel heavy or something. But it's not in a bad way."

It was my turn to laugh. "It is because you are not hollow anymore, Eli! Humans are given the will to seek Adonai out, because He hopes that each of His children will seek Him. Before you sought Him, you were empty, waiting to be filled. Now that you have seen Him, you are whole. It may take some time getting used to that feeling, but it feels wonderful, doesn't it?"

"It feels incredible." He answered me simply. And I knew he meant it with his whole heart.

My father's eyes lit up suddenly. "Eli, come with me. I have something for you." And he turned and started back around the tree to the door.

"Erez, you don't have to do anything else for me," Eli replied. But my father, though I knew he could hear him, continued on. I smiled.

"Let's follow him," I said to my mother.

So we pursued him inside, and we found him going towards his bedroom door. We followed him inside, and he rummaged through his armoire of clothes. Eli watched him curiously, as did I.

"Ah, here it is."

He turned to face Eli and me with a white robe in hand, the kind that the Eldurians wore. "I want you to have this, Eli, and wear it today to the celebration."

Eli took a step back, his hands up defensively. "No, Erez, I couldn't possibly. I'm a Human, not an Eldurian. It wouldn't be right."

"But you are as good as an Eldurian," Father said as he showed the robe to us. "For you, it can be that He has freed you from the darkness, so that you are as clean as the whitest snow."

"But I'm not worthy to wear it."

My father smiled. "And that belief in you is exactly why I believe that you are."

Eli looked with wide eyes from the robe, to me, to my father. I smiled encouragingly at him. He eventually took a slow step forward, and my father helped him put it over his shoulders and situate the cloth until it sat just right. My heart tightened; he looked as if he were made to wear that robe. He turned to me and he unleashed a completely uninhibited smile, as if to say *Look at me, Kerana! Look what I've done!*

"It certainly fits you well," Father said as he stood back to take a look at him. He laughed. "Yes, I think that fits you better than anything else I've given you."

"Do you think this works, Kerana?" He questioned me.

"I certainly do, Eli. I think you were always supposed to wear that robe."

He beamed. But then a flash of panic entered his eyes. "But

what will the other Eldurians think of me?"

I laughed gently. "Eli, Eldurians are not judgmental; we are not like Humans in that sense. There may be some who are wondering why you are wearing the robe, but I don't think that you have much to worry about."

The sun was bright and warm as it shone down through the trees as we walked. My father and mother walked hand in hand in front of us, and the boys talked happily in front of them. Eli and I brought up the rear. Neither of us felt the need to speak, though. So instead, I gently took his hand in my own again, and we walked all the way to the Fountain like that.

We heard everything before we saw it. I was accustomed to the noise; the loud music, the singing, the laughter, the hollering of children. Eli, I was sure, was not. His eyes widened as the trees began to thin.

"Wow, it sounds like some kind of crazy party going on out here!"

As we reached the open meadow, we saw the thousands of Eldurians all gathered there together. There were tables of every shape and size scattered around, heaped with plates of food and bowls full of the best juices. Musicians were spread out and around the entire field, seated on the sides of the fountain. Children climbed the trees and shrieked as they played. Hani and Oni immediately found some of their playmates, and ran out into the sea of Eldurians.

"You two have fun, all right?" My father called over his shoulder as he and my mother made their way towards a group of Eldurians playing wooden flutes and tambourines.

"This is what I imagine a birthday party would be like for royalty back on earth," Eli said, as a smirk danced on his face.

"I imagine so!"

"Is this what happens every time an Eldun is born?" he asked as we made our way to a long, narrow table fixed with fruits from the Winter realm. He still held my hand, and he held it tightly; I wondered if all of these people made him slightly uncomfortable.

"Oh yes," I replied. "Each Eldun born is a new brother."

"So parents here don't give birth to the Elduns?"

"They do, but it is only when Adonai has given them permission."

"Eldurians don't feel that kind of physical attraction, then? I mean, how could they control it?"

I could see we were about to venture into interesting territory. "Adonai made love, and He made love to be pure, beautiful, and fulfilling in every way. It is much as it is on Earth; at least all of the good characteristics. He made romantic love, as you Humans call it, and He has allowed us to experience that type of love. Only here, it is untainted."

"And that is why there are so many problems on Earth," he finished for me. I agreed with him by a nod of my head.

We had reached a table and looked at all of the delicious fruits laid out on platters made of sculpted ice and snow. They were all perfectly smooth, piled high with the richest berries in every color, luscious, juicy fruits that were just the right amount of cold, as well as sliced large fruits that were surrounded by thin, delicate icicles.

"This is so incredible," Eli murmured. I smiled. I was so glad that it was me who was able to show him around like this. I felt so privileged.

"How is this stuff made?" He asked as he scooped a handful of crystallized berries into his hands. I watched as he tipped them into his mouth, crunching on them.

"Oh my gosh—those are more amazing than any candy I have ever eaten back home."

"Now you don't wonder why I didn't care much for food on Earth?"

"Not in the least."

I knew it wouldn't be some time until Adonai came and presented the new Eldun; He was with the family preparing for his or her new place in our society. I looked over the various Eldurians' heads for my father. An idea had occurred to me that I thought Eli might really enjoy. But I had to find my father first because he would know all of the details that I needed to know.

"Looking for someone, I take it?" Eli teased as I stood on the tips of my toes to see over a particularly tall individual named Noam. I glared at him, but a smile tugged at the corner of my mouth. There was no fooling him, that's for sure. I returned my feet to the ground.

"My father, yes."

"I'm pretty much taller than anyone here, so let me see if I can find him." He inspected the crowd for a moment or two until recognition registered on his face. "I found him." And with that, he pulled me through the crowds of talking, laughing Eldurians.

"Kerana, Eli, we were just talking about you," Father said when we reached him and my mother. I saw they stood with the Ieoua family: Juar, Kient, and their two daughters who were friends of Hani and Oni, Frea and Leiha.

"Oh, really?" I asked. I greeted the Ieouas, and then I introduced Eli. Juar presented his hand to Eli for him to shake, and smiled at him.

"It was wonderful to finally meet you, Eli. There has been much news about you circulating through Eden since you have arrived. I hoped dearly that Adonai would give me the chance to meet you!"

"Oh, well, thank you, sir."

Kient also shook Eli's hand. "It is truly an honor to have one of Adonai's children here in Eden. I feel as if I am meeting a Human for the very first time all over again! It's been almost one hundred years since I have been to Earth," she trailed off, and sighed. Eli gave me a quizzical look. "I am so very glad that you are here. I trust that your stay has been pleasant with Erez and Aonani?"

"It has been. They are a wonderful family, and I'm probably too spoiled staying there." Juar laughed at Eli's subtle humor, and Kient smiled.

When the conversation subsided, and my mother and Kient delved into the topic of gardening, I knew it was safe for me to talk to Father.

Eli gave me a sideways glance. "Eldurians are how old now?"

I smiled. "They can live to be thousands of years old, sometimes."

"Did you need me for something, Kerana?" Father asked me, and it reminded me why I found him in the first place.

"I was wondering when the next Undalusum match was going to begin?"

"Una-what?" Eli asked.

"Oh, probably about fifteen minutes or so. They've had matches going all day. I didn't know you wanted to go, otherwise I would have taken you right over."

"I wanted to show Eli. I know he will enjoy it."

Father smiled broadly. "Oh, yes, I am sure that he will."

"Come, Eli, we are going to the division between the Summer and Fall realm to watch this match."

"Match? You mean like a sporting match?"

"Yes, but this sport is a sport worthy of Heaven, Eli."

"Lead the way!" We said farewell to my parents and to our friends.

We made our way through the crowds once more and weaved in and out and around Eldurians until we came to the path leading into the Fall realm. We walked it for a few moments before I took a smaller, less noticeable path that went towards the Summer realm. Eli followed quietly but peered over my shoulders to catch a glimpse of anything he could that might give away my little surprise.

Not a moment later, we came to a crest in the path, and it sloped downwards into a small valley. There was a large pond in the very center, and it was divided perfectly in half by the Summer and Fall realms. The half on our left side had red and yellows leaves floating on the surface, with golden glowing trees around, while the lush green and bright sunshine filtered through the trees on our right. There were rows of seats dug out of the earth as it sloped back up the valley, and many of the seats were filled.

"Uh, Kerana?" I heard Eli say behind me. "There's a big pond in the middle. Are they doing swimming races or something?"

"Just wait and see," I replied, and led the way down to seats in the second to bottom row. There were Eldurian men dressed in colored robes; one team soft blue, and the other team a mint green. We sat on the dugout rows, but Eli sat on the very edge. He intently inspected the teams.

"So Undalusum is a sport? Like football?"

"That is the sport with the pig-skinned ball, correct?'

Eli laughed out loud. His head rolled back and he closed his eyes, the laughter came from his stomach. It made me laugh a little along with him seeing him react in such a way.

"It is not actually pig skin, Kerana. It's made out of leather, but yes, that is the sport I was talking about."

"Then no, it really isn't anything like that at all."

The men who played Undalusum all lined up on the edge of the lake, and faced the water. Eli leaned closer to me. "So why are they wearing robes if they are just going to get wet?" He asked me. I smirked.

"Just wait and see."

The men all stood side by side, with one member of the opposite team on the very end of the line.

I knew that Eli was going to be astounded by this game, and that it would be far easier for him to understand if he just watched.

Just then, the ten players all took a step forward and right out into the water. But they didn't sink through; they continued across the surface of the water as if it was the grass they had just left. Their feet left ripples in the water behind it.

"What the—"Eli began, but his words were caught in his throat. I glanced over at him; his mouth hung wide open, and he sat on the edge of the row. He leaned forward and watched with open, intense eyes. I wasn't sure my smile could get any bigger.

"This is nothing like a sport from Earth, is it, Eli?"

All he could do was shake his head, but his eyes stayed on the lake.

The nine blue robed men lined up in a formation on the left, with five in the front row right behind the line that divided the two seasons, three behind them, and one in the third row. The lone green player stood at the edge of the lake. The green players lined up in the exact same way in the Fall realm.

"I can't believe they are actually walking on the water!" Eli cried. I smiled.

"Water in Eden is not limited like it is on Earth. Neither are the Eldurians."

The players were then all ready and faced one another. And out of the pockets of their robes, all of the players except the two on the ends pulled out small, red balls from their pockets. They were about the size of an apple. They all held tightly to the small round objects, and looked from one to another in anticipation.

Eli leaned over to me again. "What are they all holding, and what are we waiting for?"

"They are each holding an Undaberry. At random, these berries will expand, and that person's job is to get it across the lake and into the hands of their team's goalie. The berries expand with water, and they have roughly two minutes or less to get that berry to their team member before it bursts, or the other team steals it."

"Do all of the berries expand at the same time?"

"No, if that happened, there would be less entertainment in the sport. The berries are picked at different stages of ripeness. The riper the berry is, the less time it takes for it to expand and then burst."

"What happens when the Undaberry bursts?"

"The team doesn't get a point for that berry. And each berry has a small pit inside. When the pits are opened, there is a sweet juice on the inside that is one of the most delectable foods here in Eden. After each game, the pits are gathered and opened and used for the later part of the celebration tonight."

"So what about the players whose berries haven't expanded yet? What do they do?"

"They try to protect their teammates whose berries have grown, and defend their side from the opposing team so they don't get their berries to their goalie."

But before I could explain any more, a young Eldurian on the blue team saw his berry grow from the size of an orange to the size of a pumpkin.

And then the game began.

Cheers echoed throughout the valley as that player instantly dashed across the line to the other seasoned realm. Eldurians speeds were far faster than Humans, so the game often moved very quickly. The young Eldurian from the blue team, now surrounded by two of his teammates, ducked around one of the green players and spun gracefully in order to correct his balance. At that exact same moment, a berry expanded in the hands of a member of the green team.

"This is so fast!" I heard Eli say exuberantly.

The green player, who stood in the front lines for his team, grinned at the Eldurian from the blue team across from him, and he jumped in the air, and turned his body to dive into the water.

"No, wait!" Eli cried, and stood to his feet.

But the green player broke the surface of the water, and dove beneath the blue player, and made a perfect arch beneath him. He resurfaced behind the blue player, and quickly hopped back up on top of the water, perfectly dry.

"Whoa, how in the world did that happen?" Eli said to me, entirely bewildered. It was now my turn to laugh out loud.

"Eli, I already told you. Water in Eden is not the same as it is on Earth."

"I don't really get that, but I have to tell you: I think it's awesome."

So did I.

The blue player, who had obviously anticipated this move, was there to meet him. He yanked the berry from his hand, and turned on his heels back towards the other end of the lake. Several other players now had full sized berries, and every member of the team was participating. Some dove into the water, out of the reach of others. One blue member had his berry expand only to have it stolen when he dropped it by a green player.

The young Eldurian player who had begun the game had crossed the lake to the blue goalie, and despite one last valiant defensive attempt from the green team, succeeded in bringing his berry to the goalie.

The shouts and cheers were incredibly loud, and Eli joined right with them. I was sure I had never seen him so happy, so carefree. I was far more interested in watching him than the game, but that was a bit more subconscious.

After another minute and a half of fast-paced action, back and forth, offense and defense, in and out of the water, the game came to an end when the last berry was handed off to the green player's goalie. They counted the pits that each team had, and the blue team ended up the winners.

Eli watched in astonishment as each team member from the opposing sides went up and embraced the other players.

"So, there is no competitiveness in Eden I take it? No sore losers or poor sports?"

"No, none at all. The game is played for entertainment, not to win."

The players cleared the lake, and collected all of the remaining Undaberry pits from its surface. We watched as they all sat down on long benches for a moment, counted the pits, and passed them off to a female Eldurian for cleaning and opening.

"That was some game," Eli said, getting to his feet. "I have never seen anything like that before."

I smiled up at him.

"Hey, Human boy!" A voice called up from the lakeside. Eli and I looked down to see one of the blue players looking up at him. "You should come join us for a round! Word has it that you are quite the Earth-sports player."

"I wouldn't say that," Eli said sheepishly.

"Yeah, come on, then! One of the green team's players has to leave, so we're a player short!"

Eli looked down at me hesitantly. I returned the look, but I smiled gently up at him.

"Don't worry; we'd slow it down for you!" Another Eldurian hollered up to him.

Eli took a deep breath and set his shoulders straight. "I think I will play with them."

"Good! I think you will really enjoy it!"

He gave me one more long glance, a wide and quick smile, and hopped down to the valley floor to stand beside the Eldurians to play Undalusum.

22 ELI

The Eldurian from the green team who was leaving took off his outer robe, and revealed the stark white one beneath it. He passed it to me, and nodded his head in acknowledgment of me, and smiled.

"You think you can follow the game well enough?" He asked me. I felt my lacrosse attitude come on. Not the vengeful, I-have-to-win type of attitude. My focus became sharper, my senses grew more precise, and I felt the adrenaline kick in. The familiarity of the Eldurian's words comforted me in a strange way.

"Definitely."

He clapped me on the shoulder, and turned to leave. The other green players swarmed around me. They all introduced themselves, but I would not have been able to remember their names to save my life, and they all eagerly wanted to shake my hand. Despite being an outsider in this world, I sure wasn't being treated as one.

Each player then lined up on the side of the lake. I was to be in the second row with two other Eldurians on either side of me.

The one who stood to my left, whose name was Kouin, reminded me that my Undaberry was in the pocket of the robe. I unconsciously slid my hand into the pocket and discovered the berry. It was smooth like glass, but as soft as rubber. It fit perfectly into the palm of my hand.

All of the players then began to walk out onto the lake. They all had done this hundreds of times before, walking on water.

Me on the other hand? Not once.

I hesitantly stepped forward, right to the edge of the water. I looked down at it. It looked like water, and it moved like water. And yeah, the Eldurians could walk on it, but what if I fell right through?

I guess I'd be wet *and* a sucker.

But I decided to take my chances.

So I took a deep breath, just in case I did sink like lead, and stepped out onto the water. My foot actually stopped on the surface of the water instead of sailing right through it. I opened my eyes instantly, and looked down at my leg, wondering if maybe I was extremely lucky and somehow found a rock to stand on. But no, I definitely was standing on the water.

This had to be one of the coolest things I had ever done. I gingerly placed my other foot on the surface, and then stood up straight. It didn't feel like I was walking on the top of the water; felt like I was walking on grass or something, nothing too strange.

"Yes!" I cried, so excited that I did not care who laughed at me. Sure that I could move without a problem, I crossed the water, but not as fast as I would the lacrosse field. It was probably going to take some time for me to get used to walking on water here.

I took my position in between the other two Eldurian players in the second row, and mimicked them as they all drew the Undaberries from their pockets. I looked around me; the field sure looked different from down here. I glanced up into the rows on the valley's edge, and I immediately found Kerana. She was sitting there, beautiful as ever, just watching. Watching me, no less.

I grinned in spite of myself.

"Brace yourself, Human," Kouin said to me, a playful gaze in his eyes. "Any moment now!"

"And remember to defend this side if any blue players come this way," the Eldurian to my right added.

"But once your Undaberry expands, run for the other side!"

I nodded, and bent forward slightly. It was my favorite lacrosse stance.

A moment later, Kouin's berry grew in his hands. He looked at it, rather surprised, but wasted no time darting for the other side. A few members of the green team detached themselves from the group and ran up to help him. I was rather impressed with their incredible team work; they didn't even need to communicate to one another.

I saw a blue player out of the corner of my eye, and he ran up the right side. I followed the Eldurian to my right to try and cut him off, but as soon as we reached him, he dove beneath the water. I watched in awe as he swam like a fish beneath us and came up a few feet behind us. He clambered out of the water like it was the side of a pool, and continued towards his team member to give him his berry. I didn't even notice that I just let him get away; I was having far too much fun just watching him.

But that joy soon disappeared when the berry in my hand grew four times its original size.

"Human, run!" I heard an Eldurian, from the opposite team no less, cry out to me in amusement.

My senses returned and I made it to the line without any problems. But as soon as I crossed, three blue players were on me, completely blocked my way. I looked from one to the next, and each time I tried to dodge around them, they would move with me. I sighed.

"Dive underneath, Human boy! Dive underneath!" I heard Kouin shout from somewhere over our heads.

That thought made my nerves tingle almost painfully.

But I didn't have any choice, and I had about a minute left before my berry exploded, so I did what I was told. I closed my eyes and pretended I was diving into a swimming pool. I was pleasantly surprised when the sensation was rather close to that. The water was cool, but not cold, and I could open my eyes and see perfectly. Kerana was right; this water was nothing like water on Earth. I looked up at the surface to see the rippling shapes of the three blue team players above me. I was proud of how long I could hold my breath, and so I continued to swim farther down the lake. The lake was crystal clear, with a flat and sandy bottom. If I was able to breathe underwater, I was pretty sure I would never want to leave.

I came up for air, and I pulled myself up out of the water. Strangely enough, I grasped the edge of the water as if it were a hard surface, and hoisted myself from the lake. I expected that I was going to be dripping wet, but there was not a drop on me anywhere. Before I got too caught up on that phenomenon, I reoriented myself and saw that I was no more than ten or fifteen feet from my team's goalie. I made to step towards them, but the three Eldurians from the blue team quickly surrounded me, and I stopped in my tracks. They all just smiled down at me.

Unfortunately, before I was able to find a way around them, the berry in my hands started to shake subtly, and as I watched it, I realized it was going to burst. I was sort of afraid of balloons being popped as a kid, so I worried that this was going to be like that. I turned my face away, but instead of a loud *pop*, it just blew up like a water balloon would, and it scattered the four of us with water. The three Eldurians laughed, and even though I was slightly unhappy that I couldn't get it to the goalie, I laughed along with them.

"Go run back and help your team!" One of the blue players said as he nudged me with his elbow before he took off down the pond.

"Yes, go back and help! The game is not finished yet!" another added.

And so I ran back and helped defend my side. I was even able to successfully rescue a fallen berry when one of the blue players accidentally dropped it. The game ended with the blues winning again, but everyone still acted as if everyone was a winner. I liked that feeling, and allowed myself not to get lost in the fact that the team I played on had lost.

Kerana came down to meet us, a wide smile on her face. I had to seriously suppress the urge to run up and take her in my arms, spin her around. I figured that might not be exactly appropriate.

"You did wonderfully, Eli!" She exclaimed. She was proud of me!

"Indeed he did!" Kouin added, coming to stand beside us.

"Are you happy you got to play?"

"I'm sure that I would never play lacrosse again if I had the choice between that and Undalusum."

She beamed back at me, and I felt my heart leap. Man, I sure was in deep with this girl.

After a bit more talk here and there from the rest of the Eldurians, Kerana shared the fact that it was getting close to Adonai's presentation of the new Eldun. Excitement coursed through me. That should be interesting! I agreed to follow her back into the heart of Eden and hopefully find her family and some more wonderful foods.

The center of Eden was just as full with people as it had been before, but the atmosphere was entirely different. With the evening light fading and the starry sky beginning to create a veil over us all, the Eldurians became even more beautiful. Here, the darkness didn't mean fear or anxiety or death. Here, the night meant peace, and comfort. It meant intimacy, closeness, and the start of a new day.

What really caught my eye when we walked into the large expanse surrounding the Fountain were the balls of light that hung from the sides of the Fountain and from all of the tree branches surrounding the clearing.

"Kerana, there isn't electricity in Eden, right?"

She smiled up at me, in a way that said, *You know the answer to that question.*

"Then what are those lights?" I asked, and pointed to the spheres that were glowing with rich, white light.

She followed my gaze, and almost as if it were common knowledge, said to me, "Those are infant stars."

"Stars? Really? Like the ones that my sixth grade teacher had us memorize in clusters called constellations?"

"The very same. Those ones, however, are far older than the ones here. These were only made today. Tomorrow Adonai will take them and place them up in the sky where they belong."

I couldn't believe I was staring at actual stars.

"Can I touch one?" I questioned impulsively.

She looked up at me with a quizzical look. "I wouldn't recommend it. They would probably burn right through your Human fingers."

"Oh, right. I can't walk through fire like you can."

All I got in response was the smallest of smiles.

Music was going just as strong as it had been earlier, and there had even been a large space in the winter realm that had been cleared for dancing. I watched the Eldurians beam at one another and spin their partners gracefully and fluidly. The dances were intricate, yet simple. None like I had ever seen, that was for sure. It was like a mix between a waltz and big band swing. It was fast-paced just like the music, but it was intimate and engaging. As Kerana took a second to look over the heads of the Eldurians nearby for her folks, I took the time to watch the dancers more closely.

I took a quick look over at Kerana. She still searched for her parents. Then the insane idea came over me that I wanted Kerana to be on that dance floor with me. Pronto.

"Kerana, would you want to maybe—"

But I didn't get a chance to ask her, because all of the Eldurians erupted into cheers that could have easily deafened me if I had not plugged my ears. I looked around wildly for what they were so excited about, and as I turned around, a taller figure standing on the edge of the Fountain caught my eye.

He wore a white robe like all of the Eldurians, but there was something different about him. I knew instantly that he was not an Eldurian, but something more. He had dark hair, like many of the Eldurians here, and incredibly bright eyes. He looked to be in better shape than anyone I had ever seen, and his entire presence was perfection. It was almost hard to look at him, but I couldn't stop.

In his arms, there was an infant cradled in a blanket. It had wispy blonde hair and tiny fists. And for the first time, I noticed two Eldurians standing on either side of him.

"Kerana!" I shouted over all of the cheering and screaming. She looked up at me. "What is going on? Who is that?"

"Eli, it's Adonai! Didn't you figure that out?"

"But wait, why can I see Him?" I tried to ask Kerana, but my voice was drowned out by the clapping.

Adonai smiled down at everyone, and raised His free hand to quiet everyone down.

"Thank you all, my faithful and treasured ones. I am here this evening to present to you a new life!"

Cheers ensued once again. Kerana and I clapped enthusiastically.

Adonai smiled as he raised the child into the air for all to see. Once the noise died down, Adonai continued.

"This family will raise this Eldun to continue the legacy of the Eldurians and to serve and guard the children of Adonai! I now present this tiny boy to you, and I have given him his name. Blessings and love upon the new Eldun, Kosei!"

And the crowd erupted again.

Adonai smiled as He held the infant high above his head. He happily passed the child off to his mother, who looked at that baby as if it were the only thing in the entire world. I had no doubt in my mind that Eldurians were fantastic parents. They were a perfect society.

Shortly after, the crowds went back to eating, talking, laughing, and dancing. Kerana turned back to me.

"I'm sorry, Eli, but what were you trying to say to me before? You asked me if I wanted to do something?"

I looked back over at the couples that had congregated again in the Winter realm and were dancing. The music now matched the atmosphere; it was calm, soft and gentle. The Eldurians still spun gracefully, but more slowly, more dramatically. There was a single piano playing, but I couldn't see from where. It reminded me of the part in classic romance films when the dancing couple realizes they are in love with their partner. Very cliché, but believable here. Movies were often the best case scenario, the happily-ever-after. Eden seemed to be the best happily-ever-after. I swallowed the lump that had risen in my throat.

"I was watching the dancers." I made eye contact with her. In comparison to the starlight, her eyes were worthy competition.

"Would you like to dance?" She asked me.

"Actually, yes I would."

She grinned at me as I had just given her everything she had ever wanted. Without a word, I felt her fingers lace through my own. I instantly felt that slow burn start in my chest, but I let it come. I didn't know if I really wanted to hide how I felt anymore. I had hidden from everything and everyone too long, and it was all thanks to Adonai that I was different now.

She led me over to the Winter realm, and as soon as we stepped into the powdery snow, I was shocked when I found that it wasn't bitter and cold.

"This is so unbelievable!" I said, more to myself then anything. Kerana heard me though, and looked over her shoulder at me.

"What is, exactly?"

"The snow isn't cold!"

"Is the snow supposed to be cold?" she questioned, circling around a particularly long table.

"Yes! On Earth, it is so cold that we have to wear layers of clothing and hats on our heads to keep us from freezing to death!"

"Oh, now I remember," Kerana added. "I think I learned about Earthly snow when I was younger. I've never seen it on Earth, and I am just so used to the snow here in Eden."

"Well, I have seen it many times, and I know all about how cold it is." The music slowed to stop, and so did the couples. Everyone took a step away from each other and laughed and applauded. Soon after, the music began again, but in a fast tempo. The piano was joined by a violin, a bongo drum, and a tambourine. It was lively and upbeat.

"Come, Eli!" Kerana exclaimed, and pulled me onto the snowy, starlit dance floor. She instantly pulled me in a circle until I faced her, and she threw her free hand around my neck. I both tensed and melted at the touch; we had never been this close before. Instinctively, I wrapped my free hand around her waist.

And with that, she began to dance like the rest of the Eldurians, graceful and elegant. But then, she had me as a dance partner, who was never really good at dancing to begin with. Even though I was a little embarrassed, I let her lead me. I also realized that if I just went with it, if I just let it go, I would have so much more fun and not care anymore. So I did, and I was right.

When the song ended, I slid my hand to the small of her back and drew her close to me. She looked up at me with her large, cloudless blue sky eyes and waited on me, trusted me. I then slowly dipped her back down towards the ground.

Her eyes never left mine.

She never tensed, never squirmed or made any movements that told me she was uncomfortable. She totally trusted me enough to let her all the way down to the ground, stable and protected. I hesitated before I brought her up, amazed at her trust in me. And what was stranger was that action told me more than words ever could.

I drew her back up to her feet, and color rushed into both of our faces. The song's last chords echoed across the clearing, and everyone stepped back from their partner and clapped enthusiastically. The band picked right back up with another slow song, with just the piano and violin.

Kerana looked at me curiously while I was mentally brought back to the eighth grade when I went to my first middle school dance. Kristen Glass had asked me to dance, and so I had accepted, even though I'd had no idea what I was doing. She had graciously shown me by putting my hands at her waist and her arms around my neck, and proceeded to sway side to side with me. It was easy, but I was pretty sure that that type of dancing wasn't going to cut it in Eden.

"Um, I really am not sure what to do here," I confessed as I rubbed the back of my neck absently with my hand.

"Not to worry, I'll show you. Besides, you did fantastic on the last one. This one should be even simpler for you."

She mimicked Kristen Glass very closely by bringing her arms up around my neck, so then I did all I knew how to and brought my hands to her waist. For a minute or two, it was somewhat awkward. We didn't talk to each other at all, and I wanted to kick myself. It *was* the eighth grade dance all over again.

But as we danced, I realized we were slowly closing the distance between us. Her hands were tighter around me, and my hands were closer to the small of her back. I had a mini panic attack, knowing her parents were right nearby, but then as I looked around, I realized that many of the couples were dancing like we were.

"Some things are just the same across the board, huh?" I muttered, and looked over the top of Kerana's head at the other couples. She looked over her shoulder.

"What do you mean?"

"People dance this way on Earth, too. Close like this, I mean."

I smiled at her. "So I've been thinking about something," I said to her. She shifted her gaze up to me. I took this as her acknowledgement to go on. "Well, Adonai created everything."

"Yes, He did," she agreed, a small smile tugging at the corners of her mouth.

"Well, if Humans are His children, made in His image, then are the Eldurians as well? Are you just another race that He created and never shared anything about with Earth?"

She shook her head, the beginnings of a smile still on her face. "No, Eli. We are not made in His image like the Humans are. He created us to be able to help protect you and to do His good deeds on Earth. He made us to be messengers, healers, rescuers, protectors. Long ago, when Humans were exiled from Eden, He removed all traces of Eden from the Earth. Humans were banished, never to set foot in that garden ever again."

"So it makes even less sense that I am here now," I commented. She shook her head.

"Not necessarily, because this Eden is not the same Eden that existed on Earth. This one was remade for us specifically. After the Fall of man, Adonai knew that His chosen people would need help, and would need ways of knowing Him. We do not speak in His place, mind you. We are the means, the instruments, if you will. Here is the key, though, Eli. *He does not need us.* He needs nothing to accomplish His will. He is all-powerful, and can very well do it on His own. However, He created new beings," and she gestured to herself and those around her, "Us, to help to forward His plans. While He doesn't need us, He uses us."

I thought through what she said. "I grew up hearing about angels, that they are messengers and guardians and such. Are you—are you an angel?"

"No, no, no. Not at all. Angels are higher beings than we are. They are Adonai's most loyal servants. They are far more powerful than we are. Angels arrive with the stars and the trumpet sounds and the glorious shows. When Adonai shows off, He certainly knows how to," she said, a quiet laugh in her words. "We, however, do everything unseen. They do as well, but it is not always necessary for them like it is for us. Adonai has asked us to work without the knowledge of Humans. And that is the way it should be; otherwise Adonai would not be getting all of the reverence. We deserve none of the acknowledgement, nor do we want it."

"That's why you ran from me the day you—" I still had a hard time saying it, let alone believing it. "Saved me."

"That is precisely why I did. You were not to know what had happened. I was simply..." her words came up short as she stared intently at something over my shoulder. "...doing my job."

The music continued to play, and as it did, she smiled at me and returned her arms to up around my neck. This time around, we didn't feel the need to talk at all. We just listened to the music, myself especially. Adonai's music for me the night before had been incredible, and even though this music was good, it didn't even compare. As I lost myself in the melody, I felt a pressure on my chest. Confused, I looked down at realized that Kerana had leaned forward and put her head on my chest. Elated and panicking all at once, I looked around wildly. Everyone else was either engaged in conversation or entirely lost in their own dancing.

I returned my gaze to Kerana, or rather to the top of her head. Not wanting to upset her, I kept my hands where they were on her back, but I pulled her a little closer to me. In response, she tightened her arms around my neck.

When the song ended, I felt her disentangle herself from my grasp, but she was nice about it. She smiled up at me, her eyes extra bright, and we heard clapping from beside us. We both looked over and saw Adonai standing on the edge of the dance floor smiling at Kerana and me.

Thinking I had just misbehaved, I took a relatively good-sized step backwards away from Kerana. Adonai laughed out loud. "Dear Eli, you are an extraordinary dancer!"

"Thank you, sir." I replied. I felt like I was talking to someone different now that I could see Him. He had a face, eyes, a smile, and a body. It's not that it made it harder for me to believe in Him, it just made it different.

"Kerana, you did splendid as well. I am so glad that you have taken Eli around today and showed him all that Eden has to offer during one of our many celebrations."

He smiled at Kerana, and I saw nothing but love in His eyes. Then He turned those loving eyes on me.

"Eli, would you like to take a walk with me?"

"Sure," I replied and glanced at Kerana quickly. She nodded at me, and disappeared into the crowd in what I assumed was the direction of her parents.

Adonai turned from the dance floor and headed straight for the forest. I caught up with Him quickly and fell into step beside Him.

"Good, I'm glad you chose to walk beside me instead of behind me. I want to walk with you, Eli, so we can talk and have a relationship. I will lead you when the path gets tricky or dirty, so you know which way to go and where it is safe. But when the path is smooth, I want you to stay right where you are right now."

Then He was silent again. As we walked, the noises and music from the forest grew softer and softer, but the forest grew more peaceful and calming. Unsure of what to do or say, I continued to be quiet too.

"There is something you've wanted to ask me," Adonai said after a little while. I shifted my gaze to Him to find Him looking at me intently. I swallowed hard. I still wasn't used to Him knowing *everything*.

"Yes, I know it can be hard at first. But even though I do know everything, it helps if you actually talk it through with me. I want to hear your voice, hear exactly what you have to say. We have to have conversations for this relationship to work. It can't all be one way, Son." He gave me a look that I assumed most fathers would give their sons when they are trying to teach them an important life lesson. "Now, what was it that you wanted to ask me?"

"Okay, well I was wondering, when you were introducing the new Eldun, how come I can see you? I mean last night I couldn't, but now I can?"

"A good question, Eli, and one that has both a simple and a complex answer."

"What do you mean?"

"What you see before you right now is the part of me with an actual body, like an Eldurian or a Human."

"Wait, the part of you? You mean there are more?" I asked.

"Three, to be exact. There is this part, in the form of a man," He gestured down at Himself and His white robe. "Then there is the part that you met last night, which is the part that cannot be seen. It is the form of a spirit, and it is what lives inside of you now that you have answered my call on your life."

"And what is the third part?" I continued.

"That part is the Father."

"So instead of you being one," I struggled with the right word, "being," *No, that's not right.* "Entity?" *Still not right.* "Instead of just being one whole Adonai, you are three?"

"No, I am still one. I just have three parts."

"I am so confused," I concluded, looking at me feet. Adonai smiled.

"Watch this."

He bent to the ground, and with a swipe of His hand, brushed away the snow, revealing a green patch of grass. He tugged at a three leaf clover, which seemed to be in abundant supply beneath the snow, and stood to His feet.

"Do you see this clover, how there are three leaves that make up the same plant?"

I nodded at Him as I too looked at the clover.

"These three leaves, though their own leaf, are a part of the same plant, and they all connect here," He pointed, "At the stem. They are three parts to one whole."

I must have been focused on the clover very intently, because I heard a small chuckle. I looked over at Adonai, who was smiling at me.

"I think both of our eyes were crossed for a moment, there." He said.

For some reason, the idea of the Creator of the Universe with His eyes crossed was incredibly funny to me. I couldn't help it; I started to laugh. It wasn't until I heard Adonai burst out laughing that I let it all out. We had to stop walking so we could laugh together. Once we gained control of ourselves, Adonai looked at me, the aftereffects from the laugh still showing in His smile.

"So you understand what I mean, then?"

"Yeah, I think so."

"Good. And I wanted you to be able to see me so we could talk more freely like this. When I told you I had sent my son to Earth, I was telling the truth. But in the same sense, I was sending the Human form of myself to Earth. Granted, I am not in a Human body anymore; it is more like an Eldurian's body."

"I have to be honest, I never imagined you with such a good sense of humor."

"I created laughter too, didn't I? Where do you think all of the humorous people in the world came from?"

I laughed. Adonai turned and looked at me. "I'm glad that we got to talk like this," I said to Him. He smiled wide.

"I am too, Eli. I am too."

23 KERANA

The sun rose the next morning strong and clear. I woke up to sunbeams that pierced through my windows and fell onto my face. I rolled over away from them, but sighed contentedly.

The night before had been wonderful. Celebrations in Eden were always fun and entertaining, but there was something about having Eli by my side that made it so much more special. He had enjoyed himself as well, and didn't even seem bothered by the present circumstances. Maybe he was just hiding his thoughts well. Or maybe after last night, it really didn't matter to him.

I rolled over onto my back and looked up at the ceiling of roots tangled above me. There was only a few days left until his condition completely took over, until his body disappeared. And then what would happen to him?

Adonai, I know you are in control of this. Please help us to be patient as we await your answer.

I got to my feet, stretched, and crossed to the door. I stepped out into the hallway, and discovered Eli walking towards the bathroom. He stopped as he heard me leaving my room.

"Good morning, sleepy head," he said to me, a small smile on his face. "You must have needed it, though. I'm even awake before you are today."

I smiled. "Yes, it would appear so. How are you this morning, Eli?" I asked him. He looked down at his hands, which clutched a towel. All I received in response was a single hand raised to my eye level.

As I looked closer at his hand, I realized that it was hard to look close at. It appeared as if I were looking through sheer fabric; I could see his chest and shoulder through the flesh.

"Oh, Eli," I said. He shrugged, and casually tossed the towel over his shoulder, holding tight to one end.

"What's weird, though, is that my face and my middle are still solid. But it has spread up my arms and legs. The white robes help to disguise the change, so I'm pretty glad for that."

I nodded. "I see."

He held his gaze at me for a moment or so longer. Then he looked down. "Well, I probably should go get cleaned up. I need to bathe like no one's business."

I laughed softly. "All right. I will leave you alone, then."

And with that, he proceeded to the bathroom.

When I walked into the kitchen, I found my mother, father, and little brothers. The twins greeted me with happy smiles and laughter, and my mother came and kissed me gently on the cheek.

"So you saw Eli?" Father asked me. I nodded. "The process is indeed happening quite quickly."

"I am worried about him." I answered flatly, yet honestly. Father put his hand on my shoulder.

"I am too, but we know that Adonai loves Eli and is only doing what is right. So we must trust Him."

"I know," I replied.

"I am going to be speaking with the Elders again this morning. They have called a meeting since Adonai met with Eli. Your mother is bringing Eli down after he has had a chance to wash up, but they wanted to see me before they spoke to him."

"I want to come with you, then." I responded immediately. My reaction even surprised myself, but I didn't want to just sit at home wondering what was being said down at the Council Hall. "Please?" I added.

My father smiled. "I appreciate your enthusiasm. Yes, you can come with me. I don't think they'll have a problem since you sat in with us earlier. Adonai is still asking us to just wait. I am not sure anything would have changed since last night. If it had, we probably have heard."

He smiled then at me in a way that I was not familiar with. "There is something quite different about you, my dear daughter."

I returned his gaze. *What was so different?*

Mother looked at me as well from the sink. She smiled the same way at me. "Indeed there is. You've changed in the last few days, Kerana. Adonai has affected more than just Eli's life while he has been here."

I felt my face color at the mention of Eli's name. I hid my eyes from them by looking at the boys who played on the floor of the living room. My mother laughed ever so softly that I questioned if I even heard it at all.

"Come, Kerana. We can stop at the Fountain and see what is left in regards to food from last night. I am sure that the Heraos or the Yeuis will be happy to part with some of their abundant foods."

I followed my father out of the doors and down the path towards the center of Eden. We walked with little conversation, for my thoughts were scattered. I think he knew this.

Father was right when he said that the Heraos would be willing to share their food from the festivities the evening prior. We took a few perfectly red and round apples and a few crystallized berries from the winter realm. We thanked them graciously, and proceeded towards the Council Hall.

"The Fountain is particularly full today," My father noticed curiously as we walked beside it. He was right; there were so many petals on the surface of the glassy water that the water couldn't even be seen.

"Eli met so many people last night," I reflected.

"He did, yes. Many people have shared their prayers with Adonai this morning for him, if I were to guess."

My heart both leapt and fell at those words.

The Council Hall was relatively quiet that morning. It was still early, but everyone was resting from such a late night the night before. We walked right into the very same room that I had gone to many times as I grew up, but I felt heavier with memories of what had transpired here just a few days before. The fear in Eli still hung in the air; dark feelings didn't disappear quite so easily.

Eight of the other Elders were sitting at the table already. "Erez, Kerana. Good morning to you," Faris greeted us, his green eyes peaceful and calm.

"Good morning to you all as well," Father replied. "Where are the other three?" I noted that Kobe, Kimo, and Ovid were missing.

"I believe they went to the Fountain one last time before we began our meeting."

We didn't have to wait very long at all. All three men in their long white robes strolled into the room and took their seats.

"Now, assuming that Kerana's presence involves our discussion, I believe that we should just get right to the point." Kobe looked around at everyone, sighing heavily. His dark eyes were fixed on his hands that were folded in front of him on the table. "Adonai still has not given us an answer as to what to do or what is to happen to the Human."

"To Eli," I replied flatly. "He has a name."

Kobe, as well as the rest of the Elders, looked at me closely. I had spoken out of turn, which was disrespectful, but I realized that this matter was far more than respect and manners.

"Is he still fading, Erez?" Seoras asked. Father nodded.

"Yes, he is. And at an alarming rate. I do believe that you were correct in your assumption, Dru. He probably only has the next few days left. And when they end—"

I shuddered. I didn't want to think about that.

"Well, at this point, we are looking at two different possibilities, and we need to be prepared for both of them." Ovid stepped in.

"What are those possibilities?" Keon asked. "At this rate, there seems to be only one."

I glared at him. I have always had the highest respect for these men, knowing Adonai hand chosen each of them, but right now my own personal feelings were being tampered with in a bizarre, obscure way.

"No, Keon, there are two. The first is that Adonai reopens the Portal before the seventh day comes. Has anyone checked the Portal?" Ovid looked at my Father.

"I took Eli early this morning. It was still closed, unfortunately."

Ovid hung his head, exhaling. "All right, then we still must be patient. Our next possibility is that at the end of the seventh day, Eli will—well, he will disappear."

I closed my eyes and willed the pain rising in my chest to recede. Adonai wouldn't take him away, would He?

The sun shone through the windows, and I wished more than anything that Adonai was here right now, and would provide us with the answers. I so badly wanted the answers.

Tedros looked up at us all. "We will get an answer. I just hope that it is soon."

"We've never had to deal with anything like this before. We've never once had to feel any sort of anxiety about a decision or a discussion. We've always trusted Adonai, and He has always come through." Teom added.

"So then why is this time so much more difficult?" Kimo asked, a bit too aggressively for my liking.

"I'll tell you why." Kobe said, as he got to his feet and a harsh tone coated his voice. "It's because of that black-souled Human—"

"Kobe!" shouted my father, who stood as well and looked across the table at Kobe. "That's enough!" I was grateful that he had said something, because if he hadn't, I certainly was going to.

"Enough of what? It's true! That is all Humans are! I don't know why Adonai wastes His time with them anymore. Before the Human, everything was fine! Then he came and destroyed our order!"

"Do you even hear yourself right now?" Conan piped up, a look of utter disbelief shadowing his usually gentle face. "How could you say any of that?"

"Has anyone been to Earth recently? When I was, not a single one cared for another, no one believed in Adonai, and everyone was killing everyone else. That world is a waste of time, if you ask me."

"And no one did ask you, Kobe." Ovid retorted, his tone stern and final. Kobe looked over at Ovid. They were both very serious.

"Kobe is right, though! All the Human brought with him was chaos and evil. It shouldn't have happened!" Kimo added. I was appalled with what these men were saying. All these men who so strongly relied on Adonai were now turning their backs on their own words and wisdoms. I could clearly see the division in the room. And that was when I couldn't take anymore.

"Shouldn't have happened?" I cried. I got out of my chair and stared at each of the Elders, especially Kobe and Kimo. "What has happened here? You are falling apart! You say before Eli came, things were perfect. And maybe that is correct, but perhaps things were too comfortable, too perfect. Has anyone ever thought of that?"

The Elders were entirely focused on me now. I felt a flood of strength rush into my veins, and so I continued on. "You say Eli brought evil and anxiety into our midst. I know I have only been on Earth for a fraction of the time that all of you have been, but in those few months, I learned that the Humans suffer with this anxiety *every single day of their lives*. And being there, being in a Human's shoes, I felt that anxiety, that fear. And isn't that what it is all about? Isn't that what we were *created* for? Adonai made us to be His helpers, His hands and His feet on Earth, to *help* His children, to *protect* His children. And what are we doing here? We are just sitting here in Eden, living perfect lives. It is wonderful, but aren't we being selfish? Our entire purpose on Earth is to *help* them. And we have one here, in our midst, and you are *upset*?"

Many of them looked away from me. Perhaps my words were too much for them to hear. But I couldn't take it. I wasn't going to listen to a single one of them speak another word against Eli or the situation. "We have the chance to help one of Adonai's own in our very home. We don't have any idea what we are doing, but when we went to Earth, did we have any idea? It is the same with Eli coming to Eden; Adonai had prepared us for this, even if we don't recognize it as that. He had Eli come to Eden for a reason. We may not know the outcome of it, and I can promise you that I am scared out of my mind for Eli, but I trust Adonai more than I am afraid. That is a lot of trust on my part, but He has never, *never* let us down, any of us. Has He?"

Heads around the table shook side to side; no.

"You say that this shouldn't have happened. Well, I can stand here and tell you that I am glad that it has happened. I have discovered that Humans have so much more to offer than just being watched over. They have hearts that need mending, and they need Adonai just like we do. They have the same capacity to love as we do, and Adonai is what ties us all together. Eli's presence in my life has changed it forever, and no matter what happens, I won't regret taking the time to know him and care for him. Adonai placed him here, in my life as well as everyone else's in Eden, for a reason. I think it was about time that we just let Adonai do His job and take care of everything."

Spent now, I looked away. I swallowed hard. Dru was the

first to speak.

"Your emotions run deep, dear one."

"Yes," was all I could reply. There was no point in fighting it. Eli meant far more to me than I had ever admitted to myself. I wouldn't have defended him so much if it were anything different. I felt a hand on my shoulder and looked up to see my father, who watched me with loving eyes. Maybe they were right that Eli coming had tainted the room with the pain that only darkness can bring, but I believed with my whole heart that it was good that I was feeling *something*.

As my father pulled away, I slowly opened my eyes. I caught a glimpse of shapes over my father's shoulder, and gasped. My mother stood in the doorway with Eli. An expression of shock must have appeared on my face, because my father turned to follow my gaze.

"How long have you been standing there?" I breathed, my eyes fixed on Eli. His eyes were soft and tender, and I had my answer.

"Long enough." His voice was strained, and I knew he fought himself to keep his emotions in check. My mother's eyes were not dry.

"We have much to think about now. We will ask Adonai once again and hope for the best. *We will receive an answer.* We must believe that Adonai will not let us down. Kerana is very right; He never has in the past. Why would He now?" Ovid said. Everyone nodded in agreement.

Then, as one whole group, the Elders got to their feet and prepared to leave the room. My father was the last to leave the table. I couldn't move. I didn't have the energy to yet. He kissed the top of my head, and crossed the room to my mother, and they left hand in hand to go to the Fountain.

Eli stood in the doorway, and he could only look at me, his eyes a tornado of turmoil. "I heard everything you said, Kerana."

My insides burned. I had not acknowledged my feelings yet, even to myself. And now he knew them. I had too many emotions going through me, too many thoughts racing through my head.

"I'm so sorry, Eli," I breathed as my eyes welled up. He quickly crossed the room to me, and in one swift motion, he gently took me in his arms. I tensed, unsure of what to do. But his strong and sturdy hands on my back and shoulders comforted me in a way I had never known. He rested his head on my shoulder, and held me so close. Only a moment passed where I contemplated pushing away from him and running.

But that moment came and went, and I threw my arms around him and held him just as closely to me. I buried my face in the fabric of his robe. I could smell him past the scent of my father's robe. He held me against him for endless minutes, but I didn't care. I fought back tears, bit my lip, and eventually I just couldn't handle it anymore. It started off soft and subtle, but as Eli whispered in my ear, the tears began to come more freely.

"Shh, It's okay, Kerana. I'm not going anywhere, I promise. I'm right here."

His words made it so much harder. I was so afraid for him, and I knew that by the way he held me that his fear was equal to my own. But I wouldn't trade any of it. I didn't want anything to happen to him, but I wouldn't be standing here wrapped in his arms if it hadn't happen. That selfish thought brought on a fresh flood of tears.

Eli continued to hold me until I was physically unable to cry anymore and even afterwards he held tightly to me. When my breathing returned to normal, I released my grip on him, and he slowly pulled away from me. He left his arms around my shoulders, though. All I could do was look up into his stormy eyes and hope that I didn't have to one day forget them.

"I don't want you to be sorry, Kerana." He responded in a whisper. "I don't ever want you to be sorry."

I smiled half-heartedly at him.

"Could you take me to the Fountain? I want to send off a prayer myself."

"Yes, I can do that. We should join everyone," I added. Before I was able to step away from him, his hand returned to my face to tenderly brush a tear away from my cheek. He held out his hand to me. I smiled weakly at him, and took his hand. It steadied me as we left the room and back out into the sunshine. I breathed in the fresh air as we walked, and Eli was silent. We stepped up right beside the Fountain, and I let go of Eli's hand. I bent down and plucked a single rose petal off a rose, and cupped my hands around it. Eli mimicked me, and then I drew my hands to my mouth.

"Adonai, please bring us the answers we seek. Be with Eli, protect Him, and bring peace back to Eden." I whispered. I then brought the rose petal down to the surface of the water in the Fountain, and let the liquid crystal wash it from the palm of my hand. Eli's prayer was longer than mine, and as he whispered to the petal, his eyes were closed. When he was done, he released his petal. Before too long, I felt Eli's hand find mine again, and held onto it tightly. I squeezed it reassuringly.

We were going to be just fine.

24 ELI

We walked back to the house alone that morning.

I asked her about what the Elders had said. She was kind of short about it.

"So do they have any idea what is actually going on with me?"

She looked at me, and I saw a sadness returned to her eyes. "No, they don't. Adonai still is asking us to wait."

"I see," I replied. I trusted Adonai now too, but I was confused as to why He was letting this happen to me. I raised a hand above me and watched as the sunshine shone through it, wondering what this all meant. It was weird turning into a shadow. Or ghost. Or whatever I was now.

She hesitated a moment. "Are you in any pain?"

"Nah, I'm fine. I can't even tell its happening unless I look at it."

We reached her house, and I stopped in front of the door. She had stepped through, but before she went down the stairs, she turned back around to look at me.

"Eli? Is everything okay?"

I looked around me; all of the trees were tall, ancient, thick, and green. The dirt paths were familiar to me now. And the girl that stood before me made me feel more alive than anything ever had before.

"It's just," I struggled to find the right words. "I've never felt more at home than I do here. I don't want to leave."

Kerana's face fell, and within a moment she was at my side. "Eli, no one is saying—"

"But I am, Kerana," I interrupted, afraid of what she might say. "At the end of this, I'll be back on Earth or I will have disappeared. I'm pretty sure me hanging out here is not in the cards."

She sighed but didn't reply.

"I am not Eldurian, Kerana. You are, and I'm Human. As much as I hate it, I belong on Earth."

"It is strange, because I belong in both places." she murmured. Then she tried to smile at me, but it was a forced one. She wanted me to believe that she was okay. But I knew better; she and I would only be lying to each other.

The rest of the day was kind of weird. We didn't talk all that much to each other, and if we did, it was pretty light conversation. Erez and Aonani, as well as Hani and Oni, joined us and didn't leave us the rest of the day. We had shared lunch and dinner, and after dinner, Erez took me back to the Portal. It was still closed.

We returned to the house to find Kerana and Aonani putting the boys to bed. As I stood in the doorframe and watched her tuck them into bed and kiss their small foreheads, I felt my heart seize in my chest; there was probably no chance that I would be lucky enough to watch her like this again after the next few days were over.

I slid away from the door and walked back down the hall. I heard the door click shut behind me and heard Kerana's sweet voice.

"Eli? Are you heading to bed?"

I stopped, tried to swallow my recent disappointment, and

replied, "Yeah, I think so. All this fading away into oblivion stuff has me tired out."

I heard a soft laugh behind me, but I think it was for my benefit that she laughed, not because she actually thought my joke was funny.

"Well, I am too, I guess. Good night, Eli." She said to me, and walked past me to her room.

"Kerana?" I asked her, and waited until her sparkling eyes met mine. "Don't be afraid for me, okay?"

She looked at me very seriously. "What do you mean?"

"I mean don't worry about me. There is no reason to. You said it yourself; Adonai is going to come through for us." I wasn't sure I said that because I wanted her to believe it, or because I wanted to believe it myself.

"He will, Eli. I know He will."

I found my way to the couch and collapsed onto it. I really was drained, and I figured all this emotional roller coaster stuff was going to eventually take its toll on me. I pulled the blanket closer to me, and brought it to my face. The echo of the hug Kerana and I had shared earlier that day crashed into me like a falling tree. Nothing in my entire life had ever felt more right than that moment with her. I squeezed my eyes tighter, trying to hold onto the feeling and also trying to let it go.

I rolled over onto my back, releasing the blanket. "Adonai," I whispered into the darkness. There was no answer. But instead of being angry this time, I felt a peace wash over me. He listened, and I knew that now. "Adonai," I started again. "I'm afraid. Really afraid. I am going to need you to help me out. I want to know why this is happening to me. I know you are there and that you care, did you just bring me here to talk to me and then let me die? I trust you, and I am glad that I've found you, but being here you've given me so much. You've given me life again, and hope. I had lost all of it until I met Kerana."

My throat constricted when I said her name. It was like I

had swallowed a handful of sugar; hard to do, but there was an adrenaline rush afterwards.

"Look, it's not my place to question you or how you run things, but this has all got us a little bit confused. Let us in on what's going on, please?"

I waited in the silence for some time. I saw the moon leak in through the windows and create pools on the floor beside the couch. I rolled over onto my side to look at them more closely. "And thanks for everything, too. Being here has been the best thing to ever happen to me, even if has only been a few days."

My thoughts wandered to the fact that Kerana slept literally a matter of feet away from me. I wondered if she was lying awake too, thinking. I wondered what she would be think about, and if it was at all about me. The idea of that made me smile, and I sunk into a deep, dreamless sleep.

The morning came far sooner than I had expected it to. I woke up even before the sun had risen. But for some reason, when I woke up, I was fully awake. I sat up, noticed the blanket on the floor. *Must have kicked it off in the middle of the night again.* I listened hard, but didn't hear anything from the rest of the house. I must have woken up *really* early.

I realized I didn't want to just lay there awake anymore, so I rubbed my hands over my face and got to my feet. I clumsily crossed the room and went out into the hall, blindly looking for the bathroom. Once I found it, I found that there were still candles lit on the side of the sink. A nightlight of sorts, I guessed. I splashed some of the running water onto my face.

When I brushed my hands over my face, I opened my eyes.

And I could see all the way through my hand.

I gasped and pulled them away from my face. Sure enough, the edges of my hands had all but faded away, leaving just the transparent palm. Panic rose in me as I looked at my arms that were beginning to fade as well. I pulled the robe up over my knees and saw that my legs were totally transparent. I pulled the robe down from my neck and looked at the skin there; everything was becoming transparent. I pulled the robe more closely around me so I would avoid looking at any of my own skin and made my way to the stairs and outside. I needed to walk and think.

I didn't see very many Eldurians out. When they passed me, they all bowed and smiled at me. I felt like a prince walking around, but on the other hand, I felt so unworthy.

I didn't go towards the Fountain, but I also didn't go towards the Portal. Either place would bring me back to my mini panic mode. So I just walked alone, in complete silence, and tried to not think about anything at all.

It was at that point when I heard someone run up behind me. I peered over my shoulder and saw the blonde hair first. She was awake already?

"Eli!" she called to me. "Eli, there you are!"

"I'm here, no need to worry."

She caught up to me. "I wondered where you had gone when you weren't on the couch."

"Yeah, I needed to get some fresh air, clear my head."

"Are you all right?" she questioned.

I exhaled in a huff. "Not so much." And I showed her my hand, and then pulled up the sleeve of the robe so she could see the full extent of it. She gasped just like I had. Without a word, she reached up with one of her hands and laid it against mine, palm to palm.

"It's still there. I mean, you are still solid."

"Yeah, and that is really what's weird."

She let her hand fall to her side. "This is really getting to be serious."

"Pretty sure it was serious from the get-go, Kerana," I teased somewhat. She nodded. Then she seemed to compose herself and showed me a basket in her hands.

"What's that?"

"It's some breakfast. I figured you hadn't eaten when you left, and I was thinking we could go up to the hilltop and watch the sunrise." *A picnic? It's like a date back on Earth.*

I looked up at the sky. I could almost watch it turn shades of pink and orange. "You know, I could go for some food."

She led the way, since I hadn't exactly paid attention when I stormed off last time. We made it to the top of the hill just as the sun broke the horizon. She passed me an incredibly sweet bread with some berry spread on it and a wooden mug of sorts, pouring a bright blue liquid into the glass.

"What is all this?"

"Mother made the bread last night, the spread was from the celebration, and the juice is freshly squeezed from a berry grown in the winter realm."

As I took a sip, the liquid coated my throat in ice, and I coughed.

"What's wrong?" she asked concerned. I coughed for a moment or two, and held up my hand to her.

"I'm," I coughed. "I'm fine, really. Just," coughed again, "just wasn't expecting it to be so cold!"

"Well I did say it was from the Winter realm."

"But it's not cold in the Winter realm."

"Well, the snow isn't, but the fruit certainly is."

Well, no matter how much I loved this place, it would always confuse me. I took another sip of the juice, but was far more careful. It was good, now that I didn't feel like I had swallowed an icicle.

"So can you believe it has only been six days since everything started to turn upside down?" she asked me. I looked over at her. The rising sun had painted her hair gold and her eyes like sea water.

"Why six days? I was thinking more like four or five."

"Well, I was referring more to the night when those guys—" she trailed off. She fidgeted with the mug in her hands. It was odd to see such a graceful woman fidget. But I knew exactly what she meant. We hadn't talked about it at all since it had happened, and I didn't know what to say to her at all. So I looked away too, and bit down into the bread she gave me, avoiding the fact that she was probably looking for some kind of response from me.

She looked over at me. "I really don't know what would have happened to me if you hadn't come along. I was so afraid, and let me be honest and tell you that before that night, I had only felt fear once before. And that was on my first day on Earth. But even that was not as potent as the fear I felt that night."

"Wait, how is that possible?"

"And I could have very simply prevented them from doing anything. I just felt—"

"Paralyzed?" I finished for her.

She looked at me with wide eyes. "Yes, that is exactly it."

I sat back on my hands. "I know what that's like too. I've experienced that fear a lot in my life."

"Yes, that is what Adonai told me. I can't imagine having to live like that..."

I shrugged my shoulders, though I wholly agreed with her. "I've been there twice in the last week."

"Twice?" She questioned, taking a sip of her drink.

"Twice. Once when I was told that I was essentially turning into the invisible man, and also when I was stuck in the dorm when it was in flames." I paused, the memories vivid for the first time. It was too hard, so I just turned back to her. "And so I guess it is my turn to thank you for saving me. I have to admit, your rescue was way cooler than mine; I got punched in the face when I rescued you, and you got to walk through fire for me."

"I never would have made it out of there if it hadn't been for you. And as soon as I knew it was you, I knew—"

She smiled at me very slowly.

"I knew that I would be safe."

The equivalent of an un-Fallen Human was telling me that she felt safe around me. Talk about an ego boost, even for a guy like me who didn't care for ego boosts.

"Well, even though I was unconscious when you saved me, I am pretty sure that I can safely say that I am glad you came in to get me." I pondered for a second. "Speaking of that, how did you know I was in there?"

"To be entirely honest, I could hear you scream from outside."

"Super-hearing is one of your abilities, huh?"

She grinned at me.

"Why did you go in for me?" I asked.

"Why would you even ask me that question?"

"I just didn't know why it mattered so much, why one life mattered so much. Why I mattered so much."

"It's part of the reason why Eldurians are on Earth in the first place, and I knew it was you, and then I knew I had no choice but to get in there and find you. I don't know what I would have done if I was too late, and you are not just one life. You are an important one. All lives are important, but you—"

I just looked at her.

"What was it like?" I asked, and tried to kill my train of thought before it spiraled out of control.

"Really scary. I had no idea where you were once I got in the building, so I had to listen for your breathing."

"You heard me *breathing*?"

"Super-hearing, as you called it, remember? But it was hard over all of the flames. Fire is loud. But once I found you, I didn't know how I was going to get you out because Humans can't go through flames."

"No, that usually kills us. Not always, but usually."

"Well, Adonai certainly wanted you to live, because He opened a gap in the flames that I was able to navigate and get you out of the building right before it collapsed."

"And that was why I was covered in ashes and dust."

"Yes. My instinct was to run home and tell my family what happened, and that was how you followed me. If you had woken up with me right there, how could I have explained myself?"

"You could have lied to me, made something up."

She looked at me very seriously. "I can't lie, Eli. I couldn't do it."

"There are not enough people like you. Granted, you aren't Human, but it would be nice if there were more Human people that didn't lie out there."

"You don't lie," she observed, but stated it as if it were a well-known fact.

"Yes, I do. I would be lying if I said I didn't. Like that night with Hanley? I lied to him."

"Why did you lie to him?"

"Isn't it obvious? If I didn't lie to him, he may not have ever left you alone. I needed to lie to him in order to get him away from you."

"So you lied in order to protect me? Is that correct?"

"Kerana, I would have done anything in the whole world to protect you."

I wasn't sure I was ready for that one to slip out like it had. I looked away from her down at the wooden cup on my hand. What I had said was the entire truth, and for the life of me I couldn't figure out why I just blurted it out like I had.

I felt her warm hand on mine just then, and looked down to see her take my hand in hers. I looked up at her.

"I would have done anything to protect you," she whispered.

I felt my chest start to burn, but I smirked at her and said, "We already went over that your rescue was cooler than mine."

For probably fifteen minutes or so, we just sat there, hand in hand, and watched the sun rise into the sky. The temperature rose as we finished up the rest of the food in silence, yet she never let go of my hand, and I was glad for that.

"So where was your family when you left?"

"Mother and Father were taking Hani and Oni to their lessons that day."

"Lessons? Elduns have lessons? Like school?"

"Well, yes, it is."

"So you did that? They basically train you to be Human?" I thought it was interesting that the Eldurians even had to go to school.

She then smiled up at me. "Eli... I have a confession to make to you."

25 KERANA

He looked at me very seriously. "What is it?"

"When we were on Earth," I paused. His look encouraged me on. "I watched you play the piano for several weeks." I let it all tumble out of my mouth before I could stop myself.

His face looked amused and confused. "How did you do that? The music building, it was always closed."

"Yes, but I snuck in through a second floor window. And then I hid in the back of the auditorium along the wall so you couldn't see me with the stage lights on."

He now seemed impressed. "I never once had any idea that someone was watching me."

"It is my job to go unseen, Eli."

He smiled. "I guess so."

I looked earnestly at him. "Eli, I have never heard music like that before. Your gift of music, I know without a doubt that it is Adonai's special gift to you. And denying yourself your passion and your gift all these years has to be exhausting. Did you come up with it all by yourself?"

"Most of it. I still can't believe that you snuck in and listened to me!"

"I think I grew to know you quite well on those late nights. And now learning so much more about you being here in Eden, I understand the lyrics and the music so much better now."

He shook his head. "It's unbelievable."

"Eli!" An idea struck me. "You should play something!"

"What? How?"

"Back home, we have a piano. Haven't you seen it?"

"Of course I did; I have been eyeing it for days now."

"Then we should go back and you should play it."

He shifted uncomfortably. "No, Kerana, I couldn't."

"What do you mean you couldn't? Eli, you don't have to run anymore, you don't have to hide. You can be free to play here. I know it is what you love. I want you to do what you love."

He studied my face. "I've never played for an audience before."

"You've played for me dozens of times," I replied.

"In my defense, I didn't know you were there." He had a point. Then he sighed. "But, I guess maybe playing a little wouldn't hurt."

I was positively beaming at him.

We made our way back to our home, and we found that my family was still not around. I led him downstairs to the piano, and watched him excitedly as he sat at the wooden bench and rested his hands on the ivory keys.

"You look so natural doing that, Eli," I observed, and realized that it was out loud instead of just an internal thought. He looked over at me, and I saw light pouring from his eyes.

"You think so?"

I walked across the room, and quietly rested myself on the edge of the chair beside the fire. I could see him so much better from here. The firelight tangled with his lashes and his hair, like oil and flames. His eyes were wide and shone like the sky after a storm. I watched him as he became unaware of anything else in the room besides himself, and the piano.

His hands gingerly tested the keys. The notes vibrated inside the walls and across the floors.

He's incredibly nervous, I realized after a moment. He hesitated to play, and I couldn't quite understand why.

"The last time I played for someone was the night before my mom died."

I was startled at his words and wondered if I had heard him correctly. He trailed his right hand down the keys, playing notes that were sorrowful and heavy.

"I had a recital on Friday. The first I ever would have played in. I even remember the name of the song I was practicing."

He quickly played a series of notes, a simple strand that hung in the air like a mist over our heads.

"It was called 'Morning Light', and I had the hardest time learning the third page. 'Keep your hands steady,' she always told me, 'and your fingers loose.'"

I waited for him to remove his hands from the keys, since it was what I half expected him to do. But he didn't. It was as if he were blind, and he was relearning something that was once so familiar, and yet now so foreign.

"I've played a lot since she died, but it was always alone. I think I just forgot what it felt like to share the music with someone."

"You don't have to be afraid," I told him, my voice reserved and gentle. He didn't look over at me, but I saw the very corner of his mouth turn up in a smile.

He started with light scales to test the sound and the dynamics. Before long, he transitioned to melodies and smooth songs. I sat there completely still, and simply listened. Nervousness continued to inhibit his playing for some time, but once he found his way around the keys, I believe he truly forgot I was even there. His songs turned from quiet melodies to loud and joyful sounds.

After about an hour had passed, my parents returned home. They heard the music, and Hani and Oni came in quietly. They stood in the doorway, their eyes wide as they noticed Eli playing. They were transfixed by the music, their small mouths opened in amazement and their eyes wide. They seemed to be entirely at a loss for words. Mother and Father had similar reactions, though I sensed that they weren't entirely surprised.

It was a few moments before Eli realized they were there. He was embarrassed, I think, but my parents encouraged him, and Hani and Oni came to sit near me on the couch. Eli returned to the piano, and seemed lost. Father, as gracious as ever, crossed the room and seated himself beside Eli. He rested his hands on the keys, and then he began to teach Eli some songs he had learned as an Eldun. Eli took in everything, as if he were trying to make up for all of the lost years he never had playing in public.

The afternoon drifted into the evening, and I joined Mother across the room to help make dinner. Father and Eli continued to play together. Eli seemed joyful and he never stopped smiling. Father was happy too, and they made a wonderful pair when they played. It was a mix of two worlds, and they blended beautifully.

Eventually, their fingers grew tired, and they joined us for dinner. We sat and ate together, my parents complimented Eli on his abilities. I was sure I had never seen him more full and excited. It made my heart glad.

We helped my mother with the dinner dishes, and soon after, Father took Eli to the Portal. We discovered without much of a surprise that it was still closed. When they returned, the twins were put in bed. Eli waited in the hallway, and his hands played with the fabric on his robe. I walked out of the twins' room back into the hall, and he walked over to meet me.

"Would you like to go for a walk with me?" he asked.

"I would, yes."

We left the house and just walked side by side, not headed in any particular direction. I could see he was tired from the expression on his face, but he was also very happy.

"Kerana, I can't thank you enough for what you did for me

today."

"What did I do today?" I questioned.

"You were able to open me up, and in more ways than anyone else before you ever has been able to."

"Well, I just knew that those things would help you. No one had told you before, and I know that it is what Adonai would want."

He stopped and turned to look at me. "Kerana, since I met you, things have changed so much for me. Before you, my life was a mess. I was running. I didn't want to, but I had no other choice. When I met you, everything changed. You confused me, frustrated me. Captivated me. I have never met anyone like you."

He rubbed the back of his neck. "Look, I've never been any good at this kind of thing, and I am not even sure if this is right. I just know that I can't go on thinking or feeling these things if something is going to happen to me."

I could feel my heartbeat increase, though I wasn't exactly sure why. I felt like I couldn't breathe, but I needed him to continue. I needed to hear everything he had to say.

"Kerana, you are amazing. Yes, that is a given, because you aren't Fallen or anything. But, Adonai has changed me so much since I met you that I don't even know who I was anymore. I just know that since Adonai brought you into my life, I've been me."

He hesitated, looking around wildly, having a hard time keeping eye contact with me. "I just—what's between us doesn't happen every day. In fact, I'm pretty sure it's never happened before. But we aren't all that different. Maybe we come from different places, or maybe we are technically two different races, but essentially we can feel the same things, think the same things, be a part of the same things—"

"Eli, what are you trying to say?"

"I'm crazy about you, Kerana. I have been since the moment I laid eyes on you. You are beautiful, incredible in every way possible, and you just make so much sense to me."

I just stared at him. Had I heard him correctly? Did everything I had ever felt for him just come out of his mouth, about me?

I took a step closer to him. And he took a step closer to me.

"Eli, I don't know what to say," I whispered. He was mere inches from me now, and I felt a slow burn start in my chest.

"I'm not expecting anything in return. I just couldn't live any longer without telling you. Adonai has blessed me immeasurably with you in my life, and I can't... I can't even imagine my life without you anymore."

It was everything I could have ever even hoped to hear, and I was frozen, completely immovable. I could only look up into his eyes, his beautiful, midnight blue eyes, and lose myself in them.

"Eli," I murmured. "You've changed me so much. You startled me, surprised me, and you protected me. You have made me feel safe, even when it is me who should be making you feel safe. I've never felt anything like this before, but I know what it is. I was afraid to admit it to myself for so long. It seemed so crazy. I think I ignored it longer than I have admitted to it. I've been so afraid, so unsure—"

"I know, I know. I mean, how crazy is it that a Human and an Eldurian fall for each other?" He whispered to me.

"It has never happened before."

His eyes bore into mine with such heat, such intensity, that I knew deep inside me what was about to happen. He slowly lifted his hands and placed them behind my neck, in my hair. He looked at me one last time before drawing my face to his, and gently, ever so gently, he kissed me.

I had never known what a kiss was, but I knew in my heart that I never would have wanted to kiss anyone besides Eli. He held me as if I was glass, and I could feel the kiss from the top of my head all the way to my toes. I unconsciously wrapped my arms around his neck, and returned the embrace we were now wrapped in.

He slowly pulled away from me, and I felt his lips touch the tip of my nose. He left his hands behind my neck, and I opened my eyes to see his shine down at me. For a few moments, we could only look at each other.

"So what happens now?" Eli breathed. My mind was blank; the kiss had erased any train of thought I once had.

"I'm not sure."

"This has really never happened before?" Eli asked. "An Eldurian and a Human together?"

"No, never. Before you, Humans didn't know who we were." I looked around, I grabbed Eli's hand and suggested we head back to the house; it was getting late.

He looked at his feet, and didn't answer me for some time. "I thought about this, you know. My options, or possible outcomes at this point. And neither of them is staying in Eden."

I felt my heart sink. "No, it isn't, unfortunately."

I heard him swallow rather hard. "I really don't like this."

I choked back the tears. He was right; he was either going back to Earth, or he was going to disappear. "Eli, I am so glad you shared your feelings with me; you know I feel the same way, that I want this."

"But I just don't know how it could work."

I nodded.

"If staying here was one of my options, I would choose that. You know, that, right?"

I looked at him. "Yes, I do."

We arrived back at our home. Silently, we walked down the stairs together. I turned and looked at him. Without a word, he wrapped his arms around my shoulders and pulled me closer to him. I fell into him, and rested my head on his chest, the scent of him calming me down. I felt him press his lips to the top of my head.

"Why does this have to be so impossible?" I heard him whisper. I squeezed my eyes tighter, discouraging the tears from coming.

"I don't know, Eli. But I wish it wasn't."

He held me for a few moments longer, and then he released his hold on me. He took a step back from me, and I could see that he was trying to recover himself. "Well," He looked over his shoulder at the doorway to the living areas. "It's late."

I felt my heart breaking. *Adonai, why?*

"I suppose so."

I turned to my door and heard him slowly and reluctantly turn around too. But I couldn't stand it. I turned on my heels, ran across the hall to him, threw my arms around his neck, and kissed him hard on the mouth.

It didn't last long, and I wasn't entirely sure why I did it. I just knew I had to. I had to reassure him somehow, and reassure myself. I didn't know why this was happening, but it was happening for a reason. I let go of him, and I saw a small smile cross his face.

"Good night, Kerana. I'll see you in the morning."

"Yes, Eli. You will see me in the morning."

He bent down and kissed my forehead ever so gently, and then seemingly forced himself to turn around and walk into the living areas. I closed my eyes. I had never felt anything like this before.

I went to my room and slowly closed the door behind me. I hated to leave Eli. Everything was the same, everything an echo of the other. We were both connected, both felt it, and both knew it. So why was it created to just fall apart?

I lay in bed, tears falling freely from my tired eyes, asking Adonai over and over again:

Why?

26 ELI

I was relieved when morning finally came. I ached and my eyes stung. My dreams had been awful, terrifying. I shook my head, and faster than I would have liked, the night before came back to me.

I had told her how I felt, and how I have felt all along. Had that been the dumbest decision I ever made? Or was it the best one?

Of course it wouldn't work, I thought bitterly. I closed my eyes. *It's like we're Romeo and Juliet, I'm gonna die at the end of the play. And she won't even get the chance to drink the poison.*

That, at least, I guess I was thankful for.

But I had been honest; there was no way I could have met possible destruction without telling her. I had one day left. One day! When a person is faced with death, I could see why they usually make such rash decisions. Decisions like I had made.

Everything was changing, everything was different. I mean, it had been as soon as I came into Eden, but now not just my immediate life had changed.

Stop it, Mattison, stop it! This can't work, this won't work.

I heard footsteps coming into the kitchen and found Erez strolling in, a glass cup of water in his hands.

"Eli, you're awake."

"Yeah, though I kind of wish I wasn't," I replied honestly. I got to my feet and stretched, feeling my muscles move and work. There was no sense in lying on that couch anymore; my thoughts kept getting away from me there.

And then there was the matter of how much of my body was actually left. I could barely see my hands any longer, my legs were just barely visible, and as I looked down at my chest as I pulled the robe away from myself, I realized that I was fading away there, too, finally. I closed my robe around my chest. I decided it would be best if I just stopped looking.

"Well, since you are up, we should take another walk to the Portal. I would not be surprised if it was open finally."

"I'm not getting my hopes up, but I'll be happy to go."

And I did, because I knew at least out of the house, I could put some distance between Kerana and myself. I wanted to be near her, but I knew it wasn't going to work. I needed to forget her before my feelings deepened. Erez could probably sense something was off about me, but he didn't pry, and I was grateful for that. I was reminded of Steven in a strange way.

Oh, Steven. Even though it had been only days since I had seen him, it felt like centuries. Was I ever going to see him again?

"Here we are," Erez said, and at the perfect time too. It distracted me enough to make me forget everything for a minute or two. He gestured towards the Portal, and I took a step towards it.

"You know, it's getting kind of tiring walking here and back all the time," I said, without even really realizing I did.

Erez laughed, but it was sort of hollow. "I know. But it is what must be done."

Erez walked around the other side of the arched frame of trees, and I took a deep breath.

Please let this be the last time I do this, I prayed, knowing that I really didn't fully want it to be true in some kind of sick and twisted way.

I closed my eyes and lifted my arm that was almost entirely invisible. I pushed it through the Portal and waited for something to change. And just like every time before, nothing did.

Erez shook his head. "No, Eli, I'm sorry. It's still here, it didn't pass through."

I sighed. "I figured as much."

Erez walked back around to me and clapped me on the shoulder in a fatherly manner. I wondered what it would have been like to have my actual father do something like that.

"Should we head back and get you something to eat?" I nodded.

Just as we were about to return to the main path, we heard someone greeting us.

"Good morning, gentlemen."

I looked up to see Adonai strolling up the path the opposite way. His appearance astounded me just as much as it had the first time I had seen Him. He was strong, confident, yet gentle and calm. He was a warrior, but also a peacemaker. He was everything, and I was immediately humbled by His presence.

"Adonai," Erez said, bowing before him. "I see you were checking the Portal once more?" Adonai asked us. We both nodded.

"Yes, Adonai. And it is still closed. Why?" Erez asked. Adonai held up a hand to stop him, a gentle, small smile crossing his face.

"Be patient, Erez. The answer will come." Then He looked at me. "The answer will come; you just need to trust me."

And of course He knew I was doubting it. But could He honestly blame me?

"Not at all, Eli. Your reasons for doubting are perfectly understandable. All the same, I am asking you to put them aside and to trust me."

"It's way easier said than done," I replied. I internally kicked myself for being so disrespectful, and I was sure Erez wasn't impressed with that comment either. It should be "Yes, sir," and "No, sir." But how honest with that be?

Adonai smiled, and looked amused. "Again, that is very true and I understand it completely."

He then turned to Erez. "I have a proposal for today. I would like to take you, your family, and Eli to the Throne Room."

By the look on Erez's face, I realized that the Throne Room had to be kind of a big deal. His eyes were wide, and his mouth was hanging open slightly. He was really in awe. Now I was curious.

"Why of course, Adonai. It would be an honor to come to the Throne Room!" He responded enthusiastically. Adonai smiled at us.

"Good. We will head back to your home, collect the others, and be on our way."

And so we did. We went back to the house, grabbed Kerana and Aonani, and dropped off the twins to the neighbors, who were happy to watch them for the day.

When Kerana walked out of the house, we looked at each other for one long, hard moment. It meant something so much more than what words could say, because at this point, words were just not gonna cut it. She smiled at me, but it was halfhearted. She was still dwelling on the same facts I was; I only had one day left until something happened, whether it was good or bad. But in regards to the two of us and our relationship, neither outcomes was promising.

Adonai watched our interactions closely. I knew that He knew what had happened between us last night. Part of me felt dirty, like I had done something wrong. But I knew I hadn't. He looked at us curiously, but His face betrayed nothing of what He was really thinking. I was wondering why He didn't call us out on it; maybe He didn't want to do it with Kerana's parents around. Or maybe it just wasn't the right time.

Was there ever a right or wrong time for Him?

I saw Him glance over His shoulder at me and smirk. He

thought that was funny.

He led us down to the center of Eden, to the Fountain. Kerana, Aonani and Erez were all so worked up and excited about this Throne Room that I had to finally ask.

"What exactly is the Throne Room?"

Kerana looked up at me with those beautiful blue eyes. "It is the one place that we have never seen as Eldurians. It is the most high place, the most holy place."

I got it. It was where Adonai lived.

And that's when I got nervous. I asked Adonai, "So is Eden a realm that connects Heaven and Earth?" He smiled at me and nodded His head.

"Very good observation, Eli. That is true. Since it is out of reach of the Humans, it is connected more to Heaven, but since Eden is also not a part of the city of Heaven where I am, and it is also a way in which the Eldurians get to Earth, it is connected to Earth. All three tie into each other, but they all still have their separate purposes."

His gaze softened my nerves. Communication with Him was easy since He could read my thoughts. He then turned around and climbed into the Fountain. He waded through the knee-deep water until He reached the pillar in the center of the Fountain. And before our very eyes, a smooth, white stone staircase started to spiral out from the water in the Fountain. It twirled up and up over our heads like a giant spiral beanstalk, dripping water from the Fountain down back into the pool. It continued for what seemed like forever.

Finally, it stopped, but the top of it was so far out of sight that I was sure I would pass out just walking up them.

"Come, my friends. Let us go to the Throne Room." Adonai said, gesturing to the white stairs. Aonani and Erez followed Adonai to the steps, and Kerana and I were right behind them. As soon as Kerana and I had reached the first step, they started to go up again on their own, like an escalator. I lost my balance for a second, startled by the motion, and Kerana grabbed my arm to steady me.

"Thanks," I breathed, clutching at my chest. She simply smiled in return.

And instead of letting go of her, I grabbed for her hand. I needed it, and I needed her. I needed her to know that. She tensed for a second or two, unsure if she should. But when I didn't let go, didn't slip away, she gave in. It may have been really dumb for me to do, but I just couldn't do this without her anymore.

We rode the stairs up and up for quite some time. Eden disappeared below us, and before I knew it, we were surrounded by what I could only assume were clouds. I had never been in a cloud before other than in an airplane, so it was kind of cool to be able to reach out and touch one.

I was disappointed when it wasn't fluffy, and I was sure that it couldn't support my weight to bounce on it.

Eventually, the stairs sort of slowed down, and before I knew it, the clouds dissipated, and gave way to brilliant light and gold and crystal. I saw Adonai and Aonani and Erez step off the staircase, and it wasn't long until I was able to get a good look around me.

I was in the center of a huge city, but it was unlike any city I had ever been in before. It was more beautiful than Eden. Everything sparkled; everything glowed. It was like I was stuck in a city made entirely of candy and jewels.

The streets weren't dirty like in a city, but were beautiful and clean. And I stared in wonder as I realized that each paving-stone was a brick of solid gold.

And yet the city was not all buildings. It was full, but it didn't feel crowded. There were trees everywhere, and somehow the rural seemed to blend with the urban here in a way that would never work on Earth. Flowers were everywhere. I could smell every one of them, and I nearly fell over as I realized that I had never smelled a fresher or cleaner place in my entire life. It was astounding.

But I had never seen a more alive environment. There were people everywhere, both Eldurians and Humans, living and seemingly working together. There were houses galore, along the winding river that ran straight through the heart of the city and down lanes that stretched as far as I could see in all directions. I heard animals barking and playing together happily, dogs, cats, birds.

"Oh my," was all I could mutter.

"Welcome." Adonai said, spreading His hands wide, "To my home."

Adonai started to walk down a gold-bricked street, and He had to call my name in order to get my attention again; it had wandered to a nearby building that looked like it was made totally of emeralds, and I was trying to figure out *how*.

Kerana, Aonani, and Erez joined me in following Adonai down the wide, stretching street. I finally glanced over at Kerana, who was also awe struck. "You've really never been here?" I asked her. Her face was even more radiant in this light. And as I looked around, I realized that the light wasn't coming from any particular location. There was no sun anywhere, but the entire city was filled with beautiful and bright light. It totally baffled me.

"No, I haven't," she breathed, looking at all of the Eldurians and Humans walking side by side along the river's edge, in and out of houses, and sitting beneath trees together. "This is where Eldurians come when their time on Earth and in Eden is over. Adonai calls them home, so to speak. This where we will spend the rest of eternity."

"This is a pretty nice place to retire," I replied, looking around as well. "And all of the Humans; is this Heaven?"

"I believe that is what the Humans call it, yes."

"But how is that even possible? I'm not supposed to be here until I'm dead, and even then I'm not sure I'm good enough to be here!"

"I do not think you are dead, Eli, because we are with you too."

"So I'm not dead?"

Adonai glanced behind Him and looked at me. "No, Eli, you are not dead. But you are getting an opportunity that very, very few before you have."

Adonai turned a corner, and suddenly, we were walking up a hill. And then we saw these other beings. They looked like they were standing guard, but there was nothing to guard against. "Kerana," I hissed in her ear. "What are those things?"

Her eyes were wide as she looked at what I pointed at. "Eli, those are angels."

I felt like I was going to swallow my tongue. "You're kidding, right?"

She shook her head. "No, I'm not. Those are angels, Eli."

The strongest and most loyal servants of Adonai.

The street leveled off up ahead, and seemed to lead to a huge, domed building, with a set of golden doors that were thrown wide open to all, and blinding light was pouring out of it.

"What's up there?" I called out. Adonai looked over His shoulder at me and smiled.

"You'll see," was all I got in reply.

As we got closer, the buildings became less and less the focus, while the doors grew in splendor and majesty. I knew whatever was inside that room was more awesome than I could ever imagine.

Before we crossed the threshold, I had to hold up my arm to block the light coming out so I could see Adonai speaking to us.

"Inside, you will find that your life has meant little compared to what it will mean in here."

That line alone struck a chord in me that made the hair on the back of my neck stand up. It wasn't bad, but I knew that He wasn't kidding. And that thought freaked me out.

He walked into the room, and slowly, the four of us followed Him.

I blinked hard against the white light and had to squint in

order to see anything. I could just make out reflective, white floors, and what looked like a pool of water that like a mirror, totally still, but I could see all the way through it to the bottom. As my eyes adjusted to the light, I saw that there was a large white throne seated at the far end of the room, and seated on that throne, was a man whose face I could not see; the light was making that impossible.

Around the room were several lamps, all lit with brilliant white flames, and behind the throne there were four creatures that blew my mind. They each had a different shape, and had many eyes that all seemed to stare at me as we walked farther into the room. One looked like an ox, with wide horns and a rough hide; the next looked like a lion, with a mane as gold as the streets; the third looked like an eagle, majestic and powerful; and the fourth shocked me most of all: it looked like a man.

Adonai stopped right before the pool and turned to see us. He bowed to us, which seemed to be an odd gesture in my mind, and then turned and walked around the pool, coming to a stop beside the large throne. It was at that moment that I saw another throne, but it sat to the right of the large, dominant throne.

"Kerana—" I began, but a booming voice cut me off.

"You have come to see me, dear ones. For this, I am very glad."

I recognized that voice instantly.

"Adonai?" I cried out, looking at Him sitting on the chair. He had not moved; the voice had come from elsewhere. It was then that I realized the incredibly large shape sitting on the dominant thrown was Adonai as well; it was the Adonai was who everywhere.

"Yes, Eli, you would be correct. You have come to the place where I reside. This is the Throne Room. Welcome, all of you."

His voice echoed throughout the whole room. I could only stand there and stare at the shape that I knew had created me. I had felt His spirit the night I found Him, seen His son who was Him in the flesh, and now here He was; the first and last part of the trinity, the one that everything was tied to. The Father.

I felt movement beside me, and when I looked, I saw Kerana, Aonani, and Erez all down on bended knee, bowing before Him. Looking up frantically, I instantly went to my knee too.

"Please, stand to your feet. We have much to talk about."

"Why do we deserve this highest honor, Adonai?" Erez asked a minute or so later. I heard soft laughter in the air.

"I love each of you, and I needed to see you. There are many things that have changed, as I know you all have witnessed. And each of you has handled the situation bravely and whole heartedly. For that, I must say well done, my good and faithful servants. Now, my faithful Eldurians, I have some things I would like to share with you."

I looked over at the others. Aonani was trembling, Kerana was so still I thought she was a statue, and Erez's mouth was open in awe.

"Each of you has taken the task I have set before you and handled it incredibly well. I would like each of you to know that I am proud of you all. You never lost hope, and even though questions and doubts have risen since Eli's arrival in Eden," hearing Him say my name made those chills run down my spine again. "You still trusted me. For that, I am very proud of you. I always love you, but I do appreciate it when I am trusted. After all, I do work everything out. Never fear that."

There was a pause. "And now Eli. What do you think of it here?"

"It's incredible," was all I could say. It was the truth, but the words definitely were not sufficient.

"I'm glad you think so. Eli, I wanted you to come here because I have a surprise for you. Something that I think you will be very happy to receive."

"What is it?"

Just then, I heard footsteps behind me. I turned around and saw a group of people standing at the entrance of the room, and they stretched out way into the street. But there was a woman just inside the door who looked incredibly familiar.

And that was when I realized I was staring at Mom.

"Mom?" I whispered, my legs turning to jelly and my arms turning to lead. Her long brown hair was the exact same way it had been when she left our house the day she died. Her eyes were bright, alive, and well. There was nothing but love on her face, and with a single nod of her head, I knew this wasn't a dream.

"Mom!" I cried, and dashed over to her. I didn't stop until I reached her, and I wrapped my arms around her. She was about a head shorter than I was, so when I hugged her, I had a hard time pretending to be the six-year-old that had lost her so long ago.

But everything else was the same; the smell of her, the way she held me against her, and even her voice.

"Oh, Eli... my Eli..."

And then I lost it, and cried as hard as I had when Adonai had told me she was safe. I believed Him, but seeing her here now, getting to hug her when it was all I had wanted for years and years, just made my heart swell.

After so much time had passed that I had lost count, I finally let go of her and took a step back. Her eyes were shining too, but she was smiling so widely that I was sure that I had never seen anything more satisfying in my entire twenty-two years.

"Adonai, thank you! That doesn't even cut it, but thank you! I don't even know what to say!" I said, turning to face the throne again. I could feel Him smile down on me.

"I knew you would want this, Eli. I knew that this would make you happy."

"Eli," my mother said. I immediately looked at her. "I just wanted you to know how much I love you, and how proud of you I am."

"Mom..." I said, and she reached up, cupping my cheek in her hand.

"Eli, you have endured bravely over the years. There are times when you play alone at the university and your music reaches me and I feel connected to you on Earth, even though we are apart. You are so talented—so handsome! I am so glad you are my son. But there is something else back home that needs to be addressed, dear one."

"What is it?"

"Your father."

I hung my head and nodded. She was right.

"Eli, he needs Adonai. He needs Him just like I do, just like you do, and just like everyone else does. And I don't want you two to suffer anymore. You need each other, and Adonai will help you through this."

"But, Mom, what if I don't ever make it home?"

"That is something we must discuss, Eli." The booming voice resounded in the room. I turned to look at the throne once again, standing beside my mother.

"What do you mean, Adonai? Am I going to go back to Earth?"

"I will tell you again, Eli. You must trust that what I have planned is best for you. I do know you better than you know yourself, so you must trust me. I know you trust me most of the time, but I wanted to bring you here to ask you if you trust me with your whole heart, body, and mind, if you trust me with your life. And if you do, then I ask that you hand over control to me."

Relinquishing control scared me. I had no control over anything when I was a kid, and because of it, my dad took advantage of it and beat me senseless. I swallowed hard. My mom took my hand gently in her own and used her other hand to turn my face to hers.

"Eli, I trusted Adonai with my life. And even though I am not on Earth anymore, I know it was for a reason. I know you and your father have suffered in my absence, but I can promise you that we can all be together again one day. I am not saying that if you trust Him He will take your life from you, because that is not the case. If you give Him your life, He will not disappoint you."

I sighed, exhaling heavily. I looked around me; at my mother, at Kerana, and at the throne. Everything else depended on this one decision.

"Let me put it in two different ways for you, Eli. The first is the idea of your hand. Please hold out your hand in front of you," Adonai said.

I did as I was told.

"Now, close it into a fist." And so I did. "All right. Let's pretend that your hand represents your trust in me, or your control over things. See how your fist is closed? I can't give you anything that I want to give you, Eli. I long to give you things, to prosper you and to make you grow. But if your hands are closed to me, I won't ever be able to fill them with the things I want to. The downside is, even if they are closed, I can still take the things away that I need to."

I didn't like the idea of that. He basically had just explained my whole life since my mom had died. I hadn't ever really gotten anything, but He had taken her away. I was so bitter towards Him that I didn't even think that He could give me anything good after that.

"Now open your hand back up. Good. When your hand is open, and you trust me with what is in your life, I can take things, but I can also give things. And if you let me, those good things will outweigh the bad. I am not saying your life will be easy, but it will be full and worthwhile."

I nodded. I understood Him. Ever since I had come to Eden, my life had changed. I had met people who really cared about me, I had fallen in love with music again, I had found Kerana, and most of all, I had found Adonai.

"The second way I wish to convey this idea to you is this. Imagine that you and I are in a car, Eli. I am driving the car, and you are sitting in the passenger seat. As you grow older, you learn that you can try and take the wheel from me. You seem to think that you know the roads and the trip better than I do, so you again try to take the wheel back. I don't fight you, because I know eventually you will realize we are lost, and you will ask me to take back the wheel." He paused. "I know that sometimes it is hard and it is tempting to try and take control back. After all, it's scary going into foreign territory. But if you give me the control, Eli, the only thing that you will have to do is sit back, put on your favorite pair of sunglasses, and enjoy the ride. You won't have to worry about a thing, because I will have it all covered. I'll cover the expenses for gas, I will make all the stops, and I will find the right places for you to rest. But overall, it is my route, because I know the best route for you."

I had never heard it put in terms that I could relate to so well.

As I looked up at Adonai sitting on the throne, I realized that everything He was saying bit me down at my core. I looked all around and saw all of the glances and gazes of people around me. Everyone was waiting for me to open my hand, or keep it closed.

Letting control go would have been out of the question a week ago.

But standing here in this throne room, looking at the Creator of all things, I realized I would be an idiot not to say yes to Him.

I crossed over to the poolside, and I bent down to my knees. I closed my eyes and then said, "Adonai, I give you my life. You can take it, and do with it what you want. I am done running, and I am done trying to do it all on my own. I know you will be there with me through it all. If at the end of all this your will is for me to die, then I will have confidence knowing I will join you here. If you need me to continue your work on Earth, I will do that too. But everything that I have is yours."

And then the entire room erupted in cheers.

27 KERANA

Morning came, and I woke up with the color, voices, and faces of Heaven still close to my heart. I lay back and rehearsed each step, each nuance. I wanted to imprint the entire experience into my memory forever.

I opened my eyes slowly, and realized I still lay in the same position, with my head propped on the couch pillows.

Eli walked into the room and cleared his throat. I motioned him closer and he lifted my head so that I could rest on his lap.

"Morning." I said to him. He closed his eyes and pulled me close to his face and kissed my forehead.

I smiled. For this moment in time, I could believe that things could stay this way, that I could stay with him.

He rubbed my back with his hand, and I knew that he was trying to salvage as much time as he could with me. I heard someone open the door from upstairs, and instantly I sat up and away from Eli.

"Someone's here." I looked over Eli's shoulder at the windows. The sun was bright, so I realized I must have slept in. "What time is it?"

"I don't know. I just got up myself. Who would be here?"

His question was shortly answered when my father walked into the room, his eyes wide and bright.

"It's open!" He cried. Eli stopped yawning and stood to his feet. I felt my stomach drop.

"It's open? The Portal? Really?!" He seemed ecstatic.

I felt my heart constrict. His body was almost entirely gone. His face was just visible, and I couldn't even see his hands or his feet. Today was the last day for him, the day he was supposed to disappear.

"Yes! The Elders are already there. Come, let's get going!"

Eli looked at me and beamed. "It's open! I'm not gonna die!"

I laughed, but my heart wasn't filled with joy for him. I didn't want him to leave. I was glad he was safe. More than glad, actually. But that meant he would leave.

I was being selfish. I should be happier than anything that he was going to be alive, even if that meant he wasn't with me.

He grabbed my hand and pulled me off the couch, and we followed Father outside. Eli was beaming, and that made my selfish feelings dissipate. Father ran all the way to the Portal, so we picked up our pace and caught up to him.

As we reached the small grove where this Portal was located, I saw all twelve of the Elders standing by. Mother was there too, and as we approached, everyone swarmed around Eli.

"Come see!" Mother whispered, appearing at my side. She pulled me towards it, and I was baffled when I saw that the Portal had turned into an open doorway. As I walked towards it, I could see straight through to the forest near the university. It was just as I had remembered it; less green, less alive. I had forgotten how Earth had looked since I had been there a week prior.

"How did that happen?" I asked Mother. She looked at me and shrugged.

"We aren't sure. We just know that Adonai opened it sometime before this morning."

"So what does this mean?" I asked her. She put her hand on my shoulder, and in that simple gesture, I realized she knew more than she was telling me.

"I am not sure, dear. The Elders are trying to ask Adonai, but He is staying silent. Come over here, so we can listen."

We turned from the Portal to the circle of Eldurians that had formed some distance away, and we went to stand beside my father and Eli. I just caught the end of what Conan was saying.

"—must mean that He wants us to send him back. If He was intending for him to disappear, then He wouldn't have opened it."

"So what do we do?"

"Well, if we send him through, we are going to have to wipe his memory or something."

"Wipe my memory?" I heard a hitch in Eli's voice. His nerves had returned.

"Well we can't very well send you back to Earth with everything you know now."

"Why not?" I asked. Kobe and Kimo turned to look at me, their eyes turning stern and serious.

"Because then everyone will know who we are, and we can't have him betraying us. You know that Kerana. We must remain a secret to the Humans."

"I wouldn't tell anyone!" Eli cried, anxiety coating his words.

"We can't risk it, Eli. I'm sorry." Ovid said quietly.

"What if we did let him go back without changing his memory? He would just seem as if he had lost his mind, as if he had gone crazy. No one would believe him. To Humans, it would be a farfetched tale," Seoras said, almost offhandedly.

"Well, then he might actually become crazy. If no one would believe him, and once he goes back to the world of the Fallen, his mind will become tainted once more, and corruption will take over. He will lose his mind if we allow him to keep these memories," Ovid continued.

Eli hung his head, seemingly defeated. After just being so elated that he was going to stay alive, he had discovered he could no longer retain anything he had seen or heard or known here.

My heart fell.

And that meant he would have to forget everything that had happened between us.

"Well, what if instead of sending him back with a clean memory, we send him back in a sleep state? It could have all been an incredibly vivid dream."

"No! I want to go back with my memories here! I can't forget this stuff."

My father turned to Eli, and placed a hand on his arm. "Let us go through our options before we choose one."

"Erez, we have no choice but to make him believe it was some sort of crazy dream, or either that get rid of his memory all together."

"I'm telling you, I wouldn't tell a soul."

I believed him; if he were going to go back to Earth, I knew he would keep his word. "Well, we know this much: Adonai wants us to send him back."

I sighed. Even I couldn't deny that; the Portal was obviously open before us, and Eli had been right when he said that he was Human and he belonged on Earth. I felt tears rise, and I blinked them away, looking at the ground. I had to be strong and supportive for him right now. He needed me to stand beside him in this, not oppose him.

Dru put his hand to his face for a moment. "The dream idea seems to be a good choice, but I fear that too much of it could linger when he wakes up. It would be a dream, but he still might have a hard time drawing the lines afterwards, especially since it will seem so realistic."

It seemed we were back at the option of completely ridding him of his memories here. Eli did not like that option at all; I could see it in his eyes. I didn't like that idea either.

The Elders then began to discuss any options as to what they would do with him once he arrived back on Earth.

"We could put him in the local hospital, and he could wake up there after having been in a coma for a week after the fire." Tedros commented.

"We would need to affect all of the doctors' memories, the nurses' memories, and many of the student's memories from the college to match that story if we do that." Dru replied. Nods went around the circle.

"No, I think if we are going to use that approach, then we need to put him back in his dormitory at the university, that way we only need to affect the memory of his roommate and some of his friends. As far as the Humans knew, no one had been in that building when it collapsed." Teom said. Eli looked at him.

"How do you know all of that?" Eli asked. "I didn't think that anyone went through."

Teom smiled. "I've been teaching at that university for some time, Eli."

Eli gawked at him. "What? I've never seen you before!"

"I am a teacher in the religion department."

"Go figure," Eli replied. He shook his head. "So no one thinks that anyone was in the building?"

"Well, no, at this point no one seems to think there was anyone in it. There were no bodies, and the only whisper of rumor I have heard was that there had been a fight on campus the night prior and a student was so injured that he was rushed to the hospital."

I gaped at Teom.

"But for injuries from a fight, it would be easy enough to put him back on Earth with just the memory of having a concussion; that way, any memories that might leak through could be a side effect. Loss of memory could be explained by that as well. He could have been back at school for days after being in the hospital, and no one would be any wiser. Eli would wake up, and then go on with his life."

"I don't like the idea of you manipulating what I know actually happened."

"To you, it will never have happened."

"What about Kerana? What am I going to do when I see her again?"

Dru's eyes furrowed. "I hadn't thought about that yet. If you saw her, this could all come undone."

"It could affect his mental stability, and we will need him to return to Earth in mint condition. If he saw her, his mind might snap." Eneas added.

"Or he could look at her and not remember her at all," Conan added.

"No," Dru finished. "We can't risk it. We are going to have Kerana finish her term on Earth in a different location."

"Wait!" I gasped. That had been my only hope, that I could actually see Eli more was that I would keep attending the school with him. "I have to go back; it wasn't just Eli that knew I was there."

"We can fix that, Kerana. Eli's memories of you will all just disappear, and that will apply to everyone else who knew you as well."

I felt sorrow seep into my veins. After all this, Eli was going to forget about me and I was never going to see him again.

"No, no, I don't like this. I don't like any of it." Eli's back was tense again, and even though I couldn't see his hands, I assumed they were curled into fists. His arms were shaking.

Kobe looked at Eli and crossed his arms over his chest. "Look, Human, it is either go back and live your life or disappear here. Adonai opened the Portal, so that means it is time for you to leave Eden. You have to trust Him."

Those words echoed what had been told to Eli yesterday. But coming from Kobe, they were far less comforting.

Eli hung his head. "And I guess I can't argue with Him," he answered quietly, but the anger still tinged his voice.

"No, I suppose not," we heard from behind us. We all turned to see Adonai approaching our group, His hands clasped behind His back.

"Adonai," Eli murmured. All of the Elders, my parents and I bowed as He approached.

"Adonai, we were just discussing the best means of sending Eli back through the Portal." Conan chimed in with a bow of his head. Adonai approached the circle and stood beside Eli.

"Yes, I know."

"Is this the best option?" Conan asked. Everyone waited for His answer.

"The way it will all turn out will be revealed."

"But the Portal is open. Doesn't that mean you wish for us to send him through?"

"It does indeed."

"Then tell us what the best way to do it is!"

He shook His head. "Choose wisely," was the only thing that He said. He then turned to Eli.

"I would like to speak to you before you leave, Eli."

Eli's face contorted; he was trying to be brave, I could see it. Adonai looked at the Elders who were eagerly listening in.

"I suggest you start to put your plan in motion and give me some privacy with him."

The Elders nodded in unison and pulled their circle tighter. Father joined the Elders. When I made to leave Adonai and Eli, Adonai reached out and gently touched my arm.

"You may stay, dear one. I know this is just as important to you."

I nodded.

He turned back to Eli and smiled at him, but it wasn't a smile of joy; it was a smile that was fatherly and concerned. "How are you feeling?"

"Terrified. I don't like this. I am happy that I am not going to die, but in all honesty, I don't want to go back without my memories."

Adonai remained silent. "Keep talking, let it all out."

Eli's eyes furrowed. I could see sadness growing in them. "I don't want to forget everything I learned here. I don't want to forget it. I've learned so much here, discovered so much. I finally know who I am, and finally know what I love. I don't want to forget the people that I met, or the things I've seen. I don't want to forget the celebration, I don't want to forget Undalusum, I don't want to forget the way that the food here tastes. I want to take it all with me."

He then looked over at me. "Adonai, I don't want to forget Kerana. I don't want to forget all that she has taught me and all that I've been able to do because of her. You brought her to me and me to her, but now you are just going to take her away? I don't want to lose her."

His eyes turned from mine and looked at the ground. I felt my heart rip into pieces slowly. I couldn't take this.

"And you, Adonai. If I forget everything, forget you, where will my faith be? It's going to be like it never happened."

Adonai placed His hand on Eli's shoulder. "Eli you will find me again because I love you, and you love me." He paused, looking Eli directly in the eye. "Have faith, my child. You *will* find me again. I promise you that. And it will probably be sooner than you think."

He nodded, but I felt as if I was looking at a small boy and his father. Eli's demeanor had changed and he was humbled, even if he was afraid. Adonai was showing him the deepest form of love, and the only way that Eli knew how to respond was to reach forward and embrace Adonai.

Adonai hugged him in return, and squeezed extra tight. I felt rude intruding on their private moment, but it was only a moment. When Adonai pulled away, he said, "I was like you, Eli. I was facing death, and I knew what was to come. It may not have been the exact same situation you are in now, but I was in a foreign place about to head back home where I belonged. I felt torn, because I knew I belonged in both places. But I was there, I was *Human* just like you. I felt the things you feel, saw the things you've seen."

"But you are Adonai's son! You are so much different than me. Next to you, I mean nothing."

Adonai looked him straight in the eye. "You do not mean nothing. You are Adonai's child. Because I came to Earth to save my people, *you are worth something*. Because I love you and you are mine, you have great worth. Never forget that. Even when you pass through that Portal, I will be there. Even if you don't know what is happening, I do."

Eli took a deep breath and exhaled. He nodded. "I understand. And Adonai?"

"Yes, my child?"

"Thank you."

Adonai smiled. "I love you, son."

Eli smiled, tears shining in his eyes. "I love you too."

And their smiles brought one to my face.

"And now Eli, it is time."

I saw his smile disappear as quickly as it had come. I saw him swallow hard, and he looked over at me.

"Adonai, do I have time to..." he choked on his words... "to say goodbye?"

Adonai nodded, a solemn look coming on his face. "Yes, I'll just give you two a moment."

I watched Adonai retreat and go stand beside my mother and father. The Elders' heads were bent together and they were still discussing everything in hushed whispers.

"Kerana, I don't know what to say right now," He began in a whisper, looking down at me with wide, sad eyes. I felt the tears sting my eyes, but I allowed them to come.

He reached out and wrapped his arms around my waist and pulled me to him. I buried my face into his chest and breathed deeply, trying to calm myself.

"I don't want this to be goodbye," I whispered in answer. He held me more tightly against him.

"I want you to know that I am so glad that I had all this time with you. I wouldn't have wanted it to be anyone else. You've shown me so much, made me believe in so much."

"I know. You've made me realize so much, Eli. So much about life that I never knew before."

I felt him smile as he brought his lips to the top of my head.

"Kerana, I have debated about what I would say to you if this were to happen, what I would want the last thing I said to you to be."

I waited for him to continue.

"I finally decided right before I fell asleep last night that I would tell you that if things were different I would want it to be you, to always be you." He hesitated, and I felt his heartbeat increase.

"I love you, Kerana, and that I always will."

I closed my eyes and felt those words seep into my bones. I debated bringing up the fact that in a matter of minutes, those words wouldn't hold any meaning any longer because I would no longer exist in his life. Not wanting to ruin the moment, wanting to imprint it in my heart so I could cherish it always, I only held him tight and said, "I love you too, Eli."

And without any hesitation, he bent down and kissed me hard on the mouth. My bones melted beneath my skin and my heart broke and swelled at the same time.

Just then, Adonai came over to us again. Reluctantly, Eli and I slowly stepped away from each other.

"The Elders are going to need you, Eli. It is time for your memories to change." Eli looked down, but Adonai continued, "Remember, Eli, just because things change doesn't mean they aren't true."

He nodded his head, and Adonai gestured for him to walk

over to the Elders. As he walked away, the tears came down in a flood, and I let myself go. I felt arms wrap around me, and they were the only other arms that could comfort me aside from Eli's at this point. Adonai held me close as I cried. I couldn't bear to look over at Eli. I didn't want to see what the Elders were doing to him to make him forget about me, or change who I was in his mind. I must have cried as silently as I could for quite a long time.

"Love is never easy, Kerana." I heard Adonai whisper. I nodded against him. "Can you let me tell you something?" Adonai added.

I looked up at him, trying as hard as I could to hold the inevitable tears back.

"Love never fails."

With that, He turned and walked over to where the Elders were standing with Eli.

I took a deep breath and followed Him over.

They were standing right beside the Portal. Eli was looking around wildly, and his entire attitude had changed. He seemed curious yet vaguely indifferent. He was dressed in the clothes that he had worn when he had come through the Portal with me. It was strange not seeing him in the robe; I had grown so used to seeing him in it. Father appeared at my side and put his arm around my shoulders. I didn't have to tell him what happened. From our goodbye, he must have known.

"Teom is going to walk him back to the building that the school has been using as the boy's dorm. It is crucial that he stays in this state until he wakes up. If Teom is with him, they can go unnoticed by other Humans."

I could only nod. I didn't want him to leave.

"It is ready, Adonai. He is in a state in which he can travel through. All of his memories have been altered so that when we lay him down to sleep, he will wake up without recollection of Eden or anyone here."

Adonai nodded. "And are you ready, Teom?"

Teom nodded. I knew my heart couldn't break anymore. All of the pieces just ached in my chest as I watched Eli look from one of the Elders to the next.

He was no longer upset, no longer sad.

My father squeezed my shoulders. "I'm going to miss you, Eli," I whispered softly.

Teom stepped through the Portal first, and it was strange that we could see him on the other side. Eli followed him through quite willingly.

And as soon as he stepped through, his body became solid and whole again. My heart leapt as I saw him that way again, and realized just how much I loved him at that moment.

Eli looked down at himself and smiled mildly. It didn't seem to bother him that he was fully intact once again, nor did it particularly surprise him. He shrugged and looked over at Teom.

"Come Eli, we must be going."

Eli, who was still looking around him, didn't seem to hear him or to care. He looked down at his feet, up above him, and straight ahead of him.

Adonai, my father, my mother, and I all approached the Portal. I really wanted to watch him walk away, knowing it could very well be the last time I ever saw him. My father let me take the last few steps until I was right in front of it, peering through. Adonai came to stand to my right, and crossed His arms over His chest, watching.

I tried as hard as I could to be brave. I didn't want to cry because then I wouldn't be able to see him clearly.

"How incredible it is that so much can change in seven days," Adonai murmured beside me. I glanced over at Him, but His eyes were still on Eli.

I looked back to the Portal, and realized that Teom was trying to coax Eli on, trying to get him to walk forward. But he wouldn't for some reason; he just kept looking around. His memory loss must have been confusing him.

The Portal in front of us started to shimmer, and it became more and more difficult to see through. I held my breath as Eli's face became harder to recognize.

I could still see the dark shades of his hair, the way that the sunlight caught the strands and made them look like glass. I could see the tension in his neck, though I was sure that he probably wasn't aware why he was tense. I could see his hands free at his side, and I felt I could have laughed, knowing that soon they would be slipped deep into the denim pockets of his jeans.

I felt Adonai's arm reach around my shoulders, and He pulled me gently to His side. I could feel His peace in my heart, but my sadness was so raw and painful that the peace only served to prevent me from breaking down immediately. He was giving me the strength I so desperately needed, the only willpower that could be strong enough to get me through this moment.

I wondered what it would have been like if Eli had never followed me through the Portal. Perhaps I never would have learned about his past, or about his father. Perhaps I never would have been brave enough to reveal how I listened to him play.

Perhaps I never would have chosen to love him.

And just before I couldn't see him anymore, just before the Portal completely closed up, I saw him look over his shoulder.

And it was like he was looking straight at me.

And his eyes lit up, recognition changing everything. He no longer looked indifferent, confused, or lost. He knew what he was seeing, and he was seeing me.

Before I even had a chance to wrap my head around that fact, and before I could blink once, there was a pair of arms around my shoulders, holding me tight.

Eli had come back through the Portal before it closed!

The tears came freely at that moment, and this time they weren't sad tears. Eli's arms were tight and strong around me, and I felt him trembling as he held onto me.

"Kerana, it's you! I know it's you! I could never forget you."

It was the Eli that was awake, alive. It wasn't the Eli whose memory had been altered; he was the Eli who had held me just minutes beforehand. He knew what he was saying, and knew what he was doing. I clung to him as if it were for my life.

"Eli, you remembered."

I opened my eyes, and Eli and I both looked over at Adonai who was standing beside me. Adonai smiled at Eli and I, and Eli returned the smile.

"Adonai, you were right!" He left me to embrace Adonai.

Adonai laughed. "I told you that you would find me again, son. I told you to trust me that everything would work out the way it was supposed to."

"I remembered everything when I looked over my shoulder and saw you and Kerana. It was like watching a movie in fast forward. I knew it was all real, that it was all true! All of my memories, they came rushing back to me!"

"You can't erase love," Adonai repeated.

"What happened?" I heard behind us. We turned and saw Kobe standing with the rest of the Elders and my parents. "I thought he was supposed to go back to Earth! We altered his memory, it was all going to work."

"Yes, but this was what I had planned all along."

Kobe, and several of the other Elders, looked dumbfounded.

My father laughed. "You answered our prayers, Adonai. It just wasn't in the way that we expected."

He smiled. "No, certainly not. You just needed to trust me is all." He looked at the Elders. "See, my intent was for him to go back to Earth. He did. But it was also my intention that he would come back. He loves me, and he loves Kerana, and he loves many others that are here. Love is important and conquers all things. It was never my intention to take that away from him."

Eli turned back to me, and he scooped me up in his arms again, picking me up and spinning me around. I laughed joyfully, and felt all of the pieces in my heart coming back together.

"So I can stay?" Eli asked when he finally returned me to my feet.

Adonai laughed when he saw how happy we were. Everyone else seemed speechless.

"Yes, Eli. You may stay. Know that your time on Earth is not over yet, but you may come and go as you please. Your duty to Eden has just begun."

Eli shouted for joy, and ran over to my mother and father, embracing them both. He kissed my mom on the cheek, and then returned to my side.

"Kerana, I don't have to leave you again."

"No—no, you don't have to."

He kissed me with so much fire and passion that it left me breathless. Adonai placed a hand on each of our shoulders.

"How can I ever thank you, Adonai?" He questioned, his face shining and bright.

"You thanked me by trusting me. Well done, my good and faithful servant."

Eli sighed, closing his eyes blissfully. I wrapped my arm through his and took his hand in my own.

"I think this calls for a celebration!" My father cried. My mother agreed enthusiastically, along with a few of the Elders. They then turned around and walked away, back down the path towards the center of Eden.

Adonai looked at Eli and me then, with all the love and joy in the world.

"I never lead those astray who follow me." He said.

28 ELI

The Colorado air was cool on that early December afternoon.

I drove up the deserted back streets in my Stratus, past the towering pines and spruces. There was a light dusting of snow on the banks of the street, and the sky overhead was grey and swirling.

Suddenly, an old house came into view. I slowed the car down, and pulled into the driveway. Looking through the windshield, I noticed the one-story, white house looked deserted. The bay window out front was dark, and the red front door off the driveway was sealed tight.

An old, beat-up, black Ford Ranger was sitting in the open garage, and the old, red work bench was strewn with tools, nails, and unfinished wooden projects.

I sighed heavily. It had only been a couple of months since I had been home, but it had been years since I had come home for any of the breaks the university had.

I felt the hand I was holding squeeze mine gently. I looked in my passenger seat to see Kerana smiling encouragingly at me.

She was wearing a sweatshirt, gloves, and jeans, and her eyes were bright in the winter light.

"You can do this, Eli. I'm right here with you."

I smiled at her. "Yeah. I think I can. Let's go before I turn right around and head back."

I grabbed the handle on the inside of my car, and opened it, stepping out into the cool air. I pulled my black jacket closer around me and I saw that my breath hung in the air around us, following us around like shadows. I smirked as I looked over at Kerana, whose hands were wrapped around herself, trying to keep the heat in.

"See, Kerana? This is what the winter I know feels like."

I saw her shiver. "I like winter in Eden better."

I laughed heartily.

We reached the front door, and now that we were close, I could see that the paint was chipping around the handle and on the edges. The gold knocker was tarnished and faded. I chewed on my tongue until I tasted blood. What was I going to say to him?

Kerana squeezed my hand again. My eyes met hers and she nodded at me.

I held up my hand, put it to the door, and knocked three times, slowly.

I took a step back and waited with my free hand in my pocket.

Not even ten seconds later, the door was opened.

A man with a balding head, dark blue eyes and a rough expression met us. As he looked outside to see who was bothering him, he saw me, and his entire face changed.

"Eli?" He asked, the shock obvious in his voice. I shifted my weight back and forth from the front of my feet to the back of them.

"Hey, Dad," I answered, unable to look at him in the eye for longer than a second or two. He pulled the door open more and looked at me with unguarded curiosity.

"What are you doing here?"

I shrugged my shoulders. "I was in the neighborhood and, uh, thought I'd drop by. You know," I hesitated. This was not going as well as I wanted it to. "See how you were doing and everything."

He folded his arms across his chest and looked at his feet. "I'm fine, I guess."

"Good, that's good."

An awkward silence fell around us for a minute or two, and I finally cleared my throat.

"So, Dad, this is Kerana," I finally said, trying to keep the conversation going. She smiled at him. He slowly and cautiously held out his hand to her, and she took it.

"It's nice to meet you, sir." she said.

"Nice to meet you. You uh, you Eli's girlfriend?" He asked, looking over at me.

"Yeah, she is. I wanted you to meet her."

"Look, if you are coming to me for permission or something, I don't think..."

"No, no, that's not it—" I interrupted. My mind raced. I had to get this out before I lost the will to.

"Dad, can we come in and talk? It's kind of cold out here, and Kerana is not used to the Colorado temperatures."

"Oh, yeah. Of course. Um," He turned around. "Come on in." He was rubbing the back of his neck, something I did when I was nervous.

He turned around and led us into the house. I looked at Kerana when his back was turned and she gave me an encouraging smile.

We followed him inside the house, and I was hit with a weird sense of vertigo when I saw the living room off the left. It was full of furniture straight from the Eighties; an old, yellow sofa, two leather arm chairs, and a dented and scratched coffee table. The walls were covered in ugly floral wallpaper, and the television was playing *Wheel of Fortune* on mute. The bay window was the only source of light in the room. It was all exactly as it had been my entire life.

My dad went and stood in the middle of the carpeted room and awkwardly gestured to the sofa. Kerana and I went and sat down together, and my dad clapped his hands together.

"Can I, uh, get you something?"

"No, Dad, it's fine."

He shrugged his shoulders, and walked over to the armchair beside the television, and sat down. He put his hands on the arm of the chair, and rubbed his fingers nervously over the aged and worn leather.

"Um, so how's school going?" He asked.

Even the small talk was hard to do. I knew driving here that this was going to be hard, but sitting here, my heart pounding in my ears, I didn't think I would have considered just getting up and leaving.

"It's good, I guess. Nothing too exciting."

"Well you got yourself a nice girl, here," he commented, looking at Kerana. "And you go to school with him?"

She nodded. "Yes, I do. We met back in August."

"Ah," he replied, nodding his head.

I couldn't take the suspense anymore.

"Dad, I had a reason for coming to see you."

He returned his gaze to me and his eyebrows furrowed. "Oh, okay, well. Go ahead, then."

I saw the piano on the wall opposite me, resting against the staircase. The dining table where he had sat listening to Mom and me play was in the exact same spot as it had been since I was born. For a moment, I could almost swear she was still in this house, and that things had not turned out the way they had.

I knew that both Adonai and Mom wanted me to fix the way things were, because who knew when I would have another chance?

"Dad, I..." I looked up at him, and I mustered up all the strength I could find. "I know that things have been really rough since Mom died."

"Is that what this is about?" He said, his voice turning cold.

"No," I said, a knee-jerk reaction. Then I shook my head. "Well, not exactly."

"Why are you here, Eli?"

"I—"

"Why," he emphasized, crossing his arms over his chest, "are you here?"

"I wanted to talk. That's all," I replied honestly.

He looked at me, the possibility of openness in his eyes now shielded. "Talk about what? I doubt it was just to catch up and tell me that school has been good."

"I want to talk to you about Mom, about what happened."

"Don't you bring that up, Eli," He cut in, the anger and volume of his voice rising. He got to his feet and turned away from me, his arms folded over his chest. "Don't bring that up after so long!"

I got to my feet too. "Dad, look, if you don't think that this is hard for me to talk about too, you're wrong."

I saw his jaw working, and I could tell he was trying to figure out what to say next. "Look, I know things have been tough. Especially between you and me, but Dad, she wouldn't want this."

His back was still to me, but he was so still the only movement I saw was the rise and fall of his chest; he was breathing quickly, but he was letting me talk.

"I've been thinking a lot about stuff, and I know that you and I have both struggled since she's been gone. Things have been said, stuff has happened—"

"She was everything to me, Eli!" he cried, finally facing me again. I saw his eyes were bloodshot, but there were no tears. His cheeks were red and his hands were curled into fists.

I held up my hands cautiously. "I know, Dad. I know. She was everything to me too."

I could see him trying to fight back his emotions. He was a tough guy, but this was obviously something he repressed. "I just miss her so much," He whispered. I felt a knot form in my chest. I knew exactly how he felt. And that had to be the first time I had ever felt I shared something in common with him.

I took a hesitant step towards him. "Dad, all these years we've fought each other because we didn't have Mom. I don't know if we blamed each other or what, but—"

"Don't you understand? You were your mother, in so many ways. It destroyed me every time I looked at you," He closed his eyes and bent his head. "But I treated you so wrong."

I wasn't sure if I had heard him correctly.

"All these years this house has been empty, dead. Ever since you grew up and knew how to get away, it's been like living as a ghost. And I only had myself to blame for it. You are the only thing I had left, and I've ruined it."

I gulped. "Dad, I know we have a rough history, but that is why I wanted to come back today, why I wanted to see you."

He slowly lifted his head to look at me. "I don't deserve it, Eli."

I stepped closer to him. "I won't lie to you and tell you that I wasn't hurt by what you did to me as a kid, both mentally and physically."

I saw him flinch at my words, but his mouth was set in a grimace.

"I didn't deserve that kind of treatment, especially not just because I reminded you of Mom, and not just because you couldn't control your drinking."

"Look, boy, if you came here to pick a fight with me, to ridicule me—" he started, and I saw the anger again and it burned away the sorrow that had just been there.

"No, Dad, but I can't pretend like that never happened."

The sorrow came back.

"No, you can't." He muttered.

I went and stood in front of him, and grabbed his shoulders. It forced him to look up at me, and I said, "But Dad, I want you to know that I forgive you for everything that happened."

His eyes grew wide and his mouth opened, gaping.

"What? Why?"

"Because you're my dad, and things shouldn't be like this between us. I know that Mom wouldn't want things to be like this. She may have been what tied us together, but her being gone shouldn't keep us apart. What's in the past is in the past. I know that family needs each other; I've learned that recently, so..." I trailed off.

I saw him swallow hard, and his eyes changed from hard to soft.

"And I'm sorry, Eli. For everything."

"That's good enough for me, Dad." I replied, dropping my hands from his shoulders and holding out my hand to him. He took it and shook it, gripping tight, but before I knew it, he had grabbed me and pulled me towards him and hugged me.

Startled and feeling kind of awkward, I felt as he pat my back. I had not hugged him since I was six years old.

However, I knew that this was what was supposed to happen, what I had wanted, and feeling a huge burden lift off of my shoulders, I returned the hug of a man who until ten minutes ago was a long-time stranger.

He let go of me, and we both cleared our throats, looking away from each other. We didn't want to seem too vulnerable towards the other. But then he stopped and looked at me.

"Eli... thank you for doing this. I don't deserve your forgiveness, but I think you are right; Mom wouldn't have wanted this for us."

"No, she wouldn't."

I saw a small shadow of a smile cross over his face. "And it's good to know I have a son again."

I smiled back.

"Dad?" I asked, rather quietly.

"Yeah?"

"I love you." I said, surprising even myself. I saw his eyes grow wide again, and as he placed his hand on my arm, he looked me straight in the eye and said,

"I love you too, son. I love you too."

He and I smiled at each other. Then an awkward, though not uncomfortable silence settled. My Dad looked like a different man as he stood there in the dull, afternoon light. He looked down at his watch.

"Oh, would you look at the time? I bet you guys are starving after your drive. How would you feel about some burgers? I just bought some quality ground beef yesterday to have a few of my buddies over for poker tomorrow."

"Sure, that sounds great, Dad," I said in reply. He smiled at me again. I was sure it would take some getting used to.

Kerana and I got to our feet, but my Dad waved his hands. "No, no, you two sit tight. It won't take me long. You should just relax after your ride. Here," he picked up the television remote off of the top of coffee table. "Watch something for a few. I will be back in a bit."

And with that, he retreated to the kitchen. Kerana and I looked at each other before we settled back onto the couch.

"Well, that went rather well," Kerana said as she took my hand in hers again. I leaned back into the cushions and nodded.

"I am surprised. It really did go pretty well." I closed my eyes for a second.

Thanks, Adonai. I couldn't have done that without you.

As Kerana opened her mouth to speak, we heard a tap at the window behind the couch. We both turned and looked outside and we saw a bright green bird with a long, thin blue beak peck furiously at the glass, a twig clasped in its small orange feet.

"What is that? I don't think that's native to Colorado," I said as I peered at the bird more closely.

"That's a Viridis! Eli, that's a bird from Eden!"

I gaped at her. "Is that even possible?"

She grabbed my hand and pulled me to my feet, and then

dragged me to the front door, which she threw open. We crossed to the window, where the bird still fluttered in mid-air.

"What are you doing here?" Kerana asked the bird. It trilled a high, piercing song, and flew over to us to hover in front of our faces. It shook its foot that clutched the twig, and that was when I realized the twig had berries still attached.

Kerana reached out her hand, and as if it had been waiting for that, the bird dropped the berries in Kerana's outstretched palm. Without so much as another sound, the bird sped off into the sky above.

I looked at the berries, which were obviously not from Earth, and then back at Kerana. "What does this mean?"

Kerana returned her eyes to me as she lifted the berries in between us. "I think—" she began, but seemed perplexed, "I think Adonai is trying to tell us something."

We both looked up into the sky, at the small speck of a bird nearly a mile away from us already. I smiled.

"I think it means that He wants us to go back to Eden."

Kerana reached out for my hand, and took it gently. I smiled down at her.

"He wants us to go back. Together."

ACKNOWLEDGMENTS

Reader, I need you to know something. I wrote this book for you. Truly, I did. I prayed for you as I wrote, thought of you, and always hoped for you. And you must know this too: though this is just a story, there is truth at the heart of it. God, the creator of all things, loves you the very same way He loved Eli. He loves you more than you can even understand.

Mom and Dad, you guys are awesome. You have stuck with me and encouraged me all the way through. You helped me to really follow my dreams, and I can't ever thank you enough for allowing me to chase after this!

David, you've always believed I could do this. You've shared my excitement, my frustrations, and my growth all through this experience. I appreciate your love and support, and letting me bounce ideas off of you at quite literally any time of the day. And I am especially thankful that you challenged me along the way, pushing me to be an even better writer and person.

My friends and family (because there are too many to name!), you all have helped me at one point or another with this story. Late nights discussing plot points, pointing out people that look like Eli or Evelyn, or just general excitement all the while sticking with me through it. Thank you, all of you, for being there for me!

Hope, you were one of the biggest blessings God ever gave to me. I truly wouldn't be able to write this without you. You constantly believed in this story, and believed in me, and I can't thank you enough for all of the hard work you put into Homecoming, but even more so into me!

Tim, you were also a blessing I did not expect, and I am so incredibly thankful for all of your help and your insight. You've done so much for me that I could never thank you enough for, and you have helped me learn and grow and strive towards success with my story.

To everyone at Koehler books that has touched this book, I thank you for taking the time to help me polish this to become what it is today. Thank you for finding value in it and helping me to make this dream a reality!

And most of all, I thank the Lord of all, Creator of heaven and earth. Without Him, I wouldn't even be here. He gave me a love for words, and He blessed me with the opportunity to share my gift with other people. None of this would even be possible without His doing! And for that, I am eternally grateful.